THE KENNEDY ENDEAVOR

THE KENNEDY ENDEAVOR

The Presidential Series
book II

BOB MAYER

Copyright

http://coolgus.com

THE KENNEDY ENDEAVOR by Bob Mayer
COPYRIGHT © 2011 by Bob Mayer

ISBN: 9781621251149

"Today, every inhabitant of this planet must contemplate the day when this planet may no longer be habitable. Every man, woman and child lives under a nuclear **Sword of Damocles**, *hanging by the slenderest of threads, capable of being cut at any moment by accident or miscalculation or by madness. The weapons of war must be abolished before they abolish us."* **John F. Kennedy** address before the General Assembly of the United Nations, New York City, September 25, 1961.

Footage of Kennedy and the Sword of Damocles
http://youtu.be/Xuy_9B1joTE

"When I read a book
I like it to kindle the true flame of feeling
So that, amidst our busy lives,
It will burn and burn, a constant flare
To ignite the impulses, the forces of men's heart,
So that we can fight against darkness until our death,
So that our lives do not pass in vain
For it is my duty, brothers,
To leave behind at least one fragment of honest labor,
So that in the black, sepulchral shades,
Conscience will not nag."
Nikita Khrushchev reciting a poem by a Russian miner he worked with fifty years previously: Pantelei Makhinia

FACTS: THE UNENDING CONFLICT

Thomas Jefferson believed in the inalienable rights of the people, a decentralized government and a non-interventionist foreign policy. He stood in fierce opposition to Alexander Hamilton, who feared the people, believed in a strong, central government and believed America's international might was commerce. The fight has continued unabated to the present day and will continue into our future in order to keep the country balanced and avoid extremism on either side.

We hope.

THE HISTORICAL FACTS

In May of 1783, the Society of the Cincinnati was founded. A leading member was Alexander Hamilton, and the first President of the Society was George Washington, even before he was President of the United States. The Society of the Cincinnati is the oldest, continuous military society in North America. Its current headquarters is located at the Anderson House in downtown Washington, DC. Besides the Society of the Cincinnati, Hamilton founded the Federalist Party, the first political party, which would eventually become today's Republican Party.

"Even to observe neutrality, you must have a strong government." Alexander Hamilton.

Thomas Jefferson was not allowed membership in the Society of the Cincinnati.

"Those who stand for nothing, fall for anything." Alexander Hamilton.

Strangely, in 1802, President Thomas Jefferson, well known for his strong opposition to a standing army, established the United States Military Academy, the oldest Military Academy in the Americas. In 1819, he founded the University of Virginia, the first college in the United States to separate religion from education.

In 1743, the American Philosophical Society (APS), the oldest learned society in North America was founded. Thomas Jefferson was a member for 47 years and its President for 17 years. He subsequently established the adjunct United States Military Philosophical Society (MPS) at West Point with the Academy Superintendent as its first leader. The APS has its current headquarters in Philosophical Hall on Liberty Square in Philadelphia. The MPS appears to have disappeared.

It hasn't.

"None but an armed nation can dispense with a standing army. To keep ours armed and disciplined is therefore at all times important." Thomas Jefferson.

Besides the APS and MPS, Jefferson founded the Anti-Federalist Party, which eventually became today's Democratic Party.

"Peace and friendship with all mankind is our wisest policy, and I wish we may be permitted to pursue it." Thomas Jefferson.

The battle between the Cincinnatians and the Philosophers for the soul and fate of our country and our foreign policy has continued to this day. A battle chronicled in The Presidential series.

Book One: *The Jefferson Allegiance*

Book Two: *The Kennedy Endeavor*

At the end of this book, I have a partial list of all the facts used in this book. It's not complete, but it's longer than you might suppose.

THE 16TH OF MAY, 1963

The Russian was secured flat on his back to the pallet by piano wire, which cut into his skin. The pallet was on top of a metal conveyor composed of numerous rollers. A 16mm camera was filming the proceedings. The steel door ten feet down the rollers was shut, but everyone in the room could feel the heat being generated by the crematorium on the other side of the wall.

The reading of the sentence was a formality, more for the camera than the prisoner. "Former Colonel Oleg Penkovsky, you have been sentenced to death by order of the Supreme Soviet for treason against the state."

There was no formal asking for last words. Months of imprisonment and torture had produced no words from Penkovsky; it didn't seem likely imminent death would either. More important, there were very powerful people in the government who didn't want Penkovsky to speak, and most certainly not on film.

The senior man in the room, First Deputy Chairman of the Council of Ministers of the Soviet Union, Anastas Mikoyan, walked over to the prisoner.

He wanted Penkovsky to speak, but only to him.

"Turn the camera off," Mikoyan ordered. "Everyone leave."

The camera was off and the room was emptied in less than fifteen seconds. Fear is an excellent enforced of discipline. In the short term, at least.

Mikoyan looked down at Penkovsky. "What did you do?"

Penkovsky glared up, beads of sweat covering his forehead, his lips trembling, but sealed.

"What did you do?" Mikoyan pressed. "What did you tell the Americans? Who were you really working for?"

Penkovsky remained silent.

"What is the Sword of Damocles?"

4

Startled, Penkovsky finally met the Deputy Chairman's eyes. "I worked for the people. I saved the world."

Mikoyan snorted. "Doubtful. You are only one man."

"Sometimes, Comrade Deputy, a single man can make all the difference. I am content to die. I served the Soviet and I served all of mankind."

Mikoyan rubbed his chin as he studied the other man. "Ah well. Then have your contentment. Your GRU friends are going to make a fine example of you. So you will make a difference in that at least. They will show your slow—and very painful—death to every agent. Everyone will think twice before betraying the Motherland."

"There is a greater cause than the Motherland," Penkovsky said.

"There is no greater cause," Mikoyan said without much conviction, because he was high enough, and had survived long enough, in the ranks of power to know one's self-interest had to come before anything else in order to not end up like the man in front of him.

Penkovsky disagreed. "This is not like the Great War, comrade. We now have weapons on both sides that if used, no one wins. And you know, Comrade, that what we tell the world about our nuclear strength is a lie. The Americans are far ahead of us, but we make them scared with our lies about our nuclear numbers." The words, after months of silence, were now pouring out of Penkovsky. Not so much an attempt to save his life—he knew that line had been crossed long ago—but to gain understanding. It is the driving force for some people to simply be understood, even in the face of impending death. Especially in the face of impending death. "Scared people are dangerous people. There are many in the American military that desire to launch a pre-emptive strike on us. If they did so, there would be no Motherland and very likely no world."

"Who is your contact in the American military? We know you were talking to someone in their Navy."

"Another patriot," Penkovsky said. "It is the true patriots that serve our countries and protect them not only against each other, but from ourselves."

"So you are a patriot?" Mikoyan stared down at the GRU spy. He'd seen many men, women and even children, heading to their execution over the decades. Ever since he was part of the Caucasus Trio with Stalin and rose to power on his coattails. From the Revolution to the present, Mikoyan's path had bodies littered on all sides; Penkovsky was just another in a long line.

"I'm a man," Penkovsky said. "I'm a person."

Mikoyan leaned close. "Were you really working *for* Khrushchev? What is he doing with Kennedy? What is this Sword of Damocles I have heard whispers of and Kennedy mentioned in his speech at the United Nations? And if you were working with Comrade Khrushchev, why has he abandoned you? If you were working for the Americans, why did they abandon you?"

"You would never believe no matter what I said," Penkovsky said. "One always has to assume a spy is lying. It is the bane of our trade. A spy tells so many lies; the truth is buried under them. I will never see the light of day again nor will the entire truth. Do you want to know the real reason I acted, Comrade Deputy? I do this for my son. For everyone's sons and daughters. Even yours."

Mikoyan snorted. "Your son. Perhaps he will share your fate? What can the offspring of a traitor expect? Your father died fighting for the Whites. You should have never been trusted. It runs in the blood."

"And what runs in your blood, Comrade Deputy?"

"We know who your British contact is. They promised you a nice little cottage in the English countryside, didn't they?"

A tear appeared at the edge of one of Penkovsky's eyes. It slowly slid down the side of his face and disappeared into his hair.

"Yes, yes," Mikoyan pressed, the tear fuel for his sadism. "A nice little cottage with your son playing with a pony perhaps? The British are so sentimental. And so brutal. They pretend to be gentlemen, but look where you are now. They let you get caught, and they couldn't care less about your fate."

Penkovsky didn't respond to the prodding.

Mikoyan continued. "Tell me the truth and I will have them give you the mercy of the bullet. We couldn't care less about the British. Who was your American contact?"

"Never."

"Khrushchev appeased our generals, yet he also got the Americans to back off regarding Cuba," Mikoyan said. "How did he appease the Americans? What did he work out with Kennedy? Those two are playing a dangerous game."

"They built a scale," Penkovsky said. "A very dangerous and delicate one."

"Ah!" Mikoyan leapt at the slip up. "So Khrushchev did appease the Americans beyond turning the ships around?"

Penkovsky squeezed his eyes shut. "This was inevitable. Do what you have to do. I am done."

Mikoyan tapped a finger against his lips, considering the doomed man. Penkovsky had accepted his fate a while ago. Mikoyan had seen it before. The mind snapped and all hope disappeared. It was why people stayed kneeling even as they heard the executioner walking along the line of others kneeling, hearing the shots, seeing out of the corner of their eyes, the bodies falling into the ditch. Often a ditch they'd dug themselves. They dug their own grave, listened to the executions and simply waited for their own to come.

There is only so much the human psyche can handle.

It was the person pulling the trigger that Mikoyan always focused on. They were the dangerous ones, the predators. Those who went into the ditch were just part of the herd and not to be feared.

"Perhaps you are what you say you are," Mikoyan finally allowed. "But no one will ever know the truth."

"I will. And God will."

"Ah, God." Mikoyan smiled. "Marx was right about *that* drug."

Mikoyan had also seen this before. When the victim invoked God, they were finished. He went over to the door and rapped on it. Everyone re-entered and the camera rolled once more. The steel door slid open and slowly, very slowly, the conveyor began rolling Penkovsky toward the flames.

Mikoyan waited until the traitor's feet reached the fire and the screams began. Then he left.

Penkovsky's cries of agony followed him out of the crematorium, but they didn't bother Mikoyan in the slightest. He was deep in thought, analyzing the various possibilities of Penkovsky's betrayal. Or non-betrayal. Or betrayal within a betrayal. And where did Premier Khrushchev fit in all of this? And, most important for Mikoyan, how did it affect Mikoyan?

It was never easy, this potentially fatal chess game of power.

THE 24ᵀᴴ OF NOVEMBER, 1963
Two Days After The Assassination of President John F. Kennedy

"I am sure that Chairman Khrushchev and my husband could have been successful in the search for peace, and they were really striving for that. Now the Chairman *must* continue the agreed upon endeavor and bring it to completion." The widow dropped her voice from a whisper becoming almost inaudible. "There are enemies everywhere."

Anastas Mikoyan wasn't overly surprised by Jacqueline Kennedy's words but his eyes darted about the interior of the Capitol Rotunda, a result of both standard Soviet paranoia and the sensitivity of the subject matter. Just six months earlier he'd heard Penkovsky being slowly burned alive and then watched the film; everyone in the GRU had been forced to watch it, and curiosity had finally gotten the better of Mikoyan and he'd had a private screening. Most impressive and it would make anyone think twice before betraying the Motherland.

It was much, much worse than the relative mercy of a bullet to the back of the head.

"You do not think—" he whispered back to her, leaving what he didn't know unsaid, hoping she'd step into the opening.

"I pray not," Mrs. Kennedy evaded, "but my prayers have rarely been answered."

"So the scales must remain balanced?" Mikoyan asked, watching her face carefully.

Through her veil, Mrs. Kennedy frowned. "The Chairman knows what I am talking about."

"The Sword of Damocles?" Mikoyan tried.

"Do as I ask," Mrs. Kennedy said sharply.

Looking past the just widowed First Lady, he saw an American soldier, one of the Green Beret Honor Guard hastily flown up from Fort Bragg, staring directly at him, face as hard as the marble floor on which he stood his post.

"Yes, yes, of course," Mikoyan murmured as if he understood. "I will relay your words to the Chairman." He took Mrs. Kennedy's hand and bending over, deposited a kiss of sorrow a few centimeters short of the glove that covered it.

"The change," Mrs. Kennedy said. "Make sure the Premier gets it."

Her fingers twitched and he felt a piece of paper drop into his hand. He smoothly palmed it, straightened, and nodded at the First Lady. Mikoyan moved on, as many others were lined up behind him to pay their condolences. As he strode away, he glanced over his shoulder and saw that Mrs. Kennedy, although she had her hand extended to the next diplomat, had her gaze fixed solidly upon him. He hurried past the closed coffin. A smart move by the First Lady to keep the body out of sight; head wounds were the worst, he knew from his World War II experiences and the many bullet-to-the-back-of-the-head executions he'd witnessed over the decades. They were saying it was a lone gunman, but Mrs. Kennedy's words and Mikoyan's experiences in high level intrigue, made that highly improbable.

One of the many guidelines Mikoyan lived by was to always suspect a plot and act accordingly. Better to be ruthless than sorry. One is not paranoid if people are indeed out to get you.

He left the Capitol Building, taking the stairs as quickly as his old knees would allow.

The area around the Capitol was crowded with cars and people. His driver had gotten him close, but his car was still a distance away. While order and decorum reined inside the Rotunda where the President lay in state, the rest of the capitol of the United States was in turmoil. Not just from the assassination. The transition of power to a new administration and preparations for a massive State funeral had the city churning. Not since Lincoln lay in the same place in 1865 had Washington experienced such shock.

Mikoyan was an old school Soviet, starting as a Bolshevik in 1915. When he was arrested in Baku along with twenty-five others as part of the 'Baku 26,' he was the lone survivor as all the others were executed by bullets to the back of the head. Such was his career path in a country where few who were close to power made it to old age. It was whispered in Moscow that Mikoyan was a man who could walk through Red Square in a blizzard and never have a snowflake touch him. This did not mean he was pure; it meant he was cunning and ruthless and chose his friends carefully, knowing that a friend was likely to be the one who would hold that gun to the back of his head at the latest breeze of power change. Which in essence meant he didn't believe there were such things as friends or loyalty.

There was only self-preservation.

He'd tied himself to Stalin from the very beginning, flirted with Beria after Stalin's death, then smoothly shifted to Khrushchev when it became apparent he would win the power struggles and Beria was executed. Even as Khrushchev gave the 'Secret Speech—On The Cult of Personality' denouncing Stalin and his reign, Mikoyan slipped through that round of purges as he'd slipped through many others.

At the moment, his mind was grappling with Mrs. Kennedy's words and he was tempted to immediately unfold the piece of paper she'd given him, but he'd learned patience was not only a virtue, it was a life saver. Any change in administration, even here in the United States, meant grabs for power. There was a dark side to Washington, as with any capitol city, which Mikoyan had caught glimpses of and he wished to be back in the relative safety of the Soviet Consulate before dealing with this latest development.

He spotted his bulky limousine with its dark windows and diplomatic plates, double-parked along Constitution Avenue. He squeezed between vehicles and slid into the backseat, irritated his driver hadn't seen him and gotten the door.

"Go, go," he ordered his driver as he unfolded the paper.

It was code. He didn't know what form, but he'd seen enough coded messages in his years to know what it was. Five letter groupings in a square.

Mikoyan sighed, and it was only then, as his car began moving, that he realized he wasn't alone in the back of the limo. He slowly folded the piece of paper and tucked it into his breast pocket. The man seated across from him held a suppressed pistol with the seriousness of one who understood the fundamental rule of never pointing a weapon at someone unless you were ready and willing to use it.

"Ambassador," the man said with a nod.

"I am not an Ambassador," Mikoyan said. "I am a diplomat at large representing the Soviet Union, and, as such, under the protection of international law."

The man nodded. "Yes, yes. That is what we all tell the world. That there is law and order and the world makes sense, but it's really us—we who dwell in the shadows—who keep the law and order, although sometimes it doesn't make much sense. Isn't that true?"

"I don't know who you are," Mikoyan said, "so I can't answer what *we* do." He glanced at the window. They'd just made a turn to the right, heading south.

Not in the direction of the Soviet Consulate.

There were three shadows crowded in the driver compartment, only their silhouettes visible through the opaque window that separated the passenger compartment from the front. The one in the center wore the outline of the cap of his driver.

"My driver is all right?"

"So far," the man said. "Please pass over the paper you received from Mrs. Kennedy."

"It is privileged communication."

The man waggled the bulky barrel of the suppressed pistol. "This negates privilege."

"I will not give you the paper," Mikoyan said. "And if you harm me, then—" he paused as the man rapped his free hand on the partition behind him.

The shadow in the right side of the front twisted, the shape of a gun flashed by, disappearing in front of the head of the driver. There was the chug of a suppressed round going off and red splattered the glass. The driver's head thudded back against the partition, then slumped over. A bullet to the forehead was as effective as one to the back of the head.

"Messy," the man said. "I told you 'so far.' Which part of that didn't you get?"

Mikoyan looked out the window. They were going down a side street. He sighed. "You dare not kill me. I am not some petty spy whose body can be tossed on the trash heap of dead operatives your CIA and my KGB have built in this so-called Cold War. It is not so cold for some." That reminded him of Penkovsky and the spy's fate, and he knew this was connected somehow.

The man cocked his head and peered at him. "You have no clue what is going on, do you? What you have in your pocket, it's important enough that I *will* kill you to get it. I prefer not to. But we just had a President assassinated. You think anyone is going to give a piss about you?" He lifted the barrel of the gun ever so slightly until it was centered on Mikoyan's forehead.

It was not the first time the Russian had had a gun pointed at his head.

He didn't want it to be the last.

"Is it about the Sword of Damocles?" Mikoyan asked.

Either the man was clueless or he was a great poker player. "My patience will run out in three seconds."

Mikoyan reached into his pocket, removing the piece of paper. "I will lodge a complaint. The Ambassador will be most upset about his car. And the driver."

"I'm sure," the man said as he reached for the paper.

The car slammed to a halt, and the man rocked back.

The sound of breaking glass came through the partition, along with more suppressed weapons going off and more blood splattering the other side of the glass.

The man's eyes were shifting back and forth, keeping the weapon trained on Mikoyan. Doors on either side opened and two soldiers in army dress uniforms, wearing green berets and with suppressed pistols in hand got in, sitting on either side of the Russian.

"Easy, easy," the man said. "I'll kill him," he added, nodding toward Mikoyan.

The Green Beret to Mikoyan's left shrugged. "Go ahead. You'll still be dead; we'll still have the paper. He's not what we're here for."

"Gentlemen," Mikoyan began, his brain racing through various enticements, threats and maneuvers to get out of another tight jam. "Perhaps—"

"Shut up," the soldier to the left said.

"You Philosophers can't—" the man began, but the Green Beret to Mikoyan's right fired. The bullet entered the man's forehead, a small black hole. The exit wound coated this side of the window just like the other: brains and bone and blood.

The Green Beret to the left turned to the Russian. "The message, please."

It was not framed as a question.

Mikoyan handed the paper to him. The soldier looked at it, nodded, then surprisingly, handed it back to Mikoyan. "Make sure it gets to your Premier."

"I thought I was not important." Mikoyan said, slipping it back in his pocket.

"You're not," the Green Beret said. "If he'd killed you, the message would have gotten to Khrushchev one way or another. You're just the most convenient mode at the moment."

The other soldier reached over to the body of the gunman. He flipped aside the man's lapel. There was some sort of medallion pinned there. The soldier removed it and put it in his own pocket.

"What is this about?" Mikoyan asked.

The soldier gave a slight smile. "Deputy Chairman Mikoyan, your guess is as good as ours. Probably better. We follow orders."

"Whose orders?"

The man nodded. "That's a smart question, but I'm afraid I can't give you the answer."

"How I do get back to the consulate?" Mikoyan asked as the two soldiers made to leave the car.

That also seemed to truly puzzle the soldier. "You drive. I'm sure your resident KGB friends can deal with the bodies."

"Who is he?" Mikoyan asked, pointing toward the man who'd held the gun on him.

"Just a pawn. Following his orders."

And then they were gone, leaving Mikoyan alone in the limo with four corpses.

What did old Nikita do? Mikoyan wondered, and he felt a chill, as if a snowflake had finally landed on him.

CHAPTER ONE
The Present

HERE RESTS IN
HONORED GLORY
AN AMERICAN
SOLDIER
KNOWN BUT TO GOD

Colonel Paul Ducharme stared at the panel on one side of the marble monument that marked the graves holding the unknown soldiers from World War I through Vietnam here in the heart of Arlington Cemetery. He doubted there would be any more unknowns given DNA typing. The military had even backtracked and identified the Vietnam unknown and his family had claimed his body and re-buried him at Jefferson Barracks. But that did not mean there would be an end to the dead, because as Plato said millennia ago, only the dead have seen the end of war.

Emergency lights were flashing around the Tomb of the Unknown Soldier and Ducharme knew the 'authorities' had their hands full trying to explain the night's activities and remove the bodies. Too many people with too much power needed this entire event hushed up, so Ducharme wasn't overly concerned about publicity. When the covert world wanted something kept quiet, they would go to any lengths.

The 3rd Infantry, more commonly known as the Old Guard, whose duty it was to guard the Tomb, had not only just defended it, but already had a man 'walking the mat,' even though he was dressed in camouflage, not dress blues. Arlington was shut down right now, but by daylight, all would be back to normal, the guard would be in the proper uniform and the world at large would be no wiser about what had happened overnight to save the country.

Twenty years of Special Operations duty had carved their hardship into Ducharme. Scars crisscrossed his skull underneath hair that was more white than silver. He also had a scar just underneath his right eye. Despite his age, he was fit, physical conditioning being an ingrained part of his lifestyle and profession. Physically fit, that is. His hands occasionally had a slight tremor in them, and there was little he could do about the intermittent pain that lanced through his brain. He'd worked hard in rehab to deal with the mental problems associated with his traumatic brain injury (TBI) and was still, as he liked to say, functional.

Almost all the time.

"We can't put part of the Cipher in the Tomb," Evie said.

"We're not going there," Ducharme replied.

Evie Tolliver, the curator of Monticello and former CIA agent, was of roughly the same age as Ducharme, in her mid-forties, and also fit. Flanking her was Sergeant Major Kincannon, the third leg of the group that had succeeded in beating the Society of the Cincinnati to the parts of the Jefferson Cipher and decoding it in order to uncover the Jefferson Allegiance before the SOC did, thus keeping control of it.

A powerful document, one that was a secret part of the Constitution, control of the Allegiance had allowed the country to keep the fulfillment of an Imperial Presidency at bay for two centuries. It was the ultimate weapon the Philosophers used to battle the Society of the Cincinnati. Brokered during the growing pains of the country between Thomas Jefferson and Alexander Hamilton, it was, and continued to be, the ultimate compromise between either extreme of government.

Without another word, Ducharme headed out into the cemetery and the two followed without question into the calm of the fields of the dead. Dawn was lighting up the eastern sky and the tombstones cast long shadows in the early morning chill.

Ducharme halted. "Here."

Evie looked at the newly emplaced headstone:

CAPTAIN CHARLES LAGRANGE
BORN NEW ORLEANS 6 MAY 1972
DIED 3 JANUARY
DUTY-HONOR-COUNTRY
SILVER STAR

Ducharme knelt at the foot of the grave where new turf had been laid. A raw grave was to the right: the General, murdered by the Society as part of their ploy to finally get their hands on the document that had eluded them for over two centuries. Ducharme pushed his knife into the loose soil and probed for a few moments. He struck something and pulled out the leather pouch he'd buried. He opened it and the two bulky West Point rings tumbled into his palm. He slid one on his finger. Then he took a third from a pocket—General LaGrange's, which Evie had retrieved from the Surgeon's body. He put it in the pouch next to the General's son's ring.

Ducharme buried the rings back in the hole, pressing them down deep.

Then he held out his hands to Evie. "Let me have the Cipher."

Evie removed the rods and disks. Ducharme unscrewed the end and removed 19 of the disks. He handed the rod and 7 remaining disks back to her. "You hide your seven wherever you want. Make sure it's a place where whoever you appoint as your successor can unravel the clues to finding it by knowing you. I'll hide the rest until we name the next two Philosophers. Then I'll give each one their six."

Ducharme turned back to the General's grave. He slid his commando knife into the dirt and covered it.

"Won't you be needing that?" Evie asked.

"I hope I won't need my knife. Not quite Kosciuszko's sword, but you get the idea. We need to move beyond the sword. I think the words of the Jefferson Allegiance are more powerful than any knife or sword."

Evie nodded. "They've proven to be so far. It's our duty to make sure they continue to do so."

CHAPTER TWO
The Present

"People used to spend a considerable amount of time trying to determine exactly how many animals were on the Ark," Jonah said as his small expedition stopped for the hourly break among the jumbled foothills at the base of Mount Ararat. "Along with the exact length of a cubit. There are various interpretations."

His companions, a half-dozen Kurdish porters and an American guide, paid him no heed, slumping to the ground and doing what a break called for: resting. This was a job for them, not a quest.

They were in the northeast corner of Turkey, having illegally crossed the border from Iraq to the south during the night and driving north. The area was a jumble of nations bumping into each other: Armenia to the north, a slice of Azerbaijan to the northwest, abutting both Armenia, and to the east, Iran. A couple hundred miles to the south was Iraq.

Amidst this jumble of nations, it was the Kurds who had been left without their own country, although they had practically taken over western Iraq since the Americans had invaded, and they'd always been a pestering presence in eastern Turkey. They saw little need to honor the haphazardly drawn borders that had torn apart their ancestral lands. It was a smuggler's heaven, with so many borders in so many directions, and officials who were more than open to bribes.

They'd driven from Iraq in an old Land Rover along back roads the Kurds knew of, until they reached a point last night where they hid the truck in a small Kurdish town, giving a local farmer a bit of money to hide it in his barn. From there, they'd started early this morning on foot with the bulk of Mount

Ararat looming in front of them, weaving their way along a washed out road that had long ago ceased to be able to support vehicle traffic.

Jonah didn't sit down. He wanted to keep going, to not stop until they got to his destination. It was only after the porters threatened to toss down their loads, and the guide, Haney, took their side, that Jonah finally accepted these halts. It didn't occur to him—couldn't occur to him—that they didn't share his passion. They also didn't share his secrets.

Jonah was skinny, with a slightly malnourished look he subconsciously maintained because it gave him the appearance of a fanatic; which he was, although not in the way most thought. He was ostensibly here in Turkey to discover Noah's Ark.

They were in jumbled country, not even at the beginning of the main ascent. The consensus, freely discussed in their native language among the porters, was that Jonah would never make it to the top. They were fine with that as they'd insisted on payment up front and they also knew even if Jonah could make the climb, they wouldn't be allowed up above 14,000 feet as the Turkish military had roving patrols at that altitude, since the government had long ago designated the mountaintop a military base, as the border with Iran ran along the east of side of Lesser Ararat, the mountain's smaller sister.

They would be turned back and that would be that.

Of course, they had no clue that Jonah had no desire to make it to the summit.

Jonah checked his watch. Two more minutes for the five-minute break. "Some say there are too many species to have fit aboard an ark, but I think they're taking things too literally. God works in mysterious ways, and if he'd wanted to fit every species aboard an ark, then Noah could most certainly do God's will." He knelt and bowed his head in prayer, as he had done for the last minute of every break, apparently taking sustenance from his faith.

The guide, Haney, got to his feet, easily slinging his pack containing the tools of his trade on his back. He'd climbed Ararat a half-dozen times and was known as an expert at getting people into the country and onto the mountain. Whether he believed there was an ark somewhere in this corner of Turkey was an opinion he kept to himself.

It didn't occur to those who hired him to wonder about his motivation beyond the money.

"Time," Haney said. He repeated it in the porters' native language. *'Time to move."*

The porters slowly got up and resumed their loads. Jonah was already moving, pushing forward. They were on a side of the mountain that had rarely been climbed and wasn't one of the more popular spots for speculation as to the Ark's possible resting place. How Jonah had picked his own location for the legendary vessel was something he hadn't shared, and that piqued Haney's interest. The Kurds were uneasy, not just because of the possibility of Turkish military patrols, a people with whom they had battled many times in the past, but also because this area had some special significance to them. Haney, who spoke their language, had caught snippets of their worries. They never said anything specific, but it was clear from the way the villagers had glared at them this morning when they departed that this wasn't a place one should go to casually.

As the porters filed past, Haney retrieved a set of binoculars from their case and trained them eastward, toward Little Ararat and Iran in the hazy distance. Haney was a nondescript man, one who would not stand out in a crowd, which was a very good physical description for a spy, almost a prerequisite.

He put the binoculars back in the case and looked up. Jonah was already out of sight, around the edge of a large spur. Haney shook his head as he followed: crazies. They came in all shapes and forms and nationalities. But they could be useful at times. Haney and Jonah were in Turkey illegally, but it would be Jonah whom would be the one held responsible. Haney could claim ignorance and that he was just doing a job.

And he had connections at very high levels that could get him out of a political jam.

There was a cry of alarm ahead and Haney sprinted, as best one could with an eighty-pound pack on one's back, toward the spur. He rounded it to see the six porters along a trail cutting between two high cliff walls. The trail ended abruptly about a hundred meters ahead, a cliff face making it obvious why this route wasn't used to get to the mountain.

However, it wasn't this that had caused Jonah to cry out. He was on the right side of the trail, running his hands along the rock.

Except it wasn't rock.

"We go back now," Nidar, the leader of the Kurds, called out to his five men.

Jonah was touching metal. It was dirty, rusted, and scored by weather.

"Wait," Haney ordered Nidar.

Nidar pointed at what Haney could now see was two massive metal doors, set into the cliff face, painted to match the rock on either side. The cliff went up about fifty meters, slightly over-hanging, which explained why it had never shown up on any imagery. Haney realized he wasn't surprised at finally having found what he'd been seeking for over a decade. He also wasn't relieved. The key was to uncover what was inside.

"This is forbidden," Nidar said. *"That is what they said in the village. They said one must not go this way. I did not understand and they wouldn't tell me why. But now we know."*

Jonah was moving to the left, past the two large doors, ignoring the foreign conversation behind him. As if he knew exactly what he was looking for.

"Ah!" Jonah cried out as he came to something. He threw his pack down and pulled a crowbar out of it.

"Slow down," Haney said, moving forward. "We don't know what—"

A piece of metal grating broke loose with a rusty protest and clanged to the ground, leaving a hole, waist high, about three feet square, in front of Jonah.

"Stop!" Haney called out, but Jonah was in his own world. He slithered into the hole.

"Idiot," Haney muttered as he dropped his pack and ran to the hole, pulling his headlamp out of a pocket. He turned it on and shone it down the tunnel. He saw Jonah's feet about fifteen feet down a smooth, metal shaft.

"Jonah! Listen to me," Haney called out.

And then Jonah disappeared from sight, as if the darkness had snatched him.

There was an exclamation echoing back down the tube, then a sudden scream, and finally silence.

"Jonah?" Haney called out.

"The mountain has taken him," Nadir said. *"It is Allah's will."*

"He fell through a hole in a metal tube," Haney said.

Haney leaned into what was obviously a ventilation shaft. "Jonah?"

A faint voice echoed up out of the darkness. "I have found it!"

"Are you all right?" Haney asked.

"He is redeemed!" Jonah's voice was faint and echoing as if he were in a void a distance away.

Haney pointed at one of the porters. *"Rope. Belay plate. Anchor points."* As the requested equipment was extracted from various packs, Haney supervised the installation of three anchor points on the rock wall outside the tunnel.

"Nidar," Haney ordered. *"You follow me, and make sure my rope doesn't fray on the edge of hole."*

"This is a bad place," Nidar said.

"It's built by men," Haney said. *"We're men."*

"It was built by demons," Nidar said. *"That is what the elder in the village told me. Demons went into the mountain many, many years ago with some of our people. Many did not come out."*

"Men went into the mountain," Haney said. *"And now I'm going in. If you run away, it will be known that Nidar and his men are cowards. That they can be scared off by words."*

"Do not talk down to me," Nidar said. *"Men did build this, but maybe they were bad men? Maybe this is a bad place?"*

"Do you want to leave Jonah down there?"

Nidar looked at the others. They refused to meet his eyes, which made the decision for him. *"I will follow."*

Haney slipped on a pair of gloves. Then he looped the rope through a carabineer on the front of his harness. He considered leaving his pack, but he knew the porters would go through it the minute he was out of sight. Besides, he had gear in it he might need, including a medkit. He crawled into the pipe. It wasn't overly tight, but he didn't relish the idea of backing out if he had to. His headlamp illuminated the way and he crawled forward. After five meters he glanced over his shoulder. Nidar was right behind him, one hand making sure the rope was clear and free.

Haney nodded at him. Then pushed onward.

He came to a spot where the bottom just disappeared; Jonah's surprise drop-off point.

"Jonah?" Haney called out.

"Redemption." Jonah's voice was low and tinged with something Haney had heard before: the onset of shock. But at least he was alive.

Haney peered down. He saw Jonah in the small pool of light cast by his headlamp sprawled on the ground directly below. One leg was canted at an unnatural angle. A grate was by his side—he must have crawled onto it and it wasn't designed to support a person's weight, or the years had weakened the metal.

"He's alive," Haney said to Nidar. *"About ten meters down. I need that much slack. And we're going to have to be pulled back up."*

He pulled on the rope, gathering enough slack with Nidar's help, then tossed it into the void. Haney felt the edge of the opening. It wasn't sharp. *"Put something under the rope where it goes over the edge once I'm down,"* he instructed Nidar.

"As you wish."

Haney went head first, Australian rappel, sliding down the rope, braking at the last moment, then swinging his feet down below his body. Still attached to the rope, he knelt next to Jonah.

Compound fracture in the right femur with white bone sticking through the pant legs and shock was setting in fast. "You'll be all right," Haney said automatically, his training taking over, even though he knew Jonah wouldn't be all right.

But Jonah was staring past him, eyes wide, a smile on his lips.

That's when Haney felt it, that he was in the presence of something.

Haney twisted around, still on one knee. The rock floor sloped down into a large open space. Haney swallowed hard as he glimpsed what was on the floor of the cavern, that wasn't a cavern. He forgot about Jonah as he stood. Once more training kicked in and he pulled out a small camera from a pocket on the outside of his pack and took several pictures, the flash illuminating only part of the tight space.

Looking up, he realized the roof wasn't rock; it was metal. Metal struts arced overhead, producing the roof. There had to be dirt on top, a layer to camouflage this place. Otherwise imagery would have picked it up years ago. He'd studied the imagery many times and there'd been nothing. The space wasn't too large, about fifty meters in circumference.

In the exact center, towering sixty feet, a rocket was aimed up at the metal roof. Large rusted gears indicated a portion of the roof above it could be retracted. There were six of the missiles, one upright and the other five still on flatbeds, the trucks that pulled the flatbeds also still attached. Those were parked tightly together, to the right.

The trucks were old, their tires rotted out. Over fifty years old.

As shocking as the missiles were, the row of corpses near the trucks told a sobering tale of a secret so important most of those who'd emplaced it had died with it. There were at least a dozen men, their corpses withered by time, but somewhat preserved by the dryness of the place. They were in a rough line and even from this distance, Haney could tell what had happened: they'd been kneeling in line, then a bullet to the back of the head. One was a little distant from the rest—he must have tried to run. The tattered remains of their clothes indicated they were locals.

"*It is demon's work!*" Nidar cried out from above.

Haney looked up and he could see Nidar leaning in. He must have caught a glimpse of what the cavern contained when the flash went off.

"*I'll need you to pull Jonah up,*" Haney said. But Nidar was gone.

"*Nidar! Nidar!*"

Haney knew it was pointless. The Kurd was gone and so was his lift out of this place. At least Nidar had left the rope.

Haney knelt in front of Jonah. "Why?"

Jonah was finally becoming aware of his leg. "I need to be bandaged. Splinted."

"Why did you come here?" Haney asked. "This isn't the Ark."

"It's *my* Ark," Jonah said. "My grail."

"How so?" Haney asked as he put the camera away and pulled out his medkit.

"Oleg Penkovsky." Jonah said.

"Who?"

"Soon everyone will have heard of him," Jonah said.

Haney had a bandage out. "Do you want some painkiller?"

"No."

"This will hurt."

Jonah ignored the statement. "That's the travesty," Jonah said. "No one's heard of Penkovsky. Yet, he saved the world. He was my grandfather. Ever since my father told me the truth of his own father, I swore that I would let the world know the truth. You've got to get me out of here. The world has to know of his sacrifice and bravery. You've—" his words were cut off as Haney cinched down the bandage on his leg, eliciting a hiss of pain. Jonah almost passed out, his eyelids fluttering, but then he came back into the moment.

"Oleg Penkovsky's name must go down in the annals of history as the savior of mankind."

"The whole point of this place, I believe, is that the world never know," Haney said. "You saw what they did here."

Jonah shook his head. "It's been too long. Everyone has become too complacent. The world needs to know of my grandfather and his bravery and his death."

"Americans won't care about some dead Russian," Haney said. "And what happened in here—and what's in here—can never see the light of day."

"Not for the Americans. For the Russian people who still believe my grandfather was a traitor." He reached out and grabbed Haney's coat. He flipped the collar and saw the medallion pinned inside. "A Cincinnatian." Jonah blinked, surprise piercing through the shock and his fanaticism for a moment. "How did you know?"

"We've been intercepting Admiral Groves' messages for year," Haney said. "We had a feeling his death would cause a reaction. You were the reaction. Where exactly are Aaron and the rest of the Peacekeepers? We know they're in New York City. Where?"

"They're not important," Jonah said.

"Where are the Peacekeepers?"

"I'll never tell you," Jonah said. "I took a death oath. Even though they were just a means, their mission continues my grandfather's legacy."

"O'Callaghan is dead too," Haney said. "The Philosophers have been wiped out."

"They don't matter."

"Is this the Sword of Damocles?" Haney asked.

Jonah gave a faint smile. "You have no idea what you're looking at or for."

"I think you've found what I've been looking for."

Haney put the camera back in his ruck and opened up one of the side pockets. He pulled out a Glock 20 with a threaded barrel. He screwed a suppressor onto the barrel.

He pressed the suppressor against the side of Jonah's head. "Where are the Peacekeepers hidden?"

"I'll never break that oath."

"You broke it by coming here."

"You know nothing."

Haney sighed. He reached down with his free hand and pressed the broken leg. Jonah screamed, the sound echoing off the sides of the hangar. "Where are the Peacekeepers?"

Jonah closed his eyes. "It is only pain," he whispered to himself.

Haney considered him, then pulled the muzzle of the gun away. "If you die, what your grandfather did will never become public."

Jonah opened his eyes and stared at Haney. "You must get me out of here."

Haney shook his head. "The break is too bad. You're already a dead man. There's no way I can get you out of here."

"I'm not important," Jonah said. "But the truth is."

"Tell me the truth then," Haney said. "Why are these missiles here? Why were they abandoned? We know Kennedy brokered a deal with Khrushchev using your grandfather as a go-between. These missiles were left here. We assume some of the Russian missiles were left in Cuba." Haney waved the gun toward the missiles. "But they're rusting away here. They can't be fired. There's no trace of active missiles in Cuba. This place was abandoned a long time ago. This doesn't make sense." He could sense Jonah slipping away, and with him the answers he desperately needed.

"The world must know, but not through the Cincinnatians," Jonah said. "Because you're lying to me. You would keep it secret and destroy everything he died for."

Haney pressed on Jonah's leg again, eliciting another curdling scream. "Why do the Peacekeepers exist? Why are they in New York City? Is this the Sword of Damocles? What role do they play?"

Haney felt wetness on his hand and looked down. He'd pressed too hard. Blood was oozing through the bandage. Jonah had only a few minutes of life left.

Haney changed tactics once more. "Please. I'll tell the world about your grandfather. How he brokered the deal that saved us from World War Three."

"You lie," Jonah said. "You all lie. Even the Peacekeepers lie." He stirred, his face pale from blood loss. "I couldn't tell you the truth of the Peacekeepers even if I wanted to because they never told me. The Admiral told me of this place. He knew Oleg. He helped my father escape to the United States. He got me into the Peacekeepers. But your people killed him. You're killing me. You kill. It's all you know." Jonah's head slumped down.

Haney fired two rounds very quickly. Both hit Jonah's forehead and the 10mm rounds splattered brain and blood all over the floor. It shortened Jonah's life by only a few seconds.

Haney walked forward, toward the nearest rocket. He recognized the missiles and knew their history. There was only one key question now. Haney opened his pack and took out a Geiger counter.

He didn't have to aim to get a reading, but the level wasn't dangerous. The fact he got a reading at all was the key.

He turned the counter off and put it back in its case. He realized he was breathing too quickly and forced himself to remain still for ten seconds. He walked by the bodies and noted that their hands had been tied behind their backs. Bullets to the head. They'd probably driven the trucks, off-loaded the one missile and then no longer been needed. Their secret would stay here with them.

He tied his ruck off to the end of the rope, both as an anchor point but also so he could retrieve it once he got up to the tube. Then he took a set of chumars out of the pack and clipped them and their loop stirrups onto the rope. He began the ascent, sliding a chumar up, locking it in place, 'stepping' up on the loop, then sliding the other one up.

It took a while, but he finally reached the opening in the tube. He clambered into it, then pulled up his ruck. He turned the headlamp off and crawled toward the light. He could hear voices. Nidar was arguing with his men. Just before he got to the exit, Haney pulled out the pistol.

He shoved himself out of the tube, hitting the ground, rolling and coming to one knee. His sudden appearance surprised the Kurds who'd been debating what to do.

He shot the closest man, a gut shot, the biggest target for an unsteady position. He fired as quickly as he could pull the trigger, taking out three of the five before they could even react, sending them into the afterlife. The last two reacted instinctively to the threat.

One charged.

Nidar ran.

Haney had to shoot the one charging twice and the man still slammed into him, wrapping his arms around the American.

Haney staggered under the impact and shoved the already dead man away.

He swung about, aiming at Nadir's back and pulled the trigger.

Nothing happened and the man disappeared around the bend. Haney got on his feet to give chase, pulling back on the Glock's slide, clearing it. That's when the first man he'd shot, gut shot, but still moving, swung an ax at him, Haney jumped away, falling onto his back. The wounded man lunged at him and Haney rolled, barely avoiding the strike. He fired, once, twice, both headshots and the man dropped.

Haney jumped to his feet and ran back the way they'd come. Going around the bend he had the pistol at the ready, but there was no sign of Nidar. The Kurd was running for his life, and that gave people an afterburner of adrenaline.

Haney slowly lowered the gun, knowing there was no way he could catch the man in his own terrain. He knew a Kurd wouldn't go to the Turkish authorities so the escape was not a pressing concern.

Getting news of the shocking discovery he'd just made back to his employer was.

He went back to his ruck and opened it, pulling out the satellite phone. He hooked up an encryption device and began typing in his message.

Then he hit 'send.'

*****

There is a theory that if you cut the head off an organization, the body will wither and die.

It's a nice theory.

Lucius, the Head of the Society of the Cincinnati, lay dead in his office inside the Anderson House on Massachusetts Avenue in Washington, DC, not far from the White House. His right hand man, Turnbull, was in FBI custody. His security detail were all dead, victims of Ducharme's airborne assault. There were no crime scene investigators, no detectives combing the building.

In fact, there was currently no one in the inner sanctum of the Anderson House. The battle between the Philosophers and the Cincinnatians almost always played out in private, a dark war kept from the limelight as much as possible.

They cleaned up their own messes.

Thus, other members of the Society of Cincinnati were descending on Washington, DC, intent on reconstituting the leadership and the secret inner core and resuming their anointed role.

But they weren't here yet.

As such, there was no one to answer as Lucius's secure satellite phone buzzed with an incoming text message. It sat on the desk, the only company for Lucius' corpse.

Protocol was that if a priority one message wasn't acknowledged within thirty minutes, it would be forwarded automatically to the next in line.

Sometimes protocol isn't a good thing.

*****

The man handcuffed to the table was as still and silent as a sphinx. His head was completely bald and his nose was crumpled from long ago breaks that had never been set right. He was staring straight ahead, as if something beyond the wall of the interrogation room held his complete attention.

"Nothing?" Ducharme asked, staring through the one-way glass into the room.

"Not a word," Burns confirmed.

"He won't talk," Evie said with as much confidence as if she were announcing that the sun would rise shortly. "He has no incentive to."

Burns' trademark fedora was on a peg near the door of the observation room. He was a tall black man, his hair graying from age and the job, serving in the Washington Headquarters of the FBI for far too many years.

Sometimes, in his more bitter moments, he likened being an FBI agent in DC to being a cowboy trying to control a herd of bulls while mounted on a donkey and using a lasso made of string.

"If I remember rightly," Ducharme said, "your questioning techniques left little to be desired." It wasn't that long ago that Ducharme had sat in that same room in the same chair as Burns questioned him about the death of General LaGrange.

"I do what the law allows," Burns said.

"A limitation," Evie noted. "But even extreme measures wouldn't work on a man like Turnbull. Plus, he's waiting on his friends in high places to get him out of here."

"I killed Lucius," Ducharme said. "That's one less friend in high places for him."

"They'll replace him," Evie said. "I suspect this isn't the first time the Head of the Society has been killed. As we're reconstituting the Philosophers, the Cincinnatians will reform. And their tentacles reach into all parts of the government."

"So it will go on," Ducharme said. He sat down wearily in one of the gray metal chairs.

"It's been going on for centuries," Evie said. "That's the point. Keeping the balance. It's the way our country functions. An extreme in any direction can be dangerous."

"Right," Ducharme said. "So Turnbull there will go free and back to being the lackey for whoever replaces Lucius."

"He won't be under the radar any more," Burns said. "That's something. And I doubt he'll keep his office here on the top floor."

"Don't bet on it." Evie stared at Burns. "He was never under the radar. He did have an office on the top floor of this building. Hiding in plain sight. He was, probably still is, and will continue to be, an assistant director. Come on. You've been in DC long enough to know how it works. The only way they'll get rid of him is if he becomes a liability."

"You don't think he is now?" Burns asked, gesturing toward the room.

Evie shrugged. "Being a liability and getting thrown under the bus is something I know about." She was referring to her time in the CIA. "The question is do the Cincinnatians need him more than they don't? Once that decision is made . . ."

"He had our friends killed," Ducharme said. "I don't think we let him get away with it. In fact, I hope his buddies spring him. Then it's open season on his ass."

Evie shook her head. "That's not the way this works. There are limits."

"Right."

"Hey," Evie said. "You had limits in the Army. Why didn't we just nuke Afghanistan? Take out Tora Bora with a couple of tac nukes? Solve that problem that way? Why'd we limit ourselves? It's not a perfect system, but it's a system that's functioned. We take him out, they come after us. Few people know how bloody the Cold War actually was when the CIA and KGB were going at it."

She turned to Burns. "I hate to say it, but it's more likely you're the one who's going to get transferred as far away from DC as possible."

"Don't *you* guys have friends in powerful places?" Burns asked.

"I suppose we do," Evie said, "but I have to go through McBride's files to find them. And you," she indicated Ducharme, "need to go through General LaGrange's stuff. I'm sure they've each left a file just in case, like they left the disks for us to find. We'll see what we can do for you. That's if you even want to stay in DC."

The door to the interrogation room swung open and two military officers in uniform stepped in, shutting the door behind them. The man had four stars on his collar and Ducharme recognized him immediately: the Army Chief of Staff. The woman wore Air Force blue and had two stars on her epaulettes.

"General Dunning," Ducharme said, snapping to his feet and to attention.

"At ease," Dunning said. He took in the three of them, then Turnbull in the next room. "You people made a mess at the Tomb."

"Couldn't be helped, Jim," Evie said.

Dunning nodded at her. "Evie. Been a while."

"It has."

Dunning indicated the Air Force two star. "This is General Pegram. She's Air Force A-3." He looked at Burns, noting the badge clipped to his pocket. "He cleared?"

"He knows what's going on," Evie said. "Some of it, at least. But enough that he has to be brought in all the way."

Dunning nodded. "I've been in contact with others. We took a big hit this past week. Sons-a-bitches took out some good men. McBride. Parker. Groves."

"We took out quite a few of their people, too," Ducharme said.

"Yes. I've heard about Lucius," Dunning said. "He overplayed his hand badly." He shook his head. "This bullshit is getting to be too much."

"It is what it is," Evie said.

"Keep saying that, Evie," Dunning said. "But there has to come a point where we don't need the violence." Dunning looked at Ducharme. "My condolences on General LaGrange. I understand he was like a father to you."

"He was, sir."

"I assume you'll reconstitute the Philosophers, Evie?"

"Yes, sir."

"You need anything, Pegram is your POC at the Pentagon. Outside of the Pentagon things get dicey. Hell, it's dicey inside. They've got people everywhere. Damn Cincinnatians about have the CIA locked up, as you know. They've got a lot of people in State, too. We play our game, back and forth. Rarely does it get bloody."

"This is one of those rare occasions," Evie said. "Unfortunately."

"What are you going to do with him?" Dunning asked, pointing at Turnbull.

"Not much we can do," Evie said.

"I say we charge him and—" Burns began, but Dunning cut him off.

"Where would he be put on trial, Agent Burns?" Dunning shook his head. "The amount of information he knows and could reveal would never be acceptable." He held out his hand. "Colonel. Thank you."

Ducharme shook it.

Dunning then shook hands with Burns and Evie.

"You need anything, don't hesitate to ask," he said as he left.

Pegram had yet to say a word. She reached in a pocket and extended a business card to Evie. "My direct line."

"Thank you."

And then they were gone.

"I guess that's your friend in high places," Burns said. "What's an A-3?"

"Operations," Ducharme said. "She runs operations for the entire Air Force. Dunning is Army Chief of Staff. I'd say they're your friends now, too."

"Yeah, if I worked at the Pentagon," Burns said.

"What about—" Ducharme began, but was interrupted by a cell phone vibrating on the table behind him. They all turned and stared. A clear plastic evidence bag was moving, shaken by the phone inside.

Ducharme got up and grabbed the bag.

"That's breaking the chain of custody," Burns noted without much emphasis or concern.

"You all just said he's going to be free soon anyway." Ducharme pulled the phone out and looked at the screen. "A text message for our friend in the other room."

"What's it say?"

"The phone is locked," Ducharme replied. "But it's flashing Priority One on the screen, so I'd say it's important."

"Probably informing him Lucius is dead," Burns said. "I already gave him the happy news."

"Maybe," Ducharme said. "But I didn't leave anyone alive back there." He headed for the door. "Maybe this will get our friend's attention."

The three of them entered the interrogation room. Turnbull didn't acknowledge them with even a glance.

Ducharme slid the phone across the table. "Priority one text."

Turnbull didn't blink but his eyes shifted toward the phone, a break that signified much to Ducharme, Evie and Burns.

Burns spoke up. "You already know the bad news about your buddy Lucius."

"I took him down like a dog," Ducharme said. "And Evie here, took out your little bitch with the big sword. Using a little knife."

Turnbull finally broke his silence. "No need to descend to the gutter, Colonel Ducharme."

"Got you to talk, didn't it?" Ducharme said.

"I'm an assistant director of the FBI," Turnbull said. "I've been quite patient with you, but I've committed no crime."

"You used the Surgeon, Lilly, to commit your crimes," Burns said. "Multiple murders."

"You have no proof."

"You told me."

"My word against yours," Turnbull said.

"What are we, in kindergarten?" Evie said.

"Turnbull isn't even your real name," Burns said. "You are Lieutenant Colonel Thomas Blake. Naval Academy, class of '62. Commissioned in the Marines. Two tours in Vietnam, winning the Navy Cross. You-"

"You don't win an award for valor," Turnbull interrupted. "You earn it. Isn't that right, Colonel Ducharme?"

Burns pressed on. "You were assigned to the National Security Council in 1969. Where, apparently, you were involved in illegal operations including arms and drug smuggling. You were even indicted, but the original charges couldn't stick."

"They won't ever stick," Turnbull said. "Either old ones or new ones."

"You retired from the military in 1976," Burns continued. "Still facing other indictments. But then the small plane you were supposedly piloting supposedly crashed off the coast of Florida. No survivors. No body was ever found. Then Agent Turnbull suddenly appears in 1977 in the FBI. Yet there's no record of you having ever gone through the Academy at Quantico."

Turnbull gave a chilly smile. "A nice story. Maybe tell it to your children to put them to sleep at night. Ah, that's right. You don't have any. Too dedicated to the job. I've been in this city a lot longer than you, Agent Burns." He glanced down at his watch. "I suspect someone is coming down from the top floor to arrange my release any moment."

"Likely," Burns agreed. "But you're my prisoner right now."

Turnbull shifted his gaze. "You and I," Turnbull said, pointing at Ducharme with a finger raised from his chained hand, "we're not any different. We do the dirty work. The wet work as they used to say."

"We're not the same," Ducharme said. "You use others to do your dirty work."

"You never commanded soldiers in combat?" Burns asked. "People laughed at that Jack Nicholson character in *A Few Good Men*, but they shouldn't have. They should have listened to what he was saying. Someone has to stand on the walls. A lot of people look down on it, but a lot of people aren't willing to get their hands dirty."

"So the rich can get richer?" Ducharme asked. "Isn't that what your Society is all about?"

"Hardly," Turnbull said. "The Jefferson Allegiance is just the beginning. Checks and balances, Colonel Ducharme. It's always been about checks and balances. And more than just here in the United States. Checks and balances across the globe. How do you think civilization has managed to last this long?" He raised his hands to the extent of the cuffs. "Do you want me to unlock the phone and read the message? Then release me first."

Ducharme pulled out his MK23 Special Operations pistol. He smiled at Turnbull. "My finger is the safety."

Burns walked around the table and unlocked the cuffs, stepping back quickly, making sure he never crossed Ducharme's line of fire. Turnbull picked up the phone and his stubby fingers, knuckles gnarled with arthritis from years of boxing, pecked at the face of it.

"Hmm," he finally said, putting the phone back down. He leaned back in his chair, his eyes closed. "There is indeed a problem superseding our present situation."

"Whose problem?" Evie asked.

Turnbull's eyes opened. "Everyone on the face the planet, unfortunately."

24 March 1943

Less than two months earlier, General Paulus had surrendered his 6th Army at Stalingrad after five months and ten days of fighting, the likes of which mankind has rarely seen; one of the bloodiest sieges ever with over one million casualties. For those close to Stalin, they knew that this hard-won victory was the turning point. The Germans had given up the initiative and would never regain it because their losses could not recouped.

For the Soviets, the vast Motherland could bring forth from her bosom an almost endless supply of men to be chewed up in battle. And Khrushchev knew that was exactly the way Stalin saw it playing out. A war of attrition that would only end with Soviet soldiers in Berlin, and Hitler in chains.

But as he entered Stalin's private quarters, it was not Hitler who stood in front of Stalin's desk in chains, but an aviator, an Air Force Officer, one whom Khrushchev could recognize even though the man was facing Stalin.

"Comrade," Stalin called out, seeing Khrushchev enter. He was flanked by several Cossacks: fierce soldiers who had sworn a blood oath to the Premier.

Khrushchev said nothing. He forced down his instinct to run to the prisoner and wrap his arms around his son, who'd been reported killed in action on the 11th his fighter shot down. Khrushchev walked up next to Leonid, who kept his gaze fixed to a point above Stalin, his eyes unfocused. His face was bloody and Khrushchev recognized the work of the savages in the cellars deep under the Kremlin.

"Premier," Khrushchev said with a nod of his head.

Stalin smiled and Khrushchev's heart dropped. He'd seen this smile many times before. "Ah, Comrade, this is a moment of both good news and bad news. As most news is. Your son, who we feared dead, is not. That is the good news."

Khrushchev remained silent.

"Unfortunately, he wasn't shot down. That is the bad news."

Leonid stirred, as if to protest that statement, but he'd learned well at Khrushchev's knee and remained silent.

"His wingman said he saw the plane on fire, Premier." Khrushchev said.

"Then why is he standing here alive?" Stalin asked, as if that solved the entire riddle. "He deserted. Betrayed the Motherland. Flew his plane to a German airfield and surrendered to save his own hide. He was taken when our victorious forces over-ran the column in which he was riding, not chained as a prisoner, but seated with German soldiers as one of them."

Leonid finally spoke. "Premier, with all due respect, I was shot down and taken prisoner. I was in cuffs when—"

"Did I ask you to speak?" Stalin said in a voice that chilled the room, as icy as that which blew across the Siberian tundra.

"Premier," Khrushchev said, jumping into the breech. "Leonid has been awarded the Order of the Red Banner for his bravery. He has never faltered in combat. He volunteered to fight in 1939 when he could have stayed safe at the Academy. He had been on the front lines ever since. He had proven his loyalty to the Motherland countless times by risking his life."

Stalin shrugged, shedding years of bravery like a summer squall. "One can be brave and still be a traitor." He glanced down at a piece of paper on his desk. "Leonid Nikitovich Khrushchev." He said the family name with particular emphasis and Khrushchev knew exactly what game the old man was playing. He'd seen it before; just never directed at him. "You have been sentenced to death by order of the Supreme Soviet for treason against the state. Sentence to be carried out immediately."

Khrushchev dared to rush around the desk. Two of the Cossacks made to stop him, but Stalin waved them off.

"Premier Stalin." Khrushchev fell to his knees and lowered his face. "I beg you to spare my son. Place him in prison. He is more effective to your purposes alive than dead."

"You dare presume you know what my purposes are?" Stalin hissed. "Insolent." He leaned forward in his seat, his mouth just above Khrushchev's head, whispering so only he

could hear. "You have two options: move away and prove your loyalty to the Motherland; or take your son's fate with him as a traitor as well."

Khrushchev remained on his knees for several long seconds. Then he stood. He walked back around the desk and hugged his son. "I am sorry, Leonid."

"I should have died when my plane was shot down," his son said. "I had some extra days of life. Look at it that way, Father."

There wasn't a chance for any more words as two Cossacks stepped up on either side of Khrushchev's son, grabbed his arms and led him toward a door on the right side of the office. A balcony was beyond that door.

They left the door open so Khrushchev could watch helplessly as they forced Leonid to his knees. One pulled a pistol, aimed it less than an inch from the side of Leonid's head, and pulled the trigger, all without the slightest hesitation.

A puff of red blew out the other side and the body slumped to the ground. The other Cossack swung the door shut.

Khrushchev turned to face the Premier.

"Do you have anything to say, Comrade?" Stalin asked, picking up a file folder and opening it. He glanced up over the folder at Khrushchev, one bushy eyebrow raised, awaiting his answer.

"No, Premier."

"Good. You may go."

25 February 1956

Premier Nikita Khrushchev looked out over the anxious faces of the members of the Twentieth Party Congress of the Communist Party of the Soviet Union and repressed the desire to smile.

It was not fitting for the message he was about to deliver. But it was what he felt. Revenge was indeed a powerful elixir.

The members were anxious because this was a closed session. The doors were sealed, armed guards standing ominously just inside them, men who were loyal to Khrushchev first, the country second.

He had learned well from Stalin.

He knew some feared a purge. It was not unheard of for some to be dragged out of such a meeting and summarily shot. Khrushchev had considered that and even made a list. But he'd come up with something much better. He glanced to his right and noted that Mikoyan was also scanning the faces, perhaps looking for allies? Or enemies? Who knew with the old bastard? But Khrushchev knew he could count on one thing with Mikoyan: he would act in his own self-interests, and that made him usable.

Khrushchev began: "Comrades, in the report of the Central Committee of the Party at the Twentieth Congress, in a number of speeches by delegates to the Congress, quite a lot has been said about the cult of the individual and about its harmful consequences."

He then proceeded to lay his base of reasoning using Lenin, quoting extensively from him. He moved to the transition point: "During Lenin's life in the Central Committee of the Party was a real expression of collective leadership of the Party and of the Nation. Being a militant Marxist-Revolutionist, always unyielding in matters of principle, Lenin never forcefully imposed his views upon his co-workers."

That, of course, Khrushchev knew was a lie. But it was what Lenin had spouted, and that was the point of this speech. Whose spouts should be believed?

"Lenin said: 'Stalin is excessively rude, and this defect, which can be freely tolerated in our midst and in contacts among us Communists, becomes a defect which cannot be tolerated in one holding the position of Secretary General. Because of this, I propose that the comrades consider the method by which Stalin would be removed from this position and by which another man would be selected for it, who above all, would differ from Stalin in only one quality, namely greater tolerance, greater loyalty, greater kindness, and more considerate attitude toward the comrades, a less capricious temper, etc.'."

As he finished that quote from one long dead man, about another only three years dead, it occurred to Khrushchev that it was a list of more than quality. Then again, Lenin had been very good at oration, not so much at math.

Khrushchev then launched full blown into his denunciation of the former Premier, and with every sentence he could feel the tremors of fear and confusion pass through the chamber. Stalin was considered a god amongst the Soviets, if they allowed gods. Using specific examples, he tore apart the myths about Stalin, exposing the raging beast he'd been.

He did not mention the execution of his own son.

Halfway through the speech, an older man, one who was a staunch Stalinist, shot to his feet, clutching his chest. He squeaked something, then collapsed.

No one moved to help him.

Khrushchev didn't pause, hammering home his points.

The Cult of Stalin was over. The future was going to be different.

CHAPTER THREE
The Present

"Today's Daily Reflection," Aaron said, expertly opening the well-worn leather book to the marked page with one hand, since one hand was all he had. His left arm was missing halfway down the humerus, the sleeve of his black pullover pinned up to the shoulder. *"'Since recovery from man's insanity is life itself to us, it is imperative that we preserve in full strength our means of survival'."*

There was a minute of silence, as there was every day, as each member of the Peacekeepers reflected on the message. A minute doesn't sound long, until one does nothing for a minute but think. Which is the point of reflection.

They were gathered in a dimly lit room with concrete walls. Behind Aaron was an old armchair. The others in the room were seated in folding chairs. Aaron was in his eighties, his skull hairless and his skin ghostly white, as if it never saw the sun. Which it didn't.

Aaron hadn't been to the surface in over thirty years.

It wasn't quiet underground. It never was. Millions of New Yorkers walked the streets above and worked in the skyscrapers, completely unaware that there was complex maze beneath their feet that kept the city functioning. They knew of the subways, of course. It was the lifeline of the city, where owning a car in Manhattan was as expensive as owning a second apartment.

It's a three dimensional maze of sewers, subways, five different rail lines, water and sewage, power, cable, steam, access tunnels, abandoned tunnels, caverns; so much and so many, at depths from just below the sidewalk to hundreds of feet into the bedrock on which Manhattan rested, that no one knows all of it. There is no single map that details it all. And that played into the Peacekeepers' agenda. They could remain hidden underneath one of the most crowded places on the planet. The tunnels extended in all directions, many going beyond the city boundaries. The main water line for New York goes 125 miles north into the Catskills and sinks over a thousand feet below the surface to pass underneath the Hudson River near West Point, sixty miles upriver.

There were many places and tunnels that were abandoned, their usage getting outdated, or a project never finished. The Peacekeepers occupied one of those places. But again, even here, deep under the surface, the rumble of the City That Never Sleeps penetrated, a cacophony of sounds that melded together into a muted symphony of industry and advancement.

Aaron closed the leather bound book and walked over to a glass case. He opened it and reverently placed the book inside, underneath a shelf holding another book, a first edition copy of *Fail Safe* by Eugene Burdick (who'd also co-written *The Ugly American*) and Harvey Wheeler. The cover was red with black circles coalescing into a single dot. The book was well worn, every Peacemaker having to read it once they took their oath.

Aaron closed the case and turned back to those assembled. A slight smile crossed Aaron's face as he broke the silence. "Are there any birthdays today?"

Everyone turned to the youngest member of the group, a girl at the end of her teens and about to enter her second decade. "Six months," she said.

"Six months a Peacekeeper," Aaron said. "Congratulations, Zarah."

Everyone applauded politely while Aaron held up a bronze coin. He tossed it and Zarah adroitly caught it. She tucked the coin into her pants pocket.

"You are still in probation," Aaron said. He reached into his own pocket and pulled out a silver coin. "It will take you another four and a half years to earn the Peace Dollar a full Peacekeeper carries." He held it up and the silver glistened.

It is one of the rarest coins ever minted. In fact, few knew that this original version had ever been struck, because the design had been changed prior to wider release of the coin most people knew at the Peace Dollar in 1922. The original design had Lady Liberty with the words *Liberty* across the top and *In God We Trust* along the lower middle and the year on the bottom. The reverse side was where this coin was unique: the original design had a bald eagle at rest clutching an olive branch and a broken sword with the words *United States of America* across the top, with *E Pluribus Unum* below that, and *PEACE* inscribed on the eagle's perch. It was the broken sword that had caused a great outcry when the design for the coin was made public. Many Americans saw such a symbol as indicating defeat and demanded it be removed.

It was, but not before fifty of the original design were pressed at the Philadelphia Mint. The Philosophers took control of that limited run. The broken sword was removed and the olive branch extended to cover its spot for all the rest of the Peace Dollars. Each Peacekeeper who made it through the initial five-year probationary period received one of the original coins with the broken sword, which would be worth a fortune to any coin collector.

None had ever made their way into the hands of a coin collector.

All the Peacekeepers were dressed alike: jeans, black turtlenecks, grey jackets. Unremarkable clothing, which was the point.

They ranged in age from the girl who'd just received her coin to Aaron, who was now eighty-two. His coin was so worn, the details were almost impossible to make out. He'd received it along with two others in the very first group that had gathered in this space underneath southern Manhattan.

"Let us bond in the circle of trust and commitment unto death," Aaron said, extending his arm straight ahead, his coin inside his fist. The twenty-three other Peacekeepers (four were on duty; four were always on duty, and they were also recently short one) formed a circle and gripped hands, those on either side of Aaron taking his fist in their own hands. They spoke in unison, a ritual decades in the ingraining for many of them. "We keep the Peace. We accept what we can do and what we can't. But the Peace comes before all else. Survival of man supersedes all else."

There was a pause, then all repeated. "All else."

The hands fell apart and they began to head to the door, but Aaron's voice stopped three of them. "Zarah and Caleb and Baths. A word, please."

The rest went off to do their duties. For four, it meant replacing the four on duty. Others went to train. Others had various duties related to the upkeep of the Fortress, the underground facility they called their home. And a select few would go to the surface, to continue the arduous task of finding those select few who could be recruited into the ranks of the Peacekeepers, since they needed at least one more to fill their ranks right now. Because of the need for absolute secrecy and absolute lifetime devotion to the group, their success rate made LDS recruiters look like rock stars.

They needed that number, because of the normal number of twenty-four, only three knew the truth of how they kept the peace. Which was why he had Caleb and Baths remained behind to do what needed to be done now with Zarah.

Aaron took two steps back and sat down in the armchair. It was worn and tattered. Holes were covered with duct tape. If someone stumbled across this room, they would think a squatter lived here. But one would not stumble across the Fortress without numerous motion detectors and infrared cameras picking them up well before they got close. Baths, a woman in her late seventies, with hair as white as her skin, stood by the side of the chair watching all through her thick granny glasses. Her designated name in the Peacekeepers was Bathsheba, but that was a mouthful, so by universal acceptance it had shrunk to its current form.

Aaron tilted his head and smiled as he heard the familiar rattle of the Number 6 subway rolling around the City Hall Loop close by. The station had opened in 1904 but was closed in 1945 because the station was too short to service the longer trains of that time and the Brooklyn Bridge Station picked up the slack. But the track through the station was still used as the Number 6 Train turned around on it to head back north.

"Zarah, my dear Zarah," Aaron said with a smile. "How have you felt about your time with us?"

"It is my mission, it is my life, it is my duty to keep the Peace," she dutifully replied.

But Aaron noted the way her eyes shifted ever so slightly up and to the right, even as Caleb silently moved to a position directly behind her. He was a large man, towering over the slight, young girl. His skull was completely shaved; even his eyebrows were gone, giving his head the appearance of a pale egg set atop a bulky body.

"Yes, but how do you really feel?" Aaron asked. "Do you have doubts about your vocation?"

"No, sir."

"You know our rules are absolute." It was not a question. "Did Jonah confide in you?"

She shifted her feet. "Jonah—" she didn't say more than the name.

"Yes?"

"Jonah just said he'd found something in the computer."

"What?"

She shook her head. "I don't know, sir."

"You're lying."

"He said he'd found the location of the Ark." She licked her lips nervously. "Somewhere near Mount Ararat."

"Why didn't you report this to me?"

"I thought he was just talking. The way he does. Rambling. You know Jonah."

"Apparently, I didn't," Aaron said. "Did he explain what he meant when he said Ark?"

Zarah blinked, confused by the question. "I assumed he meant Noah's Ark. Jonah has always been fascinated by that story."

"You assumed wrong," Aaron said.

Zarah scrambled, trying to find words that would sate Aaron. "He mentioned something about some sword."

Aaron rubbed his other sleeve, where he'd lost the arm many years ago, real pain fired above where real nerves no longer were. It was something he did when agitated, a movement that Caleb took note of.

"Did he say what the sword was?"

"No, sir. Really, sir, I just thought it was Jonah being Jonah. He's been like that since I've been here." She tried to smile. "Perhaps Excalibur? Jonah is into all those myths and legends."

"Don't toy with me, girl."

Zarah swallowed hard. "I'm sorry, sir. He mentioned someone named Koransky or something like that."

"Penkovsky," Aaron automatically corrected her.

"Yes. That was it."

"But then he disappeared. He broke his vows."

Zarah hung her head.

"You knew your old life was gone when you took your vows six months ago."

Zarah couldn't meet his eyes.

"You didn't report your conversations with Jonah."

"I'm sorry, sir. I thought he was just talking. It wasn't until he disappeared that I realized there was more to it than just talk."

"But even then you didn't report what he'd said to you."

"I didn't think it was important."

"That's not for you to judge."

"I'm sorry, sir."

"We don't accept 'sorry' in the Peacekeepers. 'Sorry' means a mistake has already been made."

"I'll do better in the future. I promise."

Baths finally spoke. "And then you tried to call your parents."

Zarah looked up in surprise at the sudden shift in direction and speaker. Tears began to form in her eyes. "I just wanted to say goodbye."

"You said goodbye to them when they were informed of your tragic death with your body never recovered," Baths said. "We went to a considerable amount of trouble to make you disappear. That phone call would have undone all of it. It would have made people ask questions. Questions that could bring attention to us. Tell me, Zarah. Do you truly believe we keep the peace?"

"Yes, ma'am."

"But you don't know how we do that exactly, do you?" Baths asked.

Zarah's eyes shifted over to the glass case holding the book of sayings and *Fail Safe*. "We keep the scale in balance."

The answer didn't satisfy Baths. "But you don't know what is on the arms of the scale."

"No, ma'am. I was told it was not for me to know. It was for me to believe. That some day, if I proved worthy, I would know. That I must have faith."

"And that's enough for you?" Baths asked.

Zarah met her eyes. "There has not been a nuclear weapon used since the end of the Second World War. The Peacekeepers date from the Cuban Missile Crisis when the world came closest to being destroyed. We have never been that close again. So it must work."

Aaron spoke. "It does. That is why our rules are sacrosanct."

"I'm sorry, sir," Zarah said. "It won't happen again."

"Exactly," Aaron said.

As Aaron said that, Caleb looped a wire survival saw over her head. As he pulled it tight he twisted his body, which crossed the wire and put his back to hers. He leaned forward, lifting her entire body off the ground—it wasn't much as she was a slender girl—and suspended by the wire cutting into her neck.

She might have been slight, but the wire was sharp and it sliced through skin, muscle and then both carotid arteries.

She bled out faster than she would have choked to death. An almost merciful death if there is such a thing.

The downside of this effective technique was that Caleb was drenched in her blood as he went to one knee, then rolled Zarah's body off his back. With more difficulty than it had gone in, he extracted the wire from her neck, which was half-severed. He reached into her pocket and removed the bronze coin.

He stood up, blood dripping off him. He wiped the saw off on his shirt and put it back inside a pocket.

"Any further word on Jonah?" Aaron asked.

"Negative," Caleb said. He looked at the bronze coin, made sure there was no blood on it, before tossing it back to Aaron. "We know he made it to Iraq. I assume from there he proceeded on the ground into Turkey."

Aaron sighed. "There is such a fine line between indoctrination and fanaticism."

Caleb glanced down at the body. "There's a fine line the other way, too. I would lean toward fanaticism being better than any doubt."

"That will be a decision you're going to be making soon," Aaron said.

"You have many years left to serve," Caleb said. "And Baths is next in line," he added with a nod toward the old woman.

"She is," Aaron said. He was still seated, having watched the execution with no reaction. Baths had shown a moment of distaste, for she disliked Caleb's methods, but she was also a pragmatist and accepted that they worked.

"I thought Jonah's religious focus would work well," Baths said.

"It did for eight years," Caleb said.

Aaron looked as though he'd aged in the last forty-eight hours. "Admiral Groves is dead. So is his replacement, O'Callaghan. Both killed by the Cincinnatians."

Caleb stepped over the body, closer to Aaron and Baths. "We're cut off, then. Jonah had been in contact with Groves. Could he have learned of the Admiral's death?"

"It's likely," Aaron said. "Jonah wasn't a religious fanatic like most thought. He was obsessed with Penkovsky. Maybe he thinks going to Turkey will change things."

"Should we send someone to Washington?" Caleb asked.

Aaron considered that, then looked at Baths. "What do you think?"

"I wasn't scheduled to do a coordination for two weeks," she said. "But given that Jonah and Zarah have disappeared, the others would understand if we deviate from our schedule."

Aaron nodded. "I think we need you in position in DC."

"I'll leave in a few hours," Baths said.

"And Philadelphia?" Caleb asked. "Should we see what's happening there?"

Aaron shook his head. "The Philosophers will reconstitute. They'll reach out to us."

"And meanwhile?"

"Only the oldest get to go topside," Aaron said. "We can't take any more chances. Our enemies are getting closer than they've been in a very long time."

"I can still send operatives after Jonah," Caleb said.

"It's too late," Aaron said. "And we're short two now. And any acolyte would have to be vetted extensively. We must focus on our primary mission."

Caleb remained silent, signaling his agreement.

Aaron stared off into the distance, lost in thought. "Perhaps it is all as it should be. We must let fate play out its hand now."

Caleb was surprised. "We control fate. We always have. We've kept the peace."

Aaron regained his focus. "Yes. Yes. We have. I'm sorry. Sometimes my old age makes me tired." He stood up. "But we must be prepared. If Jonah talks and gives up what he knows, there will be repercussions."

"Should we let the others know?" Caleb asked.

"No need to alarm them unnecessarily," Aaron said. "Jonah was unstable. It's more than likely he'll end up in a Turkish prison or worse."

"Agreed." But this time Caleb didn't stay silent. "If Jonah was talking about Penkovsky, who knows what he's up to? And if the Cincinnatians struck out against the Philosophers, they'll be coming for us."

"They'll always be coming," Aaron said. "But we keep the peace."

"We keep the peace," Baths echoed.

Aaron checked his watch. "Shift has changed. I'm going to check on things."

He walked out of the room, an old wooden door swinging shut behind him.

Baths looked down at the body. "A shame."

"A necessity," Caleb said.

"You are third," Baths said. "When you take command, I won't have to worry about it."

"No," Caleb assured her, "you won't."

"I need to prepare to leave."

"Safe journey," Caleb said.

Baths left, leaving Caleb alone with the corpse. Slowly he stripped off his blood-soaked clothes, tossing them on top of her, until he was completely naked. His body, like his head, was hairless. The shaving was a ritual he did every other day. He was muscular and defined, a result of an intensive workout regime. A former Marine, he was versed in martial arts and an expert with weapons. He had his own firing range alongside one of the abandoned tunnels, where the Peacekepers could fire unheard and unnoticed as a train rattled by a few feet away.

He went to a shelf and took a headlamp off a peg next to it, looped it over his skull and turned it on. He grabbed a pair of surgical gloves from a box and pulled them on.

He picked Zarah up and easily tossed her over his shoulder. He went to a corner of the room. There was another old wooden door, which he pulled open. The door was be old, dating back to when this place was first built at the beginning of the 20th century, but the hinges were well oiled and made no noise.

He entered the darkness. Naked but for the lamp, mask and gloves, he stepped into the tunnel, shutting the door behind him. He began walking, a route he'd done too many times. Unlike those who might notch their gun or their knife handle, Caleb kept no record of his kills. It was as much a part of his job as shaving, something to be done, but not noted.

Like a cunning rat at home in a maze he wove his way almost a quarter of a mile underneath Manhattan until he came to his destination. The roar of powerful engines thrummed through the concrete all around him. He put the body down. He hung the headlamp on a pipe so it lit up a rusty door. He opened the door.

He picked Zarah back up and put her over his shoulder. The space he was entering reeked of raw sewage. He walked across the freezing concrete floor in his bare feet until he came up to an eight-foot wide river of sewage running in a culvert eight feet deep. Without ceremony, he tossed Zarah in the thick, dark sludge. He waited, making sure she was going with the slow flow to the left.

Where powerful blades, as wide and deep as the culvert, were spinning at a steady pace, cutting apart anything larger than two inches that came in with the sewage. He watched the body reach the fans and be torn apart, disappearing to the other side in pieces so small they would easily be further rendered in the treatment plant at the end of the river of sewage.

Caleb headed back the way he'd come, except for a slight detour, a spot where a crack in a water main spilled a steady stream of fresh water. He stood underneath ice-cold water, washing off the blood, dirt and sewage.

He felt purified when he was clean.

*****

As Caleb performed his routine, Aaron walked down another corridor as he had every day for half a century. Fourteen paces. Then he turned left. He reached up and placed his right hand on a flat screen to the right side of a steel door.

That had not been part of security when this place was built in 1904.

There was a beep, the screen flashed green and then an optical scanner swung down from the ceiling, stopping four feet above the ground. Aaron leaned over and placed his face against it.

Throughout all this, he ignored the man standing in the shadows ten feet to the right, automatic rifle aimed at him, even though the guard had just left the meeting Aaron had presided over. The man's finger was on the trigger and the weapon was off safe.

That weapon was never placed on safe until it was turned back in to the arms room for servicing.

Aaron's eyes were scanned, he was now double confirmed, and the door rumbled open to the side. Aaron stepped inside, ignoring the second guard in a bulletproof booth to the right. The woman's hand was on a dead man's switch, keeping it depressed. If the woman let go of that switch the room would be flooded with poisonous gas. She would keep her hand on that button for her entire four-hour shift. A bank of screens surrounded her, linked to a camera set for night vision, covering all approaches to the Fortress.

Another steel door was beyond, and even Aaron could not pass through that door unless it was scheduled for inspection. Or they were called to action.

Two more guards were on the other side.

All was as it should be.

"We keep the Peace," Aaron whispered, as reverently as any priest in front of the cross.

21 April 1961
Four Days after the Bay of Pigs failed invasion of Cuba

President John F. Kennedy News Conference

"Gentlemen, I have several announcements to make," Kennedy said. "I know that many of you have further questions about Cuba. I made a statement on that subject yesterday afternoon. We are continuing consultations with other American republics. Active efforts are being made by ourselves and others on behalf of various individuals, including any Americans who may be in danger. I do not think that any useful national purpose would be served by my going into the Cuban question this morning. I prefer to let my statement of yesterday suffice for the present.

"I am pleased to announce that the United States has offered concrete support to a broad scale attack by the United Nation upon world hunger. I have . . ."

Mary Meyer watched her friend, the President, labor through his 10th news conference, trying to cover topics no one had any interest in this morning. Broadcast live, it was being followed by many.

"They're going to eat him alive," Timothy Leary remarked from the armchair where he was smoking a joint. Meyer ignored him. Leary was passing through town and she was letting him stay the night. This week she wasn't in the mood for his drugs or his observations given what was happening in DC since the failed invasion of Cuba.

Meyer had known the President since his Senate days in 1954 when he and Jackie bought a house nearby in Georgetown. With the death of her middle son in '56, and her divorce from ex-CIA agent Cord Meyer in '58, Meyer's life had been a rollercoaster; one she didn't see smoothing out any time soon. Not that she had any particular desire to. She was having a good time and enjoyed being in the swirl of Washington intrigue and politics.

Most of the time.

"Asshole," she muttered as a reporter ignored the President's request:

"Mister President, this is not a question about Cuba, it's a question about Castro."

The rest of the reporters in the room laughed and Kennedy twitched out a smile.

Leary laughed, too. *"He's not going to escape."*

Kennedy blew off the direction of the query and redirected it to the Saturn space program. He kept trying to avoid the elephant in the room and the reporters kept shining a spotlight on it.

Finally Kennedy squared up his shoulders as another question, never mentioning Cuba or Castro, still was directed at the Bay of Pigs.

"Well, I think in answer to your question that I have to make a judgment as to how much we can usefully say that would aid the interest of the United States," Kennedy said. *"One of the problems of a free society, a problem not met by a dictatorship, is this problem of information. A good deal has been printed in the paper.*

"There's an old saying that victory has a hundred fathers and defeat is an orphan." Kennedy spoke a little longer, then he took on the burden of his office. *"I am the responsible officer of the government."*

"Ballsy," Leary granted. "They can't pile on when you've already thrown yourself under the bus."

"Oh, they can do much worse," Meyer muttered. "Much, much worse. You don't know this town, Tim."

"By the time of the next election no one will even remember," Leary said.

Meyer shook her head at both his comment and as a new question drove the conference to other topics, including a country called Vietnam, which practically no one had ever heard of. Meyer walked over and turned the volume down.

"Of course, they might impeach him," Leary said, rolling another joint on her coffee table, trying, as he usually did, to see the other side, thus not taking a stand at all. A technique Meyer saw through, but was always amazed her old friend didn't understand about himself.

"They won't," Meyer said.

Leary looked up. "How do you know? You act like you know everything."

"I know."

"Ah, the old girl, or should I say young girl network. Who have you been chummy with?"

"I was married to a high ranking CIA officer," Meyer hedged, knowing there were things she could never tell such an unreliable person as Leary. "DC is a complex town. The people who really pull the strings stay out of the limelight." She shook her head. "The President was misled. Mostly by the CIA, but also the military. Bad advice. For him. Good advice for others."

"Are you giving him good advice?" Leary asked, an emphasis on the last word.

"You can leave now," Meyer said, her tone icy.

Leary paused with the joint halfway to his lips. Despite his blind spots, he was enough of a psychologist to understand the finality of a request. He put the roach in his coat pocket, stood up, grabbed his bag and went to the door. "If you'd call me a cab, I'll wait outside. Until we meet again, my dear." And then he was gone.

Mary Meyer turned her attention back to the television. "You need help, Jack," she whispered.

Then she went to the phone.

But not to call a cab for Leary.

*****

"This is getting out of control, Jim," Meyer said as they walked along the Chesapeake and Ohio Canal towpath. It was spring and the trees were budding out and the land was full of new life.

The man walking next to her, James Jesus Angleton, saw enemies everywhere, and he might well be right. Even if one didn't have enemies, being paranoid and having power was sure to produce some. As one of the founding members of the Central Intelligence Agency and having served in its predecessor, the Office of Strategic Services during World War II, he'd seen first hand the results of double and triple agents plying their trade. He'd also seen just plain stupidity at work. His official title was so long people just used the initials: ADDOCI. Assistant Deputy Director of Operations for Counterintelligence.

It meant he spied on spies…and a lot more.

"How are the children?" Angleton asked, as if her comment was like one of the old leaves left over from the previous fall being stirred about on the ground by the slight breeze. Of little consequence and certainly not worthy of being noticed.

But Meyer knew Angleton well and that his mind worked nonlinear and in compartments: one part focused on a problem deep inside while another dealt with the outside world. Her best friend from Vassar, Cicely d'Autermont, had married Angleton during World War II, and when they were stationed here in the DC area, the families grew tight. Unlike many friends from before divorce, Meyer wasn't isolated by Angleton after it, even though her ex was a comrade of his in the CIA. If anything, Angleton spent more time with her, coming on weekends to take the boys on outings.

They'd been intimate. Once. But Meyer had been with enough men to know such a thing didn't sit well with Angleton. It had almost felt like she was being auditioned for some role that had no label. She didn't feel slighted by the lack of a repeat performance. Also, she understood the strain his marriage with Cicely was under due to his long work hours, and she had no desire to add gasoline to a potential conflagration. But Meyer had also learned something since getting divorced and making the circuit among the powerful men of Washington: being intimate with them gave her a window into them that others didn't share. She'd had a glimpse into Angleton's inner world and she knew he would never allow that to happen again.

There were many other men of power in the area she could bed when she desired, whether for carnal or often more enjoyable, informational reasons. And, in a way, she and Angleton had an even more intimate relationship due to their mutual appreciation of literature and poetry.

"They're fine," Meyer replied.

"I'd like to take them for a ride on Saturday, if that's all right with you?"

"Certainly."

"Good."

The walked in silence for several more minutes.

"Kennedy is naïve," Angleton finally said. "He sees the world in black and white. There are no truths, Mary. There are half-truths and half-lies, and we must do the best we can to sort them out. Kennedy needs to learn that."

"Was the Bay of Pigs a set-up so Kennedy could take the fall?" Meyer asked.

"Oh, no." Angleton laughed. "Those idiots actually thought they could pull it off. I even asked one of them if he had an escape hatch and he looked at me as if he didn't know what I was talking about. And I'm afraid he was so naïve, he didn't."

"An 'escape hatch?'"

"A plan in case of failure," Angleton explained. "Always plan for failure because it's as likely as success in many cases. They need someone to go to Castro now and say 'you won. What's your price?' To keep things level. But they don't have anyone. They didn't plan for it. So it will get worse with Cuba before it gets better.

"Hell, even old Ike told Kennedy that this failure is going to embolden Castro. Lead him to do something he wouldn't have done before. Khrushchev, and especially the Soviet military high command, now think Kennedy is indecisive. He allowed the Bay of Pigs landing to go, but held back the air and naval support. Like trying to leap over a canyon in two bounds. We've got a report from a well-placed source inside the Soviet intelligence apparatus that they think Kennedy is too young, too inexperienced, and strangely enough, too intelligent. Apparently they view that as a weakness in a leader."

"How can I help Jack?"

Angleton paused and turned to face her. He was a gaunt man, his face sharp, and he wore thick, black-framed glasses. He was known at the Agency for his long hours and for being a brutal taskmaster, making those under him work just as long. But, of course, they could never work just as hard. No one there could. The divorce rate for those in Angleton's division was a running, if dark, joke among the wives. The assignment was a plum one, looked great in the resume for advancement in the ranks of the CIA, but no so great for the family.

"It's 'Jack' now, is it?"

"It's always been Jack. You know that."

"Yes, but he's President now." He peered at her through his thick lenses. "I've called him 'Mister President' ever since he was elected."

"I call him that in public," Meyer protested, "but this is just the two of us, Jim."

"Yes. And what do you call him in private?"

"I haven't seen him alone since the election."

"Why not?"

"I think he's been a bit busy."

"No one is too busy for you," Angleton said.

Meyer crossed her arms across her chest. "You've been."

"No. I'm here. I see you almost every week. I think Jack could use your support, Mary." He reached into his pocket and pulled out a card. "This is his private line in the Oval Office. Give him a call. Get closer to him."

"What's your scheme, Jim? You always have one."

"I'd prefer the President not see things in black and white, and I think you can help him with that. You're the smartest woman I've ever met, but not the most discreet. My not being with you again had to do with that, nothing to do with you. I've got enemies everywhere looking for any way to take me down. A man in my position can never have anything that can be used as leverage against him."

Angleton sighed. "I had nothing to do with the Bay of Pigs. I smelled the stench from the very beginning. Jack has more to worry about than just Cuba, although I have a sense that's going to turn into a huge problem. But old Khrushchev and his generals have their sights set on Berlin. Ever since the Airlift, they've been itching to have another go at it. The cards are stacked differently than they were back in '48. Berlin is a thorn in the Soviet Bloc's side."

"They won't risk a nuclear war over it," Meyer said.

"Probably not," Angleton allowed. *"But in my world, we know the Russians hate the fact that we have a base in their backyard. It would be like them having an outpost in Hawaii. A place where their spies can come and go pretty openly. They're going to do something about it."*

"Jack won't let West Berlin fall."

"Probably not, but he's going to have to give in on something there and it won't be pretty." Angleton shook his head. *"And then Hoover is all over him and his brother. I might be able to help there."*

"Hoover's a pig."

"Absolutely," Angleton agreed. *"More than most people suspect."*

"Is that what you have on him?" Meyer asked. *"What everyone whispers about? Him and that fellow that's always with him."*

"Hoover survives by having more dirt on others than they have on him. Which is a scary thought if you consider what Hoover does in private."

Angleton turned and began walking again. Meyer followed suit.

"When you talk to Jack, suggest he not go to Vienna," Angleton said.

Meyer noted he said 'when,' not 'if.' *"Why?"*

"He's not ready to face Khrushchev. That old man came up with Stalin, who chewed up Roosevelt. Ike didn't do too good with Khrushchev either. You think Jack is ready for someone like that?"

"Jack's tough."

"I know, but—" Angleton hesitated.

"But what?"

"That doctor he sees," Angleton said. *"Jacobson. He's got him on a lot of medication. For his back. Jack can't be thinking straight. He needs to clear his head if he's going to face Khrushchev."*

"All right," Meyer said, thinking of Leary sitting on his couch, rolling a joint. *"I'll talk to him about it. But he can be stubborn."*

They walked a little further in silence. They came to the walkway where they'd entered the path.

Angleton halted. *"So, I'll see you on Saturday? What time would you like me to pick up the boys?"*

"Ten will be fine."

"I'll see you then."

They didn't shake hands nor did they hug. It wasn't Angleton's way.

Meyer nodded and walked up the path, heading toward her car. As soon as she was out of sight a man came up the towpath. He wore a long trench coat and a hat pulled low over his eyes. His hands were stuffed into his pockets.

"Yes?" he asked as he came up to Angleton.

"Put a tap on her phone," Angleton said, staring off in the direction Meyer had gone.

The man nodded.

Angleton turned toward his operative. *"We're in a wilderness, Mister Racca. Do you understand that?"*

Racca knew better than to answer. He'd served with Angleton long enough to know his boss was thinking out loud, something he rarely did. He was giving insight into his thought process and there was a reason for that, one that Racca knew he would have to spend hours trying to unravel. And often couldn't.

A flash of light flickered across Angleton's face, a reflection of the sun off a window in a distant building. "Yes. A wilderness of mirrors. We don't know what the real object is, it's reflected so many times."

"You can break mirrors," Rocca said.

Angleton frowned, a furrow crossing his narrow forehead. "But then you can't track them back to the source."

Rocca knew he'd made a mistake. "True, sir."

"She's important, Mister Rocca. Very important. Your life now is her life. Do you understand?"

"Yes, sir."

CHAPTER FOUR
The Present

"What's the message?" Ducharme asked.

"Have a seat," Turnbull said.

"It's *my* interrogation room," Burns said.

"Turn off the recording devices," Turnbull ordered. "This stays in the room."

"Listen—" Burns began, but Evie put a hand on his forearm.

"Do what he asks," she said. "If he wants us to know the contents of the message, it must indeed affect us."

"It does," Turnbull said. "As I said, it could possibly affect everyone on the planet."

Burns went to the observation room and shut down the cameras and the mikes. Throughout all this Ducharme was silent, but his hand was pressed against the side of his head, an indication of the pain that was spiking through his brain from his injuries. Pain that would always accompany him—sometimes more, sometimes less.

"How's the TBI?" Turnbull asked as Burns came back in the room.

"I managed well enough to shut you down," Ducharme said as he and Evie and Burns took chairs across the table from Turnbull.

Turnbull tapped the side of his head. "Got hit a lot boxing. You have that constant ringing in your ears?"

"We're not friends," Ducharme said. "The message."

"One of our operatives has discovered something in Turkey," Turnbull said. "Some relics from the Cold War that could be rather dangerous in the wrong hands."

"The Jupiter missiles," Evie said. "Where?"

"Whoa," Burns said. "Slow down. The what?"

Ducharme was the only one who didn't seem surprised by her leap in logic after having spent several days with her and listening to her litany of history and arcane facts. Evie Tolliver was a walking font of seemingly useless information until that information was needed. She'd tried to explain it to him. She didn't have a photographic memory, but rather an eidetic one, where she could recall things with great detail by putting them in context. Turnbull had given her three pieces: danger, Cold War relics and Turkey, and she'd lined them up in an instant.

"She's right, isn't she?" Ducharme asked Turnbull.

He nodded. "How did you come up with that?" he asked Evie.

"The warheads," Evie said. "Are they still with the missiles? There's no way they'd work after all these year. The missiles or the warheads. But the plutonium. That's a problem. Is it still with the missiles?"

"Yes, it is," Turnbull said, confirming her guess. "At least some of it."

"I'm still back at Jupiter," Burns said.

"How many warheads?" Evie asked.

"My man just checked radiation levels," Burns said. "The reading was more then sufficient to indicate there were at least several."

"Is the dosage fatal?" Evie asked.

Turnbull shrugged. "Message didn't say, but those warheads were shielded. He got out of there and has taken up a surveillance position."

"I assume we're talking about nuclear weapons?" Burns said.

Ducharme ignored the FBI agent. "Who else knows?"

"No one."

Ducharme got to his feet. "We have to alert the National Command Authority. That material has to be secured. Your operative is all alone?"

"He is now," Turnbull said. "But one of the Kurdish porters from the group he was with escaped."

"Shit," Ducharme said. "The Kurds would love to get their hands on some plutonium."

"Never mind the Kurds," Turnbull said. "The border with Iran isn't that far away."

"Jupiter?" Burns asked plaintively.

"Evie," Ducharme said. "The short version."

Evie rattled the facts off. "Developed in the late '50s, the Jupiter was the first medium-range ballistic missile the United States developed, with a range of about fifteen hundred miles. Thus it wasn't exactly an ICBM. Intercontinental. Those came later. Thus, in order for it to be an effective weapon against the Soviets, it had to be based within range of Moscow for its nuclear warheads to be a valid threat. So we forward deployed two squadrons of fifteen missiles each in Italy and the one squadron in Turkey." She paused and glanced at Turnbull. "Did your man—I assume he's a man unless you have another Surgeon working for you—find all fifteen?"

Turnbull shook his head. "Six. One upright. Five on trailers. Again though, we don't know how many warheads."

"The missiles were supposed to have been cut to pieces and shipped back. The warheads flown back." Evie closed her eyes for a moment, accessing her remarkable memory. "They had megaton warheads. Just over one, I believe. The missiles were emplaced where they could hit Moscow at their maximum range." She opened her eyes. "And their deployment in Turkey, and before that Italy, is a big reason the Russians put their own missiles in Cuba. A little historical footnote few people remember. In essence, one could say we initiated the eventual Cuban Missile Crisis by taking that first step." She looked at Turnbull. "How did your man find them?"

"We received some intelligence," Turnbull said. "We checked it out. Turns out the intelligence was correct."

"Intelligence from where? Who?" Ducharme asked.

Turnbull gave him a deadeye stare. "Let's get real."

"Why should we believe this guy?" Burns asked. "He's a murderer and a liar. He's not even who he pretends to be."

"Let us see the message," Ducharme said.

"No."

"It's a ploy for him to get out of here," Burns insisted.

"I don't need a ploy to get out of here," Turnbull said. "And I assure you, this—" he held up the phone—"is real. Lucius should have gotten it over forty minutes ago. It was forwarded to me because Lucius can't answer his phone thanks to Mister Ducharme. We're wasting time."

"Where in Turkey are they hidden?" Evie asked.

"Near Mount Ararat. A bunker built into one of the foothills."

Evie nodded. "Perfect hiding spot. But near a lot of borders." She suddenly stiffened as something else occurred to her. "The Sword of Damocles."

"The what?" Ducharme asked, but he noted that Turnbull didn't seem surprised at the phrase.

"It was something McBride talked about one time," Evie said. "We were discussing the Cuban Missile Crisis and he mentioned it. I thought he was referring to Kennedy's speech at the UN, where the President used the term to describe the nuclear standoff of the Cold War. At the time I thought it was a throwaway line, but perhaps he was revealing something to me. It's something I need to check on."

"It's a code name," Turnbull said. "The Sword of Damocles."

"Where did you hear it?" Ducharme asked.

"We picked it up," Turnbull said vaguely.

"And it stands for?" Burns asked.

"We didn't know, but now we do now," Turnbull said. "The warheads."

"So you sent someone to check it out and they found it," Ducharme said.

Turnbull shook his large head. "No. We were investigating something else and the term came up. We found out that someone was going to Turkey to investigate this Sword. So we sent our man along."

"Just like that?" Ducharme wasn't buying it. "What, someone walk into Anderson House and say, 'Hey, I'm going to check out the Sword of Damocles just because it occurred to me', and you sent someone with him?"

"Again," Turnbull said, his voice taking on an edge, "don't trivialize me or the situation. Intelligence is an active, ongoing system. You know that. Lots of pieces. It takes time to fit the pieces into a pattern."

"So you poked into something," Ducharme said. "What?"

"Not relevant right now."

"The lack of intelligence in an operation can be fatal," Ducharme said. "You're withholding those pieces that we need for the pattern."

"Let's deal with the immediate problem," Evie suggested.

"All right," Ducharme agreed. "Enough history. We have to notify the National Command Authority about this and they need to get those warheads with their plutonium secured."

"No."

Ducharme blinked at Turnbull's succinct rejection. "This isn't politics. This is weapons grade plutonium sitting there for the grabbing."

Turnbull nodded toward Evie. "What supposedly happened to the Jupiters?"

"They were withdrawn from Turkey as part of the deal Kennedy made with Khrushchev to defuse the Cuban missile crisis."

"Correct," Turnbull said. "Except now we know they weren't. Not all of them. Think about the implications." He leaned forward. "Most people don't even know the public history of the crisis. They think our blockade turned the Russian ships carrying the missiles around. Yeah, the ships carrying *their* medium range missiles, ones that could reach DC, did turn around. But the Russians *already* had R-12 tactical nuclear missiles on the island. And the launch authority had been granted to the Soviet general on the ground, which was unheard of before and since. If we'd have invaded Cuba with ground forces—as the Pentagon was insisting—it would have started a nuclear exchange."

Burns had been listening to this, a spectator up until now. "If all the Jupiters weren't withdrawn, perhaps all the Russian missiles weren't either?"

"Give the man a cigar," Turnbull said. He pointed at Ducharme and Evie and then tapped his chest. "There was some deal brokered between Kennedy and Khrushchev. Supported by your Philosophers. We believe it's this Sword of Damocles thing. We, the Society, have been trying to figure it out for over half a century. Well, we just found one of the pieces. Maybe you need to check your own archives. You probably have a lot more in there about this than we have in ours. All those questions you've been asking me, I think you've already got a lot of the answers.

"This situation is a lot bigger than just those missiles on Ararat. We need to proceed carefully in the big scheme of things or else we could blow the lid off something that could be very, very bad. Both our groups have secrets those of us in this room don't even know about. But one thing I'm sure of is that these are secrets that can never, ever, see the light of day."

Burns slapped the table. "Oh, fuck you people. Fuck you! Fucking secrets. You're gonna get us all killed with your damn secrets." He put his fedora on and stormed out of the room.

The three left behind were at a loss for a moment. Ducharme had his hand against the side of his head, pressing hard, as if pushing in could act against the pain pushing outward. He was tired, the adrenaline rush of the previous evening's combat had long ago worn off, and he could use a shower, a good meal, and a couple days of sleep.

None of that looked to be likely in the immediate future.

"That was effective," Turnbull said dryly. "Now—"

The door opened up and Burns came back in. He carefully took off his hat and placed it on the table. "I apologize for my outburst."

"Perfectly understandable," Evie said.

"Listen," Turnbull said, his low, gravelly voice grabbing everyone's attention. "These secrets. This supposed 'game' we're all playing. It's kept things in balance for centuries. Since World War Two it's kept the world from blowing itself up. It's pretty amazing we haven't. So it might not be perfect, but it's what we've got, so we have to deal with it and work with it."

Evie glanced at Ducharme and took point. "I agree this is very sensitive. But we can't sit still and do nothing about what your man's discovered. We have to get that plutonium secured while we try to figure out what really happened back then."

Turnbull nodded. "My man is on top of the target site. If you allow me, I can get assets moving. But I'll need your help. We need to work together on this."

"Whoa!" Burns said, having apologized but not been placated. "An hour ago we were reading you your rights and charging you with murder."

"Catch up," Turnbull said.

The door to the interrogation room swung open and a tall man everyone immediately recognized filled it, with a cluster of lackeys behind him.

"Tom, everything all right?" the man asked.

Turnbull stood up. "Yes, sir, Senator. Everything's fine. Just discussing some strategy with my colleagues here."

The Senator raked Burns, Evie and Ducharme with a look that indicated what he thought of the colleagues. "I received a call that you'd been mistakenly apprehended over some misunderstanding. I thought you might need my assistance."

"I very much appreciate it, Senator," Turnbull said. "But everything has been worked out. Hasn't it, Agent Burns? Colonel Ducharme? Ms. Tolliver?"

Evie once more took the lead in making peace. "Everything is fine, Senator."

"Well." The Senator looked disappointed that he didn't get to chew up and spit out someone. "I'll go back to the Hill then. Give me a ring if you need anything, Tom. You have my personal line."

"I'll do that, sir."

And just as quickly as he had appeared, he was gone.

"Good timing," Ducharme said. "Except our guy got here first."

"If I'd still been in cuffs," Turnbull said, "things wouldn't have gone well for any of you." He tapped his phone once more. "I'm going to get things moving. I can access guns and the men who use them. People who will never speak about what happens. I'll need a way to get them into Turkey and do the extraction. Our best shot is to go in from Iraq. I can also get in touch with our contacts in the State Department and get us some cover for the operation."

"Mercenaries?" Ducharme asked, the disgust evident in his voice.

"Would you rather use soldiers and start a war?" Turnbull said. "There's plenty of contractors on the ground already there."

"I don't trust them," Ducharme said.

"I don't trust you," Burns added, pointing at Turnbull.

"TriOps?" Ducharme asked, the name of the contractors he'd already run into here in the States working for the Cincinnatians.

"Yes."

"I want to be on the ground with them," Ducharme said. "To keep the balance," he added. "And, frankly, because I don't trust you either. You're holding something back."

"Then you better catch a quick flight," Turnbull said. "It's going to take them several hours to get organized and get moving but they're a lot closer to the target than you are. They won't be waiting on you." He checked his watch. "Night is falling over there. Between getting the team alerted, a plan done, staged, and all the other stuff you know they have to do, the best we can hope for is time on target a couple of hours before dawn. We need to get it done before dawn or else wait through the day. I don't think the Kurds are going to wait that long. And remember, Iran is almost sitting on top of the site."

"The Kurds won't wait," Ducharme agreed.

"To get the packages out," Turnbull said, "my people will need heavy lift." He nodded. "I can arrange that too from assets in country. But only back to

Iraq. Beyond that will take some more planning. Either a civilian contract company or the military."

"Let's get the bombs out of Turkey first," Ducharme said.

"Correction," Evie said. "We don't need the bombs. They're worthless. It's the plutonium that's the key." She closed her eyes for a second. "But if we break the containment on the bombs' integrity, then we have a radiation problem. So we do need the bombs."

"Right," Turnbull said. "Get the bombs. That was the plan."

"I can arrange a fast flight for you, Duke," Evie said, holding up Pegram's card.

Ducharme turned to Evie. "The thumb drive from McBride has more than just the information we read about the Jefferson Allegiance, right? I remember there was one excerpt about Kennedy under the section about the Jefferson Allegiance."

"Yes," Evie said, "but that was well after the Cuban Missile Crisis and basically telling him not to be so aggressive and warning him about Vietnam." She glared at Turnbull. "Which the Cincinnatians were pressuring him to commit more troops and resources into."

"While I'm going to Turkey," Ducharme said, "you try to figure out what the hell happened back during the Crisis and afterwards."

"I will," Evie said.

Ducharme stood up. "Let's get moving people."

Burns didn't move. "You believe him?"

Ducharme sighed. "We can't afford not to."

*****

Haney was seated cross-legged on top of the hangar holding the Jupiter missiles and the warheads. It looked like a natural outcropping in the foothills of Mount Ararat, but since climbing on top, he could see why the site had been chosen. The very faint outline of a road, switching-back precariously disappeared into the wadi they'd come up, ending at the metal doors and airshaft. Whoever had designed this place had taken a natural depression, covered it with metal and then covered the metal with rocks and dirt. The decades since had added to the camouflage. It was only because he knew what was beneath that Haney could even make out that there had once been a road.

It was no longer a usable path for vehicles because either nature or an explosion had caused a massive landslide about two kilometers away, slicing through a ridgeline and creating an impassable crevice for a vehicle. Haney had pretty good fields of observation, able to see to the east and south, the direction from which he expected any Kurds to approach. Ararat was a bulk to the west and north.

Haney had his pistol next to him along with all the spare magazines for it. Four.

Sixty rounds.

This wasn't exactly going to be the Alamo.

He glanced at his phone. He'd yet to receive an acknowledgement of his message from Washington. He was going to give it another thirty minutes and then he would have to blow his cover and contact the CIA. Let them know what he was literally sitting on top of, because this was bigger than even the Society, even though the Society was everything to him.

He breathed a sigh of relief as the phone buzzed. He hit the encryption and a text message appeared:

> ACKNOWLEDGE YOUR SITUATION
> HELP EN ROUTE
> HEAVY LIFT AS PART OF PACKAGE
> TO REMOVE WARHEADS
> GATHER WARHEADS TOGETHER FOR EXTRACTION
> WILL LET YOU KNOW ETA ASAP
> BUT ESTIMATE PRIOR TO DAWN
> PROTECT AT ALL COSTS
> TB

Turnbull, Haney wondered. Why Turnbull and not Lucius?

Gather warheads? *Right.*

He fingered the medallion pinned to his shirt under his coat. It was silver, shaped like an eagle and hung on a tricolor ribbon. On one side, Latin words ringed an engraving on the chest of the eagle. The engraving was of two Roman Senators presenting a sword to another man: Lucius Quincitus Cincinnatus. It represented the Senate asking Cincinnatus, a former Consul of Rome, to come out of retirement and lead the army against invasion. They offered him the role of dictator, which he assumed.

However, it wasn't because of his defeat of the invaders for which history has noted him, but for his actions upon completion of the task given him: he resigned his role as dictator and went back to his farm. This was represented on the other side of the insignia with an image of Cincinnatus back at his plow. Later on, he was once more asked to be dictator to put down a planned rebellion, and once more, after succeeding, he gave up absolute power and went back to his farm.

The Latin on the front side read: *Omni relinquit servare replublican.* 'He abandons everything to serve the republic.' On the other side was simply the Latin for 'Fame.'

The silver metal meant that Haney was a full member of the Society of the Cincinnati. But since it wasn't a gold medallion, he wasn't part of the inner circle, most of who (those still alive) were descending upon Washington, DC. He was a field operative.

As important, and more necessary, he was the direct descendant of a lieutenant who'd served in the Continental Navy during the Revolution. He died shortly after starting his service, thus waiving the requirement of serving three years.

The Society at least accepted death to be worthy of giving membership to descendants. But otherwise they followed the rules of primogeniture rather strictly, allowing only one descendent at a time to be a member. Haney had no siblings so that hadn't been an issue.

His father had died of a heart attack when he was young; collapsing at the breakfast table, facedown literally in his pancakes. His mother had followed in the family tradition and joined the military.

She was killed in the first Gulf War, a conflict few remembered with all that had happened since.

The Society had then stepped in, providing for Haney, sending him to the best schools, grooming him to be a member. In Haney's world, one repaid debts of honor with honor of their own.

Haney was the last in his line. He'd been married once, briefly. Then he'd accepted the hand he'd been dealt and that was that. There would be no other wife and no children. All he had was the Society and the values it represented.

The Society of the Cincinnati is the oldest military organization in the Western Hemisphere. General Knox, chief artillery officer in Washington's Army, put together the first meeting in Newburgh, NY in 1783, even while the British were evacuating New York City, their last presence in the Colonies after signing the Treaty of Paris, ending the war. The end of that occupation, Evacuation Day, was once wildly celebrated annually on 25 November in New York City, because of the harshness of British rule. Over 10,000 Continental service members had died on prison ships in New York harbor over the years, more than died in all the battles. It was war at its most base and bitter. The last shot of the Revolutionary War was fired on that day by a British sailor lighting up a cannon on a departing ship. Although the shot fell short of the jeering Americans lining the shores of Manhattan, it was a sign of the bitterness of years of war. When the Americans tried to pull down the Union Jack nailed to the flagpole in Battery Park, they found that the British had greased the pole so it couldn't be scaled. The Colonists quickly nailed cleats to the pole so that they could replace the flag with the Stars and Stripes while the British fleet was still in sight.

But when Abraham Lincoln proclaimed the last Thursday in November to be a day of Thanksgiving, Evacuation Day faded away, forgotten by almost all. But not by the Society. And not by Haney's family, because his ancestor had been one of those to die on those British prisoner ships.

George Washington was elected the first President of the Society. It was almost prescient that he be tied to that ancient statesman/warrior because when Washington rode triumphantly into New York City on Evacuation Day, almost everyone was more than willing to make him dictator for life of the newly independent colonies.

Washington said goodbye to his troops at Fraunces Tavern and rode home.

When the country decided they needed a President, like the Roman Senators calling Cincinnatus off his farm, the country turned once more to Washington. He served his country once more and then, like Cincinnatus, rode off after his second term and retired back to his farm in Virginia.

Haney's musings were interrupted by movement to the south. He used his binoculars and spotted Nidar coming back up the trail with four other men. They were all armed with AK-47s.

Haney nodded. The man had run back to the Kurdish village, gathered help, and was returning to take revenge for the deaths.

And Nidar had also seen what was hidden here.

As a member of the Society of the Cincinnati, Haney was a student of military history. There were times when an outnumbered and outgunned force managed to prevail. Haney's goal was to gain time for the promised reinforcements from the Society. This was only the beginning.

When in doubt, like Chamberlain at Gettysburg, it was time to take the offensive.

Haney put the spare magazines in his front pocket. He left his pack where it was. Either he'd be back to reclaim it or it wouldn't matter. He scrambled down off the top of the hangar and onto the trail. He ran down the trail, pistol in hand.

When he reached the spot he desired, he slid into a rock chimney on the side of the trail and climbed up, feet on one side, his back against the other, until he was fifteen feet up.

'No one ever looks up,' his first platoon sergeant in the Marines had told him.

Then he waited.

It didn't take long. The Kurds were running, fueled by the desire for revenge.

Nidar ran by, followed by another and another and then the last two. Haney quickly reversed and let gravity help him climb down the chimney. He then chased after the Kurds, suppressed pistol held in front.

He put on a burst of speed and then saw the last man. Like Sergeant York taking out the German patrol, he fired, the bullet hitting number five in the back of the skull and dropping him instantly. The fourth was in sight a second later and Haney took him out.

This man's AK-47 hit the rock trail with a clatter, causing the man in front to turn to see what had caused the noise. This only served to have the bullet enter his temple rather than the back of the head, but the result was the same.

The second man spun about, bringing his AK up to fire, and Haney double-tapped him: once in the chest, once in the head. Nidar fired, spraying rounds.

Haney felt something hit him, staggering him back.

He fired, aiming low, a bullet into the firing shoulder and then two rounds into Nidar's stomach. The Kurd doubled over from the dual impacts. Haney ran up to him, knocking the AK out of his hands and shoving him to the ground. Haney pressed his knee against Nidar's stomach, causing him to hiss in pain.

"Did you tell anyone else?"

Nidar's eyes met his, the hatred blazing. *"More are coming. Many more. Not just for those you've killed. For what is in the cave. We know what it is worth. It could buy my people their freedom."*

"Nuclear blackmail won't work," Haney said. *"You'll get squashed like a bug."*

"We shall see."

"I don't think you will."

Nidar spit at him, the saliva mixed with blood. *"You will never make it away from here alive. This is our mountain. Our land."*

"Maybe it's no one's mountain," Haney said. He put Nidar out of his misery. Then he gathered all five AKs and the ammunition on the bodies.

Finally he paused to check his own body.

A round had torn through the muscle on the outside of his left shoulder. Bloody, but not fatal. Weapons slung over his shoulder, he headed up the trail toward his rucksack and the aid kit. It was growing dark and it was going to be a long, cold night.

With the additional weapons, perhaps the Alamo would hold a bit longer.

*****

The program had been stolen from a British software firm. At least that's what the firm claimed. The reality was the firm had sold it to the Iranians for a tidy profit, hiding the transaction through numerous cutouts, not only to avoid investigation by the authorities, but also to avoid paying taxes on it and to avoid paying their own developers their share of the profits. The two men who ran the firm were building a rather considerable fortune in overseas bank accounts selling their company's software on the black market.

Such was the underside of international commerce.

It wasn't quite as good as what the NSA used to spy on its own citizens but it was dependable and made it possible to automatically monitor all the cell phone and radio traffic along the western border of Iran. Even in this remote part of the world, the proliferation of cell phones and powerful hand-held radios produced an overwhelming amount of chatter. The program sifted through all that, searching for key words and phrases.

One of those key words triggered an alert, and a young enlisted man put on his headphones and began to listen to the cell phone conversation that had initiated it. The analyst wrote down the intercepted chatter, but when he heard a certain word again, he raised his other hand and waved wildly, still writing.

His supervisor stubbed out his cigarette and sighed, wondering what had excited the newest recruit to his listening post. Probably some sheepherder asking about some lost members of his flock and using some phrase like 'kill them all.'

He looked over the young man's shoulder. His skin went cold when he saw what was being written. He grabbed a secure line and called the nearest military post.

*****

The key to a successful military operation is planning. Most of the TriOp front line operatives were ex-Special Operations. And while they were technically *ex*, that didn't mean they'd left their training or expertise behind. The reality was that they—and tens of thousands like them—fought a shadow war, one that was rarely (if ever) reported on. One where casualties were never listed, coffins weren't sent home flag-draped, but stuffed inside the cargo hold of contract airplanes. If they were sent back at all.

Contracting out was a large part of the new way of war for the United States. Piled on top of a volunteer army, it further distanced those doing the dirty work from over 99% of the population. While the 'war' was officially done in Iraq, the battle for the country's resources was far from over. TriOp's primary mission since the withdrawal of most US Forces was now protecting corporate interests in country. With billions of dollars of American taxpayer money being poured into 'rebuilding' a country the Americans had pretty much destroyed, someone had to protect those doing the building, even though the graft, violence, and over-charging made it the equivalent of spraying a hose into an ocean. A multi-billion dollar hose of futility.

It was the epitome of Eisenhower's military industrial complex where even the military in this case was industrialized and incorporated.

The warning order from Turnbull reached the TriOp field commander at their forward operating base outside of Mosul. They immediately went into mission planning mode, unhappy, as all soldiers always are, at the incomplete information they'd received. There was never enough good intel provided: Go here in Turkey. Get someone and something. Call signs and identification codes, and that was about it. Vague. And vague in mission planning tended to get people killed.

One thing that was certain was they were going to need a ride.

And that was going to cost a lot of money. But for TriOp, bankrolled by the Society of the Cincinnati and its well-heeled benefactors, money was not a problem.

Although there were plenty of rides from various other contract companies in Iraq to choose from, the parameters laid out in the mission tasking indicated there was only one option that could haul the package out.

*****

"I don't trust Turnbull," Ducharme said.

"Duh," Evie replied, which caused Burns to laugh, breaking the scowl that had been permanently etched on his face since things in the interrogation room had taken an unexpected turn.

"I didn't know you had a sense of humor," the FBI agent said.

They were in one of the many not so innocuous black SUVs with tinted glass various government agencies drove. Heading from FBI headquarters toward Andrews Air Force Base. Ducharme was slumped back in the rear seat, eyes closed. Burns was driving and Evie was in the passenger seat.

"I was in the CIA," Evie said. "Sometimes known as Clowns in Action. Sometimes known as other things. We did some good work and some not so good work."

"Do you really think, after over fifty years," Ducharme asked, "that something about the Cuban Missile Crisis could cause such a problem that we shouldn't notify the National Command Authority about some unsecured grade plutonium?"

"Yes."

When there was nothing further forthcoming from Evie, Ducharme opened his eyes. He glanced at Burns, who shrugged, meeting his eyes in the rearview mirror.

"Duke," Evie finally said, "a bunch of people just died over the Jefferson Allegiance, a document over two hundred years old. Some of the material on Kennedy isn't going to get declassified for *another* twenty-five years. Some of it will never see the light of day.

"Let me ask you this one question: given your background and your expertise with weapons, do you believe a lone gunman, firing from that window in the Book Depository, killed Kennedy? Take out all the conspiracy theories, just look at it from an operational point of view."

Evie looked over her shoulder, not giving him a chance to answer. "Let me list just a few facts that most people don't know about the shooting. First, there was an entry wound in his neck. No one focuses on that. That was most likely the same round that took off most of the back of his head, yet we're to believe that headshot came from above and behind. You know the difference between an entry and exit wound."

"An autopsy could have confirmed or refuted that," Ducharme said.

"Yeah, except the autopsy was done by a hand-picked guy here in the DC area after they flew the body back, violating Texas law. By a guy who had never done a GSW autopsy. Why would someone like that get picked for perhaps the most important autopsy of the century? And he burned his own notes afterward. One thing I learned in the CIA is that where there are burned notes, there's fire."

"In the neck, out the back of the head," Ducharme mused. "I'd say a shooter in the sewer system, firing from the curb. Or maybe the grassy knoll. I've never been there so I don't know the fields of fire. Plus I'd need to know the angle of the body at fatal impact. I never understood why the first shot didn't knock him over."

"He was wearing a back brace," Evie said.

"That was bad luck," Ducharme said.

"And you'll agree the odds of a lone gunman are very, very low?" Evie asked.

"I always thought it was ridiculous," Ducharme said. "A moving target with a bolt action rifle at that range and that downward trajectory? Very tough even for a trained sniper."

"What Texas law was violated?" Burns asked as he drove them across the Potomac and onto Suitland Parkway.

"Removing the body before an autopsy was performed," Evie said. "They broke so many laws and rules that day on so many levels, it's pretty much statistically impossible, even given how screwed up the government could be. The usual Secret Service guards who rode on the steps on the rear of the Presidential limo were ordered not to that day. You can see film footage of them at the airport being told to get off and one of them arguing. And the guy who took that footage, David Powers, Kennedy's Special Secretary and BFF, well, I won't get into him right now."

"So more than a shooting," Ducharme said, not asking about Powers or else they'd end up on highway to information overload. "A conspiracy. And you think it's linked to these missiles in Turkey?"

"I think it's linked to something between the Philosophers and the Cincinnatians," Evie said. "We know from what we read of McBride's notes on the Jefferson Allegiance that the Philosophers threatened to pull out the Allegiance unless Kennedy backed off just three months before he was assassinated."

That got Ducharme to sit up straight. "Are you saying *we* were behind the assassination?"

Evie shook her head. "The Philosophers wouldn't do that. Not because we're so noble and good, but because we've always had the Allegiance to use."

"What are you guys talking about?" Burns said. "I'm catching up on the Jupiter thing, but what is this about Kennedy and the Allegiance?"

"I'll show it to you as soon as Duke is on his way," Evie said. Then she did what she was prone to, tuning Burns out as if he weren't even in the car, focusing on Ducharme in the back seat as they approached the main gate to Andrews Air Force Base. "You up for this?"

Ducharme nodded. "Sure. Nothing but a thing."

"What does that mean?" Evie asked.

"Nothing but a thing," Ducharme repeated with a weary smile. "I'll sleep on the flight. What kind of ride did you get me?"

Evie ignored the question. "You were bent on revenge for Charlie LaGrange when you were going after the Allegiance."

"I do my duty," Ducharme said.

"This is off the books," Evie reminded him.

"It's not the first time I've gone off the reservation."

"You buried your knife."

"That was a mistake," Ducharme said. "I'm gonna miss it."

"It isn't about the knife," Evie said as the gate guards waved them through after seeing Burns' ID and checking their clearance roster. Evie's phone calls were opening things up for them as the tentacles of the Philosopher's via General Pegram reached out into the military.

"Where am I going?" Burns asked.

"The tower," Evie said, without taking her eyes off Ducharme. "I know you're having a hard time with this as a soldier. But remember that 'war is a continuation of politics by other means.'"

"Clausewitz?" Ducharme was surprised. "You're quoting Clausewitz to me?" He seemed caught between the twin rocks of outrage and irony. "'Most intelligence reports in war are contradictory,'" Ducharme quoted back to her. "We studied Clausewitz at the Academy. Charlie LaGrange was in my Section when we had to read Clausewitz. Memorized a lot of his writings. 'In short, most intelligence is false.' What Clausewitz called the fog of war," Ducharme said. "We're in a pretty dense fogbank right now. Turnbull is holding back something, no doubt about that."

Burns pulled up to the Andrews Air Force Base tower and turned off the engine. There wasn't a band waiting to greet them, just a lonely looking full bird colonel wearing a long black coat, braced against the cold weather.

"Clausewitz fought against Napoleon and lost most of the time," Ducharme said. "Maybe we ought to be following some of Napoleon's advice?"

Evie raised an eyebrow. "How about: 'History is a set of lies agreed upon?'"

"I like that," Ducharme said.

"But Napoleon lost to Clausewitz and his allies at Waterloo," Evie noted.

"That's the best you've got?" Ducharme shook his head as he opened the back door and stepped out.

"I want you to understand that the lines are blurred here," Evie said. "Between the political and the military. Between political parties and countries. Between government and industry."

Evie joined him. The Colonel came up but didn't introduce himself, obviously unhappy with his assigned task.

"Your bird is inbound and about," he checked his watch, "five minutes out. We're going to do a hot refuel and then you'll be on your way." He paused, as if expecting some comment. "There's, uh, well no flight plan filed."

"Anything else?" Evie asked.

"No, ma'am."

"Thank you."

The Colonel meandered off to stand out of earshot as if hearing something might get him shot. He'd been at Andrews long enough and seen enough flights depart without a flight plan to know when to walk away.

"Evie," Ducharme said, "I know you're into theory and strategy and thinking things out and pithy quotes, but I'd have expected the last couple of days to have shown you the other side of this. The dirty side. Where people die."

"I've seen it before, when I was in the Agency.

Ducharme gave up on that angle of approach. "You have anything more about this Sword of Damocles? I've heard that phrase somewhere."

"Kennedy used it in a speech to the United Nations in 1961," Evie said. "He basically said everyone on the planet was living under a nuclear Sword of Damocles. The anecdote refers to something from Cicero. He wrote about a court hanger-on of King Dionysius the Second of Syracuse. Trying to suck up to the king, Damocles said that since he was king, Dionysius was a blessed man and quite fortunate. Dionysius turned the tables on Damocles and offered to switch places. Damocles, of course, accepted. Except the king had a very large sword hung over the throne, held only by a single horsehair. As you can expect, it freaked Damocles out to the point where he begged to go back to his position.

"Dionysius' point, no pun intended, was to show Damocles that great power came with great danger. A constant fear. Cicero summed it up by saying that a person who lived in great fear could never be happy. Kennedy expanded that to cover everyone on the planet with the sword being nuclear weapons."

"The Sword is still hanging there," Ducharme said.

"It's been there since 1945," Evie said. "But it has never fallen. Rather remarkable if you think about it. By the way," she added. "You know how the knife on the US Special Forces crest is a Fairbarn-Sykes commando knife?"

"Yes. That's also what I just buried at Arlington."

"The British Special Air Service have a knife in their insignia. But it's not a Fairbarn-Sykes. It's the Sword of Damocles."

"Curious," Ducharme allowed.

They were interrupted as an F-22 Raptor came swooping down, seemingly way too fast, and touched down at the end of the runway, braking hard.

"How am I going in that?" Ducharme asked as it rapidly slowed down, then turned off onto a taxiway and headed toward them. "I'm not a pilot."

"You're looking at the only two-seater F-22 ever built," Evie said. "The F-22B. For training purposes. But it cost too much, around half a billion a copy, so they discontinued the line. You get the backseat." She awkwardly put a hand on his shoulder. "Get some rest during the flight."

"Yeah, I'll have the in-flight meal," Ducharme said. He turned to Evie and her hand fell away. "I have a bad feeling about this. And with Charlie and his dad dead, I don't have much to come back to."

He waited a moment, then headed for the plane, where a ground crew was pushing a ladder up against it and the canopy was open and waiting. Ducharme climbed up and got in. The plane was moving even as the ground crew pulled the ladder away and the canopy was closing.

"You were supposed to say 'you've got me to come back to,'" Burns said, startling Evie.

"I was thinking that," she said.

"Thinking ain't doing," Burns said.

4 June 1961
Vienna, Austria

The leaders of the two most powerful nations in the world sat in armchairs angled toward each other for their first, and what would be their only, meeting. It wasn't going very well for the American.

"Force will be met by force," Khrushchev said. "If the United States wants war, that's its problem. You must decide whether you want war or peace."

"Then, Mister Chairman, there will be a war," Kennedy replied. "It will be a cold, long winter."

Khrushchev snorted in derision and shook his head dismissively, indicative of his attitude toward the American President since they first entered this room in Vienna. "We have many long, cold winters in the Soviet Union. It is nothing to us."

Kennedy leaned forward so only Khrushchev could hear. "We need to work something out about the nuclear weapons."

Khrushchev also leaned forward. "It is too soon and too dangerous. You must learn how to play, how is it you say, the long con because you must not only deal with me, we must both deal with our own generals." Then he sat back and raised his voice. "Is this all you have for me? The situation in Berlin is not acceptable."

*****

Kennedy slumped down into the sofa, a hat pulled down low, hiding his eyes. The blinds were shuttered and the room was dark. Kennedy sat awkwardly, the pain in his back throbbing, despite the pills and shots Dr. 'Feelgood' Jacobson had been giving him nonstop.

"How was it, Mister President?" James 'Scotty' Weston was the only other person in the room, invited to this unprecedented one-on-one with the President, just an hour after the end of the Summit.

"Worst thing in my life," Kennedy replied. "Khrushchev savaged me."

Reston was the NY Times Reporter for the Washington Press Corps. Kennedy had been in office only six months, but Reston was getting used to Kennedy's honesty and bluntness. Still, he was taken aback by this summary, even though it had been obvious to all observers that the summit between the American leader and the Soviet Premier had been a disaster for the younger man.

While he waited for more, Reston jotted a note to himself, a first reaction, a key to writing any article. 'Not usual BS. There's a look to a man when he has to tell the truth.'

"You've got two duties," Kennedy said. "Do the job for the Times. And do the job for your friends."

"My friends?'" Reston said.

Kennedy tilted his head back slightly, and even in the dim room, Reston could see the President's bloodshot eyes underneath the brim of the hat. "I'm getting clued in, Scotty. I know you answer to the people in Philly."

Reston was uncertain how to respond to that, so he didn't.

"For your readers," Kennedy said in his distinctive New England accent. "They need to begin to understand things are going to get worse, much worse, before they get better. If they ever do."

Reston jotted some notes, even though a bead of sweat was sliding down his forehead. Kennedy seemed immune to the stifling heat in the room, but it was more than that.

"Berlin," Kennedy said succinctly. "I screwed that. That old son-of-a-bitch is going to do something there. Maybe another blockade. Who knows? I thought he'd focus on Cuba, but he brings Berlin up. What does he expect? What's his angle?"

It was obvious Kennedy wasn't waiting for an answer from Reston on what Khrushchev expected. "We'd have to run the airlift again. But the game is very different now than it was back in '48. The Russians didn't have the bomb until after that was over. They've got it now. That ups the stakes. We don't have the same leverage."

"They've lost millions of people defecting to the west," Reston said. "Most through West Berlin. And these aren't just farmers and working class. A lot of the top professionals are leaving."

"I know," Kennedy said. "It's a bleeding wound they can't ignore. But how can they stop short of attacking West Berlin and starting World War Three?"

Kennedy sighed. His next words were almost to himself. "Do I give up Berlin to keep the peace? Appeasement didn't work. Can't work in the long run, but it has a place in the short term." He stirred as if realizing someone else was in the room. "You know the title of my thesis at Harvard, Scotty?"

"No, sir."

"'While England Slept,'" Kennedy said. "Wrote it in '40, before we knew what we later learned." He chuckled, a good memory intruding. "Bought myself a green Buick with the royalties from the book. Convertible. Nice car."

The memory was gone just as fast as Kennedy sank back into the depressive hangover of the Summit. "I've got to figure out why he came on so strong. I know he thinks he won hand over me with the Bay of Pigs. But something else is going on. He's got something up his sleeve. He was hostile, as if we were already at war. Why did he even come here, then? To gloat? He had to have had a reason." Kennedy didn't wait for an answer. "Not only do I have to figure out what he's going to do, I've got to figure out what we can do about it."

Kennedy took off the hat. "That's the official, unofficial version from an unnamed source, Scotty. The rest is off the record and in regards to what we can do about it."

Reston shut the notebook. "Sir?"

"The Philosophers," Kennedy said. "What's their take?"

"The who, sir?"

"I gave you this meeting," Kennedy said. "I'm giving you headline stuff. I want something in return. I want you to go your buddies in Philadelphia. Tell them hard times are ahead. That there can't be another Bay of Pigs. They're either with me—" Kennedy paused and with great difficulty, got to his feet— "or they're against me."

Reston also stood. "You sure that's the message you want to me to give them?"

"I'm the Goddamn President!"

*****

"Anyone so young and inexperienced that he got his country into that mess in Cuba seems to be a weak man," Khrushchev told Mikoyan as they rode to the Vienna airport in the Chairman's limousine.

"He might be, but his Generals are a different story," Mikoyan cautioned.

"He let the attack in Cuba start, then failed to support it," Khrushchev said. "Held back the air and naval support they needed. No guts."

"That cuts both ways," Mikoyan said. "He might not be able to do what Eisenhower did. Keep the Generals under control."

Khrushchev shrugged. "He looked anxious. Upset even. What kind of leader is that? I came on strong, the way you must when first meeting another leader. What did he expect? A big hug? A toast together?

"I didn't mean to push him so hard, but when there is no resistance, the push goes the distance. It would have been better for him to have pushed back. For us to have gone on our ways today in different moods. But that is on him. This business we are in, the wielding of power, is merciless."

"Remember, Comrade Stalin always said the west would wring our necks like a chicken once he was gone," Mikoyan warned.

"Comrade Stalin has been gone for some years now," Khrushchev observed, "and we are still breathing. He is not. Nor is Beria," he added with a sharp glance.

"True," Mikoyan said. "Kennedy is a weak man. A weak leader."

Khrushchev shook his large head. "No. You have him wrong. Strangely, I sense more strength in Kennedy than Eisenhower. Remember, Eisenhower might have been the big commander in the West during the Great War, but Kennedy was one who was in the fight in the Pacific. Who came under fire. There is a difference in such men, as you and I know. It is easy to give orders for others to face the enemy, it is different to face them in person."

Mikoyan remained silent, a course of action that was a default mode for him when someone with more power told him he was wrong. It didn't mean he accepted the judgment, it meant he accepted the reality of the scales of power. And even though he resented Khrushchev for drawing him in to that statement, he would not bring that up. It was a strategy of Khrushchev's to put conflicting statements out to subordinates in order to see how quickly they agreed and then contradicted themslves.

"And our Generals, comrade?" Khrushchev probed.

"What of them?" Mikoyan stalled, understanding the question completely.

"How do we rein them in?"

"It is best to feed a hungry pet before it turns on you," Mikoyan said.

"Feed it too much and it thinks you are the pet," Khrushchev noted. "Berlin. We will let our pets play in Berlin and see what Kennedy does. And then . . ." the Premier trailed off. "And then, we shall see. But it is a very dangerous game we are playing now. Much more dangerous than any Comrade Stalin ever participated in. He did not have nuclear weapons."

"I don't think he would have done anything different," Mikoyan said.

"And that, my old friend, is the second time you've been wrong during this ride," Khrushchev said as the limousine came to a halt and guards opened the doors so they could board the flight back to Moscow. "Everything is different."

CHAPTER FIVE
The Present

Ducharme knew he should sleep because he was going to hit the ground running when they arrived in Iraq. The F-22 was racing eastward, across the Atlantic at over Mach 2 with KC-10 tankers stationed along the route for refueling. They'd arrive in the Middle East in just a few hours.

"Have you got a specific destination for me, sir?" the pilot asked over the intercom. He was just the back of a helmet to Ducharme. The man's voice was calm, as if a run like this was something he did every day. Piloting the only F-22B, maybe that was the case. Ducharme assumed there were people who had to get places in a hurry besides him.

"Give me a minute," Ducharme said.

He accessed the comm link and brought up a connection to the terminal Turnbull had given him. He typed in his query.

>DESTINATION?

Turnbull was on station, as Ducharme expected, with an immediate reply.

<AL ASAD

>STATUS OF TARGET?

<NO MORE INFO. WILL FORWARD WHEN I HAVE SOME

"Al Asad," Ducharme said over the intercom.

"That place was shut down," the pilot said. "Marines pulled out at the end of 2011, stripped everything they could take with them."

"Looks like it will be open again."

"Roger that," but there was a note of skepticism in the pilot's voice. "Relax and enjoy the flight. I'd send the flight attendant back to you, but things are a bit tight."

"Haven't these planes been grounded because the pilots black out?" Ducharme asked.

"I've heard that story," the pilot said. "Haven't experienced it myself. Here's hoping it doesn't happen on this trip."

"What's your call sign?"

"Stretch."

"Paul."

"Nice to meet you, Paul. Most of my passengers don't talk much."

"Doubt I will either," Ducharme said. "I've got to get some rest. Not that I'm being rude."

"I'll try and stay awake up here."

Ducharme leaned his head back and closed his eyes. He thought of Evie quoting Clausewitz. He hadn't known her long, but he had a feeling he didn't know her at all.

"Hey, Stretch," Ducharme said.

"Yo."

"Women don't make any sense, do they?"

"Sure don't. That's why I like flying. The machine does what you make you do. Except this lady. It *has* blacked out pilots and we still don't know why. A test pilot and one of our own have been killed. So this little baby can be quite the bitch and do the unexpected. Much like a woman."

Much like combat, Ducharme thought, and with that came the realization he wasn't that much different than Evie Tolliver after all.

*****

Haney rappelled down the rope into the facility, his headlamp lighting the way. He assumed he had some time before the next, and most likely larger, group of Kurds showed up. It was strangely calm and quiet in the bunker as he rotated his body and his feet touched. He unclipped from the rope. Reaching into his small pack, he pulled out a flare.

He lit it and tossed it to the center of the bunker to get a more accurate assessment of what was here. The single missile was in the exact center. The other five were on flatbeds tightly parked to one side. There were various crates, boxes, and barrels scattered about. The bodies lay where they'd been executed half a century ago.

There were two trucks, large ones. One had a crane on the back, the other a large square box about eight feet square. Haney went over to it. The box was centered on the back of the truck, made of a dull grey metal. Pulling himself up, Haney ran his hand over it.

Lead.

A door like that on a safe was facing to the rear. Haney pulled out his radiation detector. Nothing, but that was apparently the purpose of the box. Had the plutonium cores been removed from the bombs and stored?

Haney knew the answer as soon as he thought it—if that had been the case, he would have gotten no reading at all. He turned the detector toward the missiles and was rewarded with a reading, indicating some cores were still in the bombs.

The flare sputtered and went out.

Haney switched on his headlamp and went over to the flatbed. He climbed up onto it, going to the nosecone of the missile.

He checked the time. While he had the Geiger counter, he didn't know squat about nuclear materials or weapons. Other than they created a lot of destruction when they went off. He'd received a briefing on the counter and told what was a safe level, but he had no idea what would happen if he opened up the nosecone and tried to get the warhead out. Or if he even could get the warhead out, although he imagined the truck with the crane was for that—not that it would run after so many years.

Haney made his way back to the ropes and quickly chumared his way back to the pipe, then rapidly crawled out into the open air. Night had fallen and the temperature was dropping. Haney shrugged on an extra sweater, then turned on his Satphone.

*****

There was a bloodstain on the floor where Major Elizabeth Peters, U.S. Air Force, and part of the next wave of Philosophers, had died. And plywood covered the window where Lieutenant General Atticus Parker (U.S. Air Force, retired), one of the Philosophers, had thrown himself out rather than give up information to the Surgeon, the Cincinnatian's assassin.

For Evie Tolliver, they were stark reminders of the seriousness of the battle between the two groups, and a contrast to their current cooperation. She and Burns were in Philosophical Hall on Fifth Street in Philadelphia. Its only other neighbor on the block was Independence Hall, where tourists flocked every day. This building was partially open to the public, but like Anderson House in Washington, that was only a cover for the real purpose: the headquarters of the inner circle of the American Philosophical Society, which Evie by default and death, was now the Chair.

"Not exactly an encouraging venue," Burns noted.

"On the contrary, Mister Burns," Evie said. "We are surrounded by history dating back to the founding of the country. Almost every notable American of the later eighteenth and early nineteenth centuries was in this room at one time or another."

"I meant the blood and the window."

"Of course," Evie said, indicating she'd barely noticed either. "If we're going to get answers," Evie said as she walked over to the desk, "this is the place." She put her briefcase down. "I've got McBride's thumb drive, and there's lots on it we need to read, but haven't had the time. But the library here, both electronic and actual documents, can't be accessed any other way than in person. The mainframe here is shielded from the outside world."

"The Surgeon was a nut job," Burns said, indicating the slashed painting behind the desk of Thomas Jefferson. The one next to it, of Alexander Hamilton, was untouched.

"It's a shame," Evie said as she pulled out her laptop. "That painting is one of only two copies that the artist, Thomas Sully, painted off his original of Jefferson. The original is at West Point, in the new Jefferson Library, and the surviving copy is at the University of Virginia." She shook her head at the irony. "The two colleges Jefferson founded, both with purposes seemingly far apart, yet not so distant when one understands his motives. West Point was the first Military Academy and UVA the first university in the United States founded without religious affiliation."

"I thought Jefferson didn't like the military," Burns said, having picked up snippets of history the past few days. "Why'd he start up a college for it?"

"Because he was a realist," Evie said. Unlike Ducharme, who'd spent more time with her, Burns hadn't learned yet to be careful of opening up the spigot of knowledge in her brain. "Jefferson deeply distrusted a standing army, but he recognized the need for one. He wanted to keep the officer corps from being filled with sycophants and men aligned with one party or the other. So in 1802, as President, he established the United States Military Academy at West Point, requiring the Corps to be made up of young men from all over the country, via allocated appointments through the federal representatives of all parties. It was actually a rather ingenious design to make sure the Corps represented the entire country.

"It's worked so far, since the United States has never experienced a coup, although it has experienced a Civil War where fifty-five of the sixty major battles had graduates of that same Academy commanding on both sides."

That gave Burns pause. "That many?"

"Almost the entire officer corps of the small standing army before the Civil War was West Pointers, most of them blooded in the Mexican War. Almost every West Pointer, both graduate and cadet, from the South chose to go with state over country and joined the Confederacy. Lincoln had even offered Lee command of the Union Army before he decided to side with Virginia."

"To side with slavery over freedom," Burns said.

"It's not that black and white, if you will excuse the poor pun," Evie said.

Before she could continue, Burns cut her off. "I don't think I can. Say what you will, but this is a subject on which we have differing perspectives."

"Agreed," Evie said and continued as if his comment wasn't even a speed bump in her train of logic and history. "It was perhaps the greatest failing of West Point, one that has barely been acknowledged, that so many of its cadets and graduates broke their oath to the Constitution at the start of the Civil War. It's also why the war was so long and bloody. Officers were fighting classmates who'd sat in the same tactics class with them. More important, they all knew each other. They knew their strengths and weaknesses not only as officers, but as people."

"Do you think that could happen again?" Burns asked.

"Most people believe it's unthinkable, but given the right set of circumstances, I think we could see great turmoil in our country. Although state's rights aren't argued as fiercely as they were then and moral and economic aspects of slavery aren't an issue, you need only to look at Texas to see a grassroots movement for secession. Hamilton and Jefferson worked hard to prevent such an event, and that's our job now." She pointed at the desk. "They brokered The Jefferson Allegiance right at this very spot. But while that was, and has been, an excellent check on the possibility of an Imperial President, it did not address slavery or state's rights. So both issues turned out to come home to roost a generation later. The Founding Fathers were smart men; they knew the festering tumor they were choosing to ignore. They decided they needed a country first, before those issues got dealt with. It was a fateful decision, one that their children and grandchildren had to resolve with blood."

"But now we're dealing with something different," Burns said.

Evie opened her laptop and turned it on. "Americans tend to wave the Constitution about and act as if it were written in stone, but the Founding Fathers—no Mothers by the way, a big mistake—had assumed that it would be changed over time as the world changed. Possibly even done away with and replaced. Jefferson, in particular, believed that the country needed to reinvent itself every generation or so. He'd be appalled that we're still operating off that same document, although we have added to it over the years. But for us, in the twenty-first century, to be arguing using words over two centuries old, strikes even me as a bit archaic."

"The Bible is older than that and people all over the world use it as the word of God. Same with the Koran."

"And they're arguing about the interpretation and going to war over it," Evie noted. "At least they're saying it's the word of God. The Constitution is most definitely the word of *men*, and not divinely inspired. And men, by the way, who were *not* representative of their society. They were quite slanted toward the wealthy and land-owners. Also, throw in a few criminals, particularly smugglers, and that's who wrote the document on which we base our country. Hancock, who signed the Declaration of Independence so boldly, was a well known smuggler and instigator of not only the Boston Tea Party, but bankrolled many other protests that supported his illegal economic agenda. He was even charged with smuggling, but was successfully defended by John Adams and acquitted of the charges."

Burns was beginning to learn what tapping Evie's font of information brought forth, but he found it fascinating.

Evie shook her head. "We live in a very different world than they did over two hundred years ago. They couldn't have conceived of nuclear weapons and the Cold War. And now the War on Terror."

Burns was looking at the other paintings as her computer booted up. "An interesting group of people."

Members of the Philosophical Society stared down at them from their perches on the wall. Benjamin Franklin, who founded the APS in 1743. His goal had been to further science in the colonies, another thing that had morphed over the years into something very different. There was George Washington, a member of both the APS and SOC, a man who could walk a razor's edge with a smile on his face and keep both sides happy. John Adams and James Madison, two more of the early Presidents. There were poets, like Robert Frost, and scientists, like Charles Darwin, indicating the wide range of interests the early Society displayed. Lewis and Clark were inducted as soon as they returned from their journey west.

Her computer ready, Evie opened a drawer and unreeled a USB connector and plugged it into her computer. "You can use that desktop," she said, indicating a flat screen monitor and keyboard set on the other side of the desk. "I'll send you the excerpt from McBride's history about Kennedy and the Jefferson Allegiance so you can get up to speed on what we already know."

Burns sat down and activated that computer.

Evie's screen blanked for a second, then the crest of the Society, featuring a Native American and a Colonist greeting an ancient Greek with a globe, sextant, and open book in between them. Along the bottom was the motto of the APS: *Nullo Discrimine*, which meant We Are Open To All.

At the very bottom of the screen was another saying in Latin: *Scientia in Bello Pax*. Science in War is the Guarantee of Peace. The motto of the supposedly defunct Military Philosophical Society, which had been founded at West Point in 1802, the same year the Academy was founded. According to history, it was shut down with the War of 1812, but Sylvanus Thayer, the Superintendent of the Academy and considered the 'father' of the institution, took it underground and thus began the secret arm of the APS, of which Evie was now the leader.

Evie plugged McBride's thumb drive into its slot and accessed the file on The Jefferson Allegiance. She copied the two excerpts about Kennedy into a document and then sent it over the system to McBride's computer.

"You'll like the first section," Evie said. "It's about your founder, J. Edgar. And McBride wrote it like a work of fiction because he planned someday to perhaps publish it, even though he knew, deep inside, most of this information can never be made public. It was a dream of his to be a novelist. It's a bit out of order for what we're looking for, occurring after the Bay of Pigs and the Cuban Missile Crisis, but it's a good starting point for you."

Then she got to work, doing a search on the rest of the thumb drive and the Philosopher's on-line archives for more information about Kennedy, the Jupiter Missiles, the Cuban Missile Crisis and the Sword of Damocles.

Burns opened the document and immediately became immersed in the history:

22 March 1962

President John F. Kennedy, as was the custom for his lunches with J. Edgar Hoover, had the Oval Office emptied of everyone, even his brother Robert. To Kennedy, today was looking to be a particularly odious session as Hoover was carrying a particularly thick file.

Kennedy had been advised by Eisenhower to continue a tradition begun by FDR: inviting the head of the FBI to lunch at the White House every month. It was under the principle of keeping your friends close and your enemies closer. Since taking office, Kennedy had stretched the interval out to every two months, and he was hoping he could eventually go without seeing the grotesque man at all. Bobby wasn't happy about the luncheons much either, because technically Hoover worked for the Attorney General, although the man never acted like he answered to Bobby. Or even the President, Kennedy reflected as he sat on the couch across from Hoover, a low, ornate, coffee table between them, Jackie's choice.

Hoover dropped the thick file onto the coffee table with great relish. Kennedy didn't rise to the bait. Instead he waited as his secretary refilled his coffee cup, offered some to Hoover, and then departed. Kennedy took a sip of coffee and waited some more, refusing to descend into Hoover's gutter.

"Interesting wiretaps," Hoover finally said. "Should I set the stage for them?"

Kennedy shrugged, knowing the old man would say what he wanted regardless. His back was killing him and he shifted, trying to adjust the brace strapped around his body. He glanced at his watch, thinking ahead to his schedule for the afternoon.

His thoughts came to an abrupt halt at Hoover's next two words: "Judith Campbell."

Kennedy tried to stay relaxed. "Who?"

Hoover gave that sickening smile of his. "Las Vegas. 1960. The filming of Oceans Eleven. *Your 'buddy' Frank Sinatra. He introduced you to her. Don't you remember?"*

"I can't recall. I don't even remember being in Vegas."

The smile grew wider. "I can assure you that you were," Hoover said. He opened the folder and on top was the picture of a woman. He slid it across to Kennedy, who didn't pick it up.

"She's quite beautiful," Hoover said. "Interesting timing. You were seeking the democratic nomination at the time. Apparently you were seeking more than that, as you became involved with Miss Campbell."

"I'm afraid your information is—"

"Incorrect?" Hoover completed for him. *"Do you know how many times I've heard that? I never share information unless I am* certain *it is correct."* He grabbed the next picture in the folder and tossed it on top of Campbell's. Kennedy's stomach tightened.

"Perhaps unknown to you at the time, but certainly known afterwards, was that Sinatra also introduced Miss Campbell to this man." He leaned forward and tapped the picture. *"Sam Giancana. A criminal. Head of what is called 'the Outfit' in Chicago. Since there is no organized crime in this country, the Outfit is a bunch of thieves and murderers."* The sarcasm was dripping from Hoover's words.

"It wouldn't surprise you, of course, to know that Miss Campbell is also Mister Giancana's mistress?"

Kennedy couldn't tell if it was a question or not, so he remained silent.

"Of course not." Hoover answered his own question. *"Since Miss Campbell calls you here at the White House using the phone in Mister Giancana's apartment in Chicago."* Hoover picked up a third picture and threw it down. *"Your father. Joseph Kennedy. He had dealings with men like Giancana, especially during Prohibition. I believe the Sinatra introduction was at his behest."*

Kennedy had not thought of that, but he knew as soon as Hoover said it that it was true. Chicago. Of course. His father pulling strings.

Hoover pursed his lips as if in thought. *"Now this part is not validated, but comes from credible sources. It seems someone from your campaign gave a bag of cash to Giancana back when you were seeking the Democratic nomination. You did win Illinois, mainly because of a huge push in Chicago. Some would say a statistically impossible push. A lot of votes from the grave."*

"What do you want?" Kennedy had had enough.

Hoover picked up the next item in the folder. A thick sheaf of papers. *"Come now, Mister President, are you really trying to hire this Giancana fellow and his 'Outfit' to assassinate Castro?"*

"What the hell are you talking about?"

Hoover blinked. *"You* really *don't know about that? Curious. Your precious CIA is keeping secrets from you, too. But, like me, they* know *your secrets."*

"What do you want?"

Hoover reached over and grabbed the sheaf of papers and the photos, making a large show of putting them back in the folder and shutting it. Kennedy didn't miss that there was a lot in that folder that Hoover had not brought out.

"It isn't what I want. It's what we *want."* Hoover lifted the lapel on the right side of his suit jacket, revealing a medallion. *"The Society of the Cincinnati, Mister President."* With his other hand he tapped the thick folder. *"We have you—and your brother—by the balls, to use a crude but appropriate phrase. If I ask for something,* we *want it. Do you understand?"*

Kennedy just stared back at the old man.

Hoover stood, tucking the folder under one arm. *"Right now, all we want it is for your brother to change his mind and sign off on the paperwork on his desk to wiretap Martin Luther King."*

"I don't—" Kennedy began, then stopped as Hoover waved the folder, as if fanning himself. "All right."

5 August 1963

"I love you, too," President Kennedy said, and then hung up the phone, severing the line to his wife in Hyannis Port.

"How is Jackie?" the only other occupant of his private dining room on the second floor of the White House asked.

Kennedy grimaced, both from the pain in his back and the recent conversation. "Not good. The heat is bad, she feels ill and she's scared."

"Of course she's scared. She already lost one child. I know how she feels."

Kennedy watched as Mary Meyer took a sip of her drink. He enjoyed her company—one of the few people he felt comfortable being alone with and simply talking, but to be honest, he still missed their affair.

"Graham shot himself," he said, referring to the Washington Post publisher who had killed himself with a shotgun just two days previously. And who, back in January, had pushed his way to the podium at a conference of newspaper editors in Phoenix—even though he wasn't supposed to speak—and drunkenly delivered a tirade that included references to the President's 'new favorite,' Mary Meyer. He had been wrong about the 'new' part, Kennedy mused. He'd known Mary since college, and she'd long been a staple of White House life.

"I heard," Mary said. "I feel for his wife. He'd just gotten out of the hospital. They thought he was better."

"He was out of control," Kennedy said. He had been intimate many times with Mary, and even though that part of their relationship had ended with the dual pressures of Graham's publicity and Jackie's pregnancy, he still felt a tight bond. He'd once smoked marijuana with her, even tried LSD—not his thing—and she'd been there with him through the Cuban Missile Crisis, Bay of Pigs, and many other significant events of his Presidency. Always someone he could confide in and count on for solid advice. "What's wrong, Mary? Is it Jackie? She's fine with your being here."

Mary Meyer shook her head. "I was approached by some men. They wanted me to give you a message and they showed me something."

"What men?"

She shook her head. "I can't tell you, except that they are for real. Three high-ranking generals and someone—let's say he's on a level with Graham."

Kennedy frowned. "What did they show you?"

"A document." Mary got up from her end of the table and sat kitty-corner to the President and took his hand.

Kennedy was surprised at the move and the look on her face. "What is it? What's wrong?"

"Have you ever heard of the Jefferson Allegiance?"

Kennedy gripped her hand tighter. "Yes. A rumor of it. No one has ever confirmed its existence though."

"It exists. They showed it to me."

Kennedy could feel his back tighten, the old injury from PT-109 coming back to haunt him as it always did when he was under stress. "Why did they show it to you?"

"They wanted me to give you a message. And they knew you trusted me."

"Go on," Kennedy prompted.

Mary's tongue snaked over her lips, a sign of how nervous she was. "They said that they respected what you did during the Missile Crisis. That it was important that one man be in charge and handle things. That it was one of those unique moments with high stakes where the responsibility and decision-making had to rest on the President's shoulders."

"But?" Kennedy prompted.

"The Bay of Pigs. The Wall being built in Berlin. Your recent speech there worried people. They felt you were continuing to challenge Khrushchev. That it had become personal. And the involvement in Vietnam greatly concerns the military men."

Kennedy scoffed. "There are only eleven thousand men in Vietnam—all advisers. And the Pentagon has promised they can be withdrawn by the end of the year after they crush the Viet Cong rebels. Vietnam is not an issue."

"That is not the way the Philosophers see it."

"The 'Philosophers?' So it's true that they guard the Allegiance." He stared at her. "Is it as powerful as rumored?"

Mary nodded. "If they invoke it, they would remove you from office. And that's just the beginning."

The silence in the dining room lasted a long time before Kennedy spoke again. "What do they want?"

"For you to use the National Security Council for advice more often. To back off Vietnam. Back off of pressing Khrushchev."

"Do they want an answer?"

"They told me they would get their answer from your actions."

"I don't like being threatened," Kennedy snapped. "I get it from both sides. The damn Cincinnatians and Hoover. Now the Philosophers. I'm sick of it."

"There's something else," Mary said.

"What?" Kennedy knew he was being short, but the pain in his back and this information along with Jackie being miserable in Hyannis Port was ruining what he had hoped would be a pleasant evening.

"Did you know the CIA is trying to use the mob to kill Castro?"

Kennedy leaned back in his chair, trying to ease the pain in his back, pulling his hand out of hers. "Hoover said something to me about that. I thought he was bluffing."

"I asked Cord," Mary said, referring to her ex-husband, who was high in the ranks of the Agency. "He said 'of course not,' which means of course they are."

"God damnit," Kennedy slammed a fist onto the tabletop, causing the crystal to jump.

"The Philosophers want you to get on top of that. After the Bay of Pigs, there can't be another Cuban fiasco. They say it's very complicated and dangerous and that the Cincinnatians are involved."

"Who the hell runs this country?" Kennedy demanded.

Mary got up and walked behind his chair. She leaned over and wrapped her arms around his chest. "I'm worried, Jack. Very worried for you. Cord didn't just lie to me. There's something going on. Something very dangerous. Promise me you'll be careful?"

Kennedy was hardly comforted by her touch or her words, but he nodded anyway. "I promise."

Burns finished reading and leaned back in his seat. He glanced over at Evie. She was making notes on a yellow legal pad. "We need something that isn't here," Burns said, startling her. "At least I don't think it's here."

Evie tore her eyes away from the screen. "What?"

"Mary Meyer's diary. If Kennedy confided in someone, it was her. And her diary is one of the great urban legends of DC. She knew everyone who was important and was intimate with many of them. She knew their secrets. If anyone knew Kennedy's secrets, it was Meyer."

Evie nodded. "I've heard of the diary." Her eyes shifted focus slightly, a look Burns was beginning to recognize as accessing her font of knowledge. "She definitely kept one. She asked a friend, Anne Truitt, who was married to a *Washington Post* reporter, to get it and keep it safe if anything ever happened to her. Unfortunately, when she was murdered, Truitt was in Japan. She called back to a couple of people, one of them Ben Bradlee of the *Washington Post* to go get the diary."

"Might as well have told the CIA and the FBI then," Burns said. "There's no doubt they had taps on Bradlee's phone."

"Exactly," Evie said. "They went over to Meyer's house the next morning and guess who they find already there, also looking for the diary? James Jesus Angleton of the CIA and his wife, both of whom were acquaintances of Meyer's. Which brings up the interesting question of how did Angleton know of the diary?

"According to later reports, they searched the house together and found the diary and some papers. Angleton took all of it under the agreement that he was to burn everything. However, as far as they knew, he only burned the loose papers. He kept the diary. Years later, he supposedly gave the diary to Bradlee's wife and she burned it in the presence of Truitt. But who knows if that was really her diary? And even if it was, Angleton had years to read and copy it. He was not the sort of man to let go of any potential piece of evidence or something he could use for leverage. He's quite the legend in the CIA. They even made a movie that was sort of about him with Matt Damon playing his character."

"So the diary, or a copy of it, could be anywhere?"

"'Anywhere' is rather broad," Evie said. "If we analyze the problem, we can narrow down 'anywhere' to possibilities."

"Then let's do it," Burns said, "because if Kennedy knew about these Jupiter missiles and warheads being left in Turkey, then there's a good chance she would have known about it. Since she represented the Philosophers in their approach to Kennedy, perhaps in death she can continue to be liaison to him." He thought about it for a moment. "You know, the part about Hoover was interesting. He was into everything. No one has ever found his files. His secret files that he used to control almost everyone." He pointed at the screen. "If he were a member of the Society of Cincinnati, then it's very likely they have his files. We need to ask Turnbull."

Evie couldn't hold back the smile. "Good luck with that."

Burns understood. "I know, I know. But we're working together on this. Turnbull wouldn't have made a deal with us if he didn't need something. The Senator would have gotten him out of there and he could have dealt with the Turkey issue pretty much on his own."

"You're correct," Evie said. "He wants information from us. And we need information from him. He knows more than he's letting on. The question is: what does he want from us?"

"If he had a spy on the Ararat expedition," Burns said, "then he knew something was up in Turkey."

"That is curious," Evie said.

Evie picked up her phone. "You go back to DC and sit down with Turnbull. Don't let him out of your sight. Like Ducharme is going to be with those TriOp guys on the op, you're on Turnbull. I'll get the chopper for you."

"What are you going to do?"

"Find information here," Evie said. "Because we need to know more, and if we're going to trade with Turnbull, we need something to trade. He's not a man who is going to give away information for free. I've got a feeling Turkey might just be the tip of the iceberg that is the Sword of Damocles."

*****

A flash of light and a lance of pain slicing through his head burst Ducharme awake. He scrambled, searching for his weapon, and hit the sides of the cockpit. He was confused for a moment, uncertain where he was, but then the roar of the engines, the steady rumble of the aircraft in flight and the soft glow of the instrument panels oriented him.

"You all right?" Stretch's voice was low and apparently unconcerned in Ducharme's helmet.

"Yeah. Why?"

"You were yelling something. Couldn't make it out."

Ducharme closed his eyes. He could feel the echo of the pain that had woken him, a throb that would take hours to dissipate. Though he wanted to deny the reality, it was getting worse and more frequent.

"Bad dream," Ducharme said.

"Yeah," Stretch acknowledged. "Have had a few myself."

They flew in silence for a few minutes before Stretch surprised Ducharme by speaking again.

"It ain't normal, Colonel."

"What isn't?"

"What we do. The things we've done."

Ducharme knew exactly what Stretch was referring to. "When I'm in the zone, in action, I do what I'm trained to do. But when things slow down, when I'm not in danger, I wonder *what was I thinking*. Then I realize I wasn't thinking."

"Exactly," Stretch said. "I flew some missions out of Al Asad, I guess that's why my brain is wandering. Sorry, Colonel. I'll get back on task."

"No problem," Ducharme said, very much knowing there was a problem.

Moscow
1 August 1961

"No one has any intention of erecting a wall!" German Democratic Council Chairman Walter Ulbricht lied to Premier Khrushchev over the phone.

Over his years in politics, Khrushchev had often wondered how not-so-bright people rose to power. Of course, in the case of Ulbricht, he hadn't risen so much as been picked for this very lack of acuity. A German who'd deserted his country's army in World War I, he'd spent the years between the wars mostly in exile, escaping the Nazi crack-down on Communists rather than dying like the rest of his Communist German brethren. He'd ended up in Russia during the Second World War and gave a speech at a Communist political rally for the German prisoners at the conclusion of the Stalingrad campaign.

Khrushchev imagined those prisoners had been as keen to listen to this man's whiny voice as he was. Of course, they were prisoners—the survivors of the most brutal campaign of the Second World War—and most were destined to die in the POW camps in Siberia.

He knew exactly why Stalin had tapped Ulbricht to head up the puppet East German government after the war: he was a spineless man who would sway in whatever direction the winds of power were blowing in Moscow. On the flip side, more than anyone else, Ulbricht was responsible for the 'brain drain' of East Germans fleeing to the West that was further crippling his country's economy.

Frankly, Khrushchev wasn't too upset that East Germany's economy was in the proverbial crapper. The last thing any Russian wanted was a powerful Germany, even a powerful half-Germany. The more the Germans suffered, the happier the Russians were. Beyond the 'brain drain' to the west, there'd been an 'factory drain' to the east as the

Russians dismantled large parts of Eastern Europe's manufacturing infrastructure and shipped it back to the Motherland.

Khrushchev had been part of the fall of Berlin at the end of the Second World War, and he'd felt then, and still did, that the utter devastation wrought by the Russians on the German people was more than justified. One reaps what one sows, and the Germans had sown millions of Russian corpses during Operation Barbarossa, their invasion of the Soviet Union. During the fall of Berlin, it was said that every woman in the city had been raped, and Khrushchev wondered how many erstwhile Berliners coming of age now had Russian blood in their veins.

"You seem to forget who you are speaking to, Comrade Ulbricht," Khrushchev said, "we agreed on this plan a long time ago. Save your propaganda for everyone else. I know you have been stockpiling the material for a wall for years."

A long silence greeted this dose of reality.

"Do I have your support, Comrade Khrushchev?" Ulbricht asked, like a child asking permission to run a prank. "Is it time?"

Why do you think I'd be talking to you about it, if it weren't Khrushchev thought. "It is."

"When?"

"The thirteenth. The Westerners feel that day bodes ill luck. We will feed into that. Plus, I am moving tank units forward in case there is a reaction by the Westerners."

"Do you think they will fight?"

Khrushchev could hear the fear in Ulbricht's voice. "If they fight, then Berlin is the least of our worries. We must make a show of strength. That's how this game is played."

"Yes, sir."

Khrushchev hung up the phone and looked across his desk at Mikoyan. "The fool spouted his same line to me about a wall that he's been telling everyone else."

Mikoyan laughed. "Beria was wrong about many things, but he was correct about Ulbricht. He called him the greatest idiot he'd ever seen."

"Coming from Beria, that might have been a compliment," Khrushchev said. "Of course, Beria should have paid more attention to his own situation."

"And the Americans?" Mikoyan asked, steering the conversation away from Beria, whose fate he had almost shared. "What do you think their response will be?"

"That will be the interesting part," Khrushchev said. "Kennedy only mentioned West Berlin during the summit, not Berlin. For him to make that distinction was either an ignorant blunder or a tacit acceptance that he would not oppose our actions there."

"And if he does?" Mikoyan dared.

"Then I will take appropriate measures," Khrushchev said.

Mikoyan surveyed Khrushchev across the table. Things were not as they seemed. There was more to this than his Premier was letting on. That put Mikoyan in a vulnerable position. "Comrade Khrushchev," Mikoyan said, treading carefully and politely, "perhaps you have a long term play in position with this maneuver in Berlin? Is this just an opening gambit?"

"Ah, you are too suspicious," Khrushchev said with a laugh.

Which confirmed to Mikoyan there was more to this than Berlin.

Berlin
13 August 1961

What a difference a day makes.

On the 12ᵗʰ of August, 1961, East Germans could simply walk into West Berlin, then take one of the safe corridors out of the city to the west. Millions had done it.

On the 13ᵗʰ of August 1961, they no longer could do so. In the decades that followed many would try; most would be caught and imprisoned and one hundred and ninety-one would die. That's the official count. It doesn't take into account all the spies trying to use the city as their crossing point to either infiltrate the other side or get back. The Cold War wasn't so cold for those captured.

The Germans could make the trains run on time; they could certainly start building a wall on time.

They didn't start with a wall, of course. East and West Berlin shared twenty-seven miles of border. Around the Allies' three sectors bordering East Germany was another ninety-seven miles. Even the Germans would have difficulty putting up a wall to cover those combined distances in one night. It took the Chinese generations to build their Great Wall. It wouldn't take that long to encase West Berlin with a wall, but it would take more than a day.

Thus the first stage was barbed wire. Ironically, it is an American invention, a result of the need to fence off the vast open spaces of the American West. While soldiers and police put the wire in place, bulldozers tore up all streets other than those leading to the official checkpoints, making them impassable to vehicles.

As dawn broke, the world could see that the Eastern Bloc had made a major move on the Cold War chessboard. Unlike the blockade of Berlin in 1948, the stakes were much higher now, as both super-powers possessed nuclear weapons.

How would the West make a counter-move?

Who would blink first?

CHAPTER SIX
The Present

Politics were being played in the conference room of the Anderson House as various senior members of the Society of the Cincinnati maneuvered to gain possession of the diamond-encrusted medallion that Lucius had worn.

Turnbull cared nothing for the games being played down the hall. As soon as he'd left FBI headquarters he'd begun making phone calls, setting in motion the long tendrils of the Society of the Cincinnati.

There was no blood on Lucius' desk. The Society was most efficient in cleaning things up, both literally and figuratively. The events at the Tomb of the Unknown were being swept away and shoved under the massive carpet of secrecy that blanketed Washington. The Surgeon no longer existed in any form.

Turnbull had no idea who would take Lucius' place, but there wasn't time to wait until the bigwigs in the conference room let loose their form of the *fumata Bianca*-white smoke-indicating a successor had been chosen.

The door to the office opened and one of the SOC's field agents came in.

Turnbull didn't waste time on a greeting or small talk. "Summarize the Sword of Damocles operation for me, Ramsay."

Ramsay was the SOC's New York field rep. His expertise was finance, his focus Wall Street. This op was outside his comfort zone, but Turnbull had been caught up in The Jefferson Allegiance issue and the Surgeon taking out the Philosophers. Ramsay had thick, white hair, a nose that would do a Roman Senator proud, and wore an expensive suit. All part of his cover as financial adviser to the Society of the Cincinnati. Except he actually was the adviser, his other duties to SOC being layered underneath his legitimate cover.

Ramsay was out of his element. While he might be able to command a boardroom on Wall Street, the chaos inside Anderson House was unsettling.

But even more unsettling was that he rarely faced someone like Turnbull in New York.

"We had to react quickly," Ramsay said, looking around for a chair. He headed toward one, but Turnbull stopped him in his tracks.

"I didn't say 'sit,' I said 'talk.' And I said summarize, not explain."

Ramsay faced the desk. "We intercepted a communication from Admiral Groves just prior to his, uh, expiration, to one of the Peacekeepers he'd been in contact with. We tracked the Peacekeeper to Kennedy Airport where he bought a ticket to Baghdad. One way. We alerted our man in Baghdad, Haney. He's also the—"

"Expert on Ararat and Turkey and Iran and a slew of other potential issues," Turnbull said. "I know that. And I'm in contact with Haney. What more have you uncovered?"

"Um, well, sir, we dug further into this Jonah fellow since we were able to finally get his real name when he was cleared through customs for his flight. Joseph Penkovsky."

Turnbull put his hand to his forehead and winced. "You gotta be shitting me."

"No, sir. His father was one Ivar Pensky, but that name was changed from Penkovksy when he immigrated to the United States in 1969. Joseph went back to the original family name of his grandfather when he was of age."

"Do you think the Peacekeepers know who he really is?"

"They vet new members extensively," Ramsay said. "But I don't think so. It appears that Pensky defected in 1969 via a classified Department of Defense program used to cover spies who gave them valuable information. He was given an entirely new cover upon arrival. It stands up to even a deep vetting process, especially after almost half a century. Everything was a paper trail back then and those can be wiped out. Joseph Penkovsky only changed his name back *after* he became a Peacekeeper, so unless they knew that, which we doubt, they'd have fallen for his cover."

"I assume Admiral Groves had something to do with Pensky's defection to the United States," Turnbull said.

"It would be logical," Ramsay said.

"So he could also have had something to do with getting Jonah into the Peacekeepers."

"Highly likely, sir. We've never been able to infiltrate them. And we've tried. I've lost three agents over the years."

"Lost?'"

"They disappeared, sir. Leaving no trace."

"And we still don't know where they are in New York City?"

"They're not *in* the City, sir. They're *under* the City. That's where my men were last seen."

"No shit. You've had all these years and you haven't been able to infiltrate or find them?"

Ramsay didn't answer because it was one of those questions where a negative answer just reinforced a negative result.

"There's no indication this Jonah, aka Penkovsky, has made contact back to the Peacekeepers?"

"No, sir. And since Admiral Groves has expired—"

"He was fucking killed," Turnbull snapped. "Get used to it."

"Since Admiral Groves was killed, the Philosophers have had no direct contact with the Peacekeepers. And Penkovsky has no point of contact with the Philosophers either."

"Will the Peacekeepers reach out to the Philosophers?"

"I doubt it, sir. They've been very security conscious over the years."

"No shit. But they screwed the pooch on Jona...Penkovsky, generation three." He leaned back in his chair. "Groves had to know. And he had a plan. Lilly killed him too soon. That was a mistake."

"Perhaps Haney can get some information from Jonah," Ramsay suggested.

"Haney killed Jonah."

Ramsay had nothing to say to that.

Turnbull drummed his fingers on the desktop. "So. We've got Penkovsky's grandson in Turkey. The Peacekeepers are cut off from the Philosophers. This must be making the Peacekeepers very anxious. Anxious people react. When you react, you tend to screw up." He looked at Ramsay. "I want everyone on the payroll, and everyone you can hire in the next twenty-four hours, on the search. We've got to find out what the Sword is. And where the Peacekeepers are."

"Yes, sir." Ramsay hesitated. "If you don't mind, sir. What exactly did Haney find in Turkey? I don't get the connection."

The Satphone buzzed on the desktop and Turnbull held up a finger, silencing Ramsay. He put the phone to his ear. "Report."

"I need information on these warheads," Haney said. "I've got low level radiation here, but I need to know what happens if I take the warheads out of the missiles. And then if I take the plutonium out of the warheads."

"Roger," Turnbull said. "I'll have someone get back to you ASAP."

He turned the phone off and pointed at the door. "Get back to New York and get to work," he ordered Ramsay. "Use Penkovsky. He had to have left a trail back to the Peacekeepers in the City. He moved fast after Groves was kid. Fast means sloppy."

*****

They touched down at Al Asad in darkness. The runway was lit by beanbag lights along both edges of the tarmac. Otherwise the place appeared deserted.

"I'd rather be in the air," Stretch said as he slowed down the plane.

A strobe light flashed to the right, moving parallel to them on a taxiway.

"Over there," Ducharme said. "The truck with the strobe."

"This is the fucking wild west," Stretch muttered. "I flew out of here during the war. You know how many billions of tax payer money they poured into the place?"

The strobe light turned toward them and then the pickup truck was in front, leading them in the darkness. "How do we know they're the good guys?" Stretch asked.

"I don't think they're good guys," Ducharme said, "but they're the guys I'm meeting." He could make out a pedestal-mounted heavy machinegun in the bed of the pickup. But the dark figure manning the gun had it pointed forward, occasionally swinging it left and right.

A tall sliver of red light appeared ahead. A hangar door was being rolled open, the interior lit with red nightlights. The pickup truck rolled in and the F-22 followed. As soon as they were inside, the door slid shut behind them.

As Stretch opened the canopy, Ducharme took in the activity inside the hanger. Piles of gear were scattered about. Men were loading magazines, others preparing combat equipment. It looked exactly like many FOB (Forward Operating Base) configurations that Ducharme had launched out of during his career. They might be mercenaries but they'd been soldiers once.

A staircase was rolled over. Ducharme got out of the plane, stretching cramped muscles at the top of the stairs, then made his way to the bottom.

A slender, dark-skinned man in full combat regalia was waiting for him. All the TriOp personnel wore black fatigues under their battle gear, with their company's red trident insignia Velcroed onto the uniforms where the American flag went on a regular soldier's fatigues. Allegiance to a company, not a country. Available for hire to the highest bidder, although Ducharme knew that wasn't quite true. TriOp had its own agenda and leanings and wouldn't work against what it saw as its own self-interests.

The merk stuck out his hand. "Colonel Ducharme, I'm Cane, Commander of this team and this operation."

Coming from most those words would be a challenge and a drawing of boundaries, but Cane said it as if it were simply a reality; which it was. Ducharme shook his hand. "Just Cane?"

"It gets my attention," Cane said with a brief smile. He looked up at the F-22. "Nice ride. Is it going to wait here for you?"

"Yes." Ducharme looked past Cane and saw a UH-60 Blackhawk with ESSS stub wings and external tanks parked in the hangar.

"We've got some fuel we can spare," Cane said. He shook Stretch's hand. "We'll have a team remaining here providing security, but we recommend you stay in the hangar. We had to run off some squatters when we rolled in. We don't think they'll try to take us on, but stranger things have happened over here. I'm sure there are some who'd love to get a hand on the aircraft and sell it to the Chinese."

"Is everything for sale?" Ducharme asked.

Cane shrugged. "Everyone has a different price. You know that bravery in battle used to be rewarded by kings and rulers by bestowing lands and riches on the best warriors? Then Napoleon came up with a nice scam: give them medals. Cheap pieces of ribbon and tin. You and I have both seen men die trying to earn those little trinkets."

"You know Evie Tolliver?" Ducharme asked.

"Who?"

"Never mind," Ducharme said. "I've seen men die fighting for their buddies. Not medals."

"Whatever," Cane said. "We all work for somebody."

"Got any chow?" Stretch asked.

Cane pointed and the pilot moved off.

"What time is wheels up?" Ducharme asked as Cane led him toward a room built into the side of the hangar.

"We secured this facility just under two hours ago," Cane said as they walked into a room that had been set up as an Operations Center. Maps and imagery were taped to the walls and a Satcom radio was on a table, manned by one of Cane's men. Cane checked his watch. "We've got six hours of darkness left." He led Ducharme to a large-scale map. "It's roughly two hundred and fifty miles to the objective. So we've got a flight time of a little over an hour and a half."

"You didn't answer the question," Ducharme said. "And one Blackhawk? Going to be crowded, and we have to bring a load back."

"No one's told me what the load is exactly other than some rather vague parameters," Cane said. "And you're getting ahead of me. You want it the official, green machine way, back in Group?" he asked referring to Special Forces. "All right, Colonel. Let's do this right."

Cane picked up a pointer and came to a position of 'at ease.' "Task Force Noah will deploy from Forward Operating Base Al Asad between oh two hundred and oh three hundred local time, infiltrate Objective Ark via helicopter fast rope insertion from one UH-60. Secure package, as yet not specified. Exfiltrate package and one personnel back to Al Asad. Flight path will be this—" he began tracing a route with the pointer along the map— "staying well inside Turkish air space and staying out of air defense range of Iran. We will maintain radio silence at all times, since the Iranians have a lot of ears pointed west."

He slapped the tip of the pointer on the map. "We've got checkpoints and rally points en route, here, here, here, here, etcetera," he said. "My team sergeant can give you the exact coordinates, call signs and all that happy shit." Cane shifted out of army mode. "I know you might not be thrilled with me and my men, but every man here served our country. Or their own country, since we got a couple of Brits, and even one Australian. We all have our own reasons for being here, but once we're wheels up, as you said, we're a band of brothers, Colonel. We have each other's backs. We have *your* back. We expect the same from you. You are not in the chain of command. You are an observer."

None of his statements were questions.

Cane turned toward the hangar, which was visible through a large plate glass window. "Yeah, we only have one Blackhawk, and we were lucky to get that, especially one that can mount the extra fuel tanks we need. But we've got a big ride en route. One that will carry the bulk of our force and can—" he paused.

Ducharme heard what caused him to stop. The deep thrum of helicopter blades. After many years of service, Ducharme could recognize any chopper in the US inventory, and he immediately knew this wasn't one of them.

"Come on," Cane said.

They walked out of the room and across the hangar. The door was open enough to allow them out. A large form hovered ahead, slowly descending. The downwash from the blades tried to shove them back into the hangar.

Ducharme recognized it as it set down. "A Halo," he said, referring to the Russian made Mi-26 by its NATO code name. It is the largest and most powerful helicopter in military service. Over forty meters long, or about half a football field, and eight meters high, unlike the US made double-bladed Chinook it had only one set of blades, but there were eight of them, each sixteen meters long. It had a massive cargo bay that could hold ninety fully armed soldiers, but as important, its two powerful engines provided excellent lift capabilities. In fact, in Afghanistan, the United States chartered a Halo to lift out downed Chinooks.

As the massive chopper settled down and the blades slowed, Ducharme could see civilian markings on the side of the aircraft.

"Does lifting work for the oil fields," Cane explained. "You don't want to know how much it's costing us to rent it and the pilots for this little excursion. Triple cost, plus hazard pay, plus a guarantee of full cost of replacement if the chopper is lost. Of course, if the chopper goes down, you and I probably won't have to worry about that, will we?" He turned to Ducharme. "I assume you want to be with me on the assault team fast-roping in off the Blackhawk."

"Roger that."

"Now that it's here, we can set a definite time for wheels up. We need to refuel it and load up." Cane checked his watch. "Forty-five minutes." He looked over his shoulder. "Forty-five minutes, Top! And remove all insignia."

A tough looking older man gave a thumbs up and began shouting orders.

Cane emphasized the last point by tearing the Velcro patch off his fatigues and tossing it on the table.

"You expect that to help if you get captured?" Ducharme asked.

"There is no getting captured," Cane said. "We come back or we die. Surrendering isn't an option. This part of the world, people like us don't get taken prisoners. We get a bullet in the brain. That's why we get paid the big bucks."

Cane turned back to Ducharme. "Do *you* know what it is we're getting, besides this guy Haney?"

Ducharme hadn't known Turnbull's agent's name. "Yes. Some abandoned nuclear warheads."

"Oh, nice," Cane said. "That's just fucking great. The men are just going to be ever so thrilled. Whose nukes?"

"Ours."

"What, some bomber crash?"

"No," Ducharme said. "They've been there for over fifty years."

*****

Haney had his back against his pack and was watching the way south, from where the next wave of attackers would come. He hoped they would hold off until dawn, but the potential of what was in the hangar might outweigh an assault in the dark. The question was: how long before the Kurds in the village realized their initial assault wasn't coming back?

His Satcom crackled. "Haney?"

"Yes?"

"Assault force is going wheels up in forty minutes. Expect them on target an hour and thirty minutes from then. Got that?"

"Roger." Haney breathed a sigh of relief now that there was a definite timetable.

"All right," Turnbull said. "I've got the guy with the information you need. You ready?"

"Yes."

There was a moment of silence, then a new voice came over the radio. "First thing you need to understand is that your Geiger counter detects radiation but it doesn't differentiate between types. The louder and faster it chirps, the more radiation. You also have the readout on the gauge. So far, you've been well under any danger level based on the reports you sent back. You're dealing with Pu-239 in those warheads. I haven't been able to draw up the specifications for the type of weapon you're dealing with, so I don't know how the plutonium is shielded, but I can assure you if it's still in the warhead, it is. Let me give you an overview so you can figure it out. We'll get you specific information as soon as we dig it up.

"You've got three types of radiation when dealing with plutonium: Alpha, Beta and Gamma. Alpha, which is a particle, is dangerous to living cells but easily blocked. A piece of metal foil can do the job. Beta's also a particle. It's smaller than Alpha so its harder to shield. A half-inch of aluminum or an inch of plastic can do the job.

"The most powerful type of radiation is Gamma. A high-energy photo. Like an X-ray you get at the dentist's office, but with much higher energy levels. Maybe six inches of lead shielding should do it. A foot definitely."

Haney cut in. "There's this large safe-like thing on a truck here. Made of lead with a large door."

"Sounds like they were ready to pull the plutonium if need be and put it in the safe. But it's best to just get the warheads intact and get them out that way. You don't want to be tampering with those cores. You get exposed, it'll kill you pretty quickly. You're safe with the warheads as long as they're intact. Naval personnel in submarines go on extended deployments living with a nuclear reactor and nuclear warheads in close proximity and they're fine."

Haney looked up at the stars overhead. "How long will the incoming party spend on the ground? Will they be able to help me gather the warheads?"

Turnbull's voice came over the radio. "They'll stay as long as needed to get that plutonium out of there, but we need you to do as much as possible before they arrive. We want them to spend as little time on the ground as possible."

No shit, Haney thought.

"At the very least, can you open up the nosecones to expose the warheads?" Turnbull asked.

"I think so."

"Do it," Turnbull said.

The other voice came back on. "Push comes to shove, and you have to remove the cores and put them in that vault, shield yourself. Body armor, extra layers of clothing. Whatever is at hand. Look around. They might have left some gear. Wear gloves. Goggles. Move it as quickly as possible."

"Right," Haney said, having his second *no shit* moment.

Turnbull must have caught something in his tone. "Listen, son. We can't let the Kurds—or anyone else for that matter—get their hands on this material. Do you understand?"

A phrase ran through Haney's head, from his time in Fallujah, the company commander passing through, shouting orders: *Hold this position at all costs*. Of course, he'd been passing through, so it was an easy order to give to the men holding the position while he scuttled back to the company command post.

"I understand, sir. I'll hold at all costs."

*****

Iran had a strong military presence in the northwest corner of its country, where it abutted Turkey. They didn't exactly fear that the Turks would invade. Of more concern was an air assault by the United States, or Israel, striking at their nuclear facilities. It was a threat that had been on the table for years, and growing likelier the more Iran rattled its saber and claimed to be closer to actually having developed a nuclear weapon.

Thus the alert from the interception facility to a unit that could react went relatively quickly. The problem was, the Iranians had a limited amount of capability to project force beyond their borders. Despite the Iran-Iraq War being over for twenty-five years, the country had never really recovered from its devastation.

Reliant on imports for most of its weaponry and military equipment, it was thus an irony of the world's arms trade that while Ducharme and his team were using a Russian Halo helicopter, two US designed CH-47 Chinooks took off from an Iranian airbase fifty miles from the Turkish border and headed toward Ararat. Even more ironic was that the US had supplied Iraq during that war while the Soviets had supplied Iran. But it was the twists of the diplomatic dance and the requirements to keep feeding the military-industrial complex that Chinooks, based on a US patent, and built by an Italian company, ended up in the Iranian Air Force. While a Halo, built in Russia, was for hire to the highest bidder in Iraq, and rented to recover downed US Chinooks in Afghanistan. A country that had absorbed much American and Russian blood alike.

The Iranians were going to violate Turkey's sovereignty, but the lure was irresistible based on the intercepted cell phone calls from the Kurds: weapons grade plutonium was sitting there for the taking.

On board each chopper were forty-five commandos. Within eight minutes of being alerted, the two helicopters lifted off and began flying west.

*****

At the same time, one UH-60 Blackhawk and the MI-26 Halo took off from Al Asad and began their much longer journey toward Mount Ararat and the hidden Jupiter missiles.

Inside the Blackhawk, Ducharme settled back, almost comforted by the familiar roar of the helicopter's turbine engines and the blades chopping air overhead. The dark figures seated all around him, geared for combat and wearing night vision goggles, could have been any Special Team he'd been a member of.

Except for the minor detail they were infiltrating a foreign country and heading toward nuclear warheads.

There was a fly in every ointment.

27 October 1961

The wall was now becoming a true Wall. Section by section, the barbwire was removed, and a wall consisting of concrete sections twelve-feet high and four-feet wide, was being built in its place. Access between East and West Berlin was restricted to a limited number of places, the most notable being the infamous Checkpoint Charlie.

Kennedy had responded to the Wall by rattling his saber, but not unsheathing it. He activated over one hundred thousand National Guard and Reserves. He forward deployed over two hundred combat aircraft to Europe.

And in Berlin, General Clay, who'd supervised the successful Airlift in 1948 and 1949, wasn't one to be cowed by the Soviets, and especially not the East Germans when they began restricting the travel of diplomats from the West to the East, clearly violating the 1945 Potsdam Treaty.

He started having diplomats escorted by military police in Jeeps to the checkpoints. For a while this cowed the East Germans into letting the diplomats through. But only for so long. The harassment resumed.

Fed up, Clay then raised the ante, throwing M-48 Patton tanks on the table, a move the General for which they were named would have greatly approved of. The next time a diplomat was denied crossing, Clay had a battalion of M-48 tanks make their way into position, with ten of them crowded in place seventy meters from Checkpoint Charlie.

Khrushchev didn't hesitate in responding. Thirty-three Russian T-55 tanks rumbled into position the exact same distance on the other side of the Checkpoint. Main guns were pointed directly at each other, live ammunition was loaded in the breeches, and the world was one twitchy finger away from the start of World War III.

For sixteen hours the two militaries who'd been allies in World War II, faced each other over the city they'd both helped defeat.

*****

"Why should we trust you?" Robert F. Kennedy asked the Russian journalist, whom Scotty Reston had just introduced him to, in a private room at an out of the way restaurant in Georgetown.

"You know I am not a journalist, correct?" Georgi Bolshakov asked.

"You're GRU," Kennedy said. "And a spy. Which makes me ask again: why should we trust you?"

"I have a direct link to the Kremlin," Bolshakov asserted. "The words I convey come from Comrade Khrushchev's lips."

"Why should my brother trust Khrushchev?" Kennedy asked.

Bolshakov smiled. He held up a bottle of vodka. "Perhaps a drink might be in order?"

Kennedy didn't acknowledge the offer, but Bolshakov poured three shots, holding two of them out. Kennedy reluctantly took one and Reston took the other.

"To peace between our great countries," Bolshakov toasted.

They downed the shots.

"I do not ask you to trust me," Bolshakov said as he slammed the glass down on the table. "I ask you to relay Comrade Khrushchev's words to your brother, the President. It is his decision whether to trust the words. Although, I am sure, your consul means a great deal to him. Which is why I implore you to listen.

"Comrade Khrushchev believes your brother to be a man of honor and, as one who has seen war firsthand, a man of peace." Bolshakov leaned forward, ignoring Reston and focusing on the Attorney General. "You must remember, we are only sixteen years removed from your country being the only one to have utilized atomic weapons. Twice. And you did not bomb military targets, but rather two cities. We make no quarrel with the method used to pursue peace." Bolshakov sat back. "Indeed, it might have been better for Berlin if we ourselves had had the bomb then and put the city out of its misery instead of leveling it with conventional forces.

"But now," Bolshakov said, raising a finger. "My Soviet Union also has nuclear weapons. We have tanks facing each other down in Berlin, inches away from firing at each other. Would it end there in Berlin? Would it stop in Europe? Or would the entire world be consumed? Neither of our countries has shown a willingness to back off in the face of war. Nothing but complete victory. Except what is victory now? What would we win? A useless planet? Where no one could live?"

Bolshakov fell silent.

"Is there an offer to solve this problem in Berlin?" Kennedy asked. "Because we do not have one. Your country began this problem. Your country must solve this problem. And don't give me that public bull your Ambassador is putting out that it's a German problem. Ulbricht wouldn't take a piss unless Khrushchev okayed it."

"I am not here to spread 'bull,' as you call it. Comrade Khrushchev wants to be up front," Bolshakov said. "But your brother invited this by his words and actions in Vienna. My Premier had to act. He had to appease the generals just as your brother has to appease your generals. So. Here is the offer:

"If you leave the Wall in place and do not attempt to destroy it, we will move one of our tanks back. You can then mirror your own withdrawal from Checkpoint Charlie. Neither side will lose face."

"You'll back down first?"

"Yes," Bolshakov said. "But it must be one move, then the other move."

"Is that all?" Kennedy asked.

"That is enough for now, Mister Attorney General."

Kennedy tapped a finger against his upper lip, considering the Russian. "Why you and not your Ambassador? Why send a spy?"

"If the Ambassador presented this, then it would be official. Read officially, it looks like the Soviet Union would be ordering the Americans to give up on Berlin while also retreating. A lose-lose. With that public, you would not be able to do it without your President losing respect nor without the Berliners claiming he is abandoning them. Doing this informally, we give peace a chance."

"My brother cares very much about West Berlin."

"My Premier understands that," Bolshakov said. "Perhaps after, as you say, the smoke clears, your brother, the President, can make some sort of gesture to the Berliners." He shrugged. "Perhaps a visit. Some day."

"Perhaps," Kennedy said, but his thoughts were elsewhere.

"It is a good solution," Bolshakov pressed.

Kennedy focused on the man across from him. "Yes, but you blew your cover by telling me your real job. You know the FBI works for me."

Bolshakov smiled. "Yes, I know the FBI works for you. But do they really? Or do they work for Hoover? That is another issue. And another reason to do this informally. As in Moscow, you have much intrigue going on here in Washington. We have had glimpses of a deeper power struggle. A group called the Cincinnatians? Am I pronouncing that correctly?"

Robert Kennedy's face tightened at the mention of Hoover and the Cincinnatians. "Where did you hear that?"

"One hears the echoes of whispers in the halls of Washington," Bolshakov said vaguely. "Comrade Khrushchev would like to keep an informal line of communications with the President."

"And that line will be you?"

"I fear not for much longer," Bolshakov said. "As you note, my cover has been blown by meeting you. But there will be someone to replace me, rest assured."

"I wasn't particularly worried," Robert Kennedy said.

28 October 1961

The message from Secretary of State Dean Rusk to General Clay was to the point and like a dagger in the heart of the man who'd defended West Berlin for so long: We had long since decided that Berlin is not a vital interest which would warrant determined recourse to protect and sustain.

Clay had been moving up engineering forces, positioning bulldozers to rip down sections of the wall; to look the Russians in the eye and see if they were bluffing. Clay was certain the Russians would back down. Despite their bluster, Clay knew in his heart that American military might could destroy the Russians, and he believed they knew it, too. Clay knew the real numbers of American nuclear weapons, and he didn't believe for a moment the numbers the CIA was throwing about for Russian nuclear capability. They could barely feed their own people, never mind match the United States in nuclear capability.

Finding out that Washington had folded infuriated the General. He went forward to Checkpoint Charlie to see if the rest of the message would unfold as Washington had predicted.

Sixteen hours after moving into position, a Russian tank, spewing black smoke and with that unmistakable high pitched squeal of tread, backed up five meters.

Clay nodded at his adjutant. Much like Longstreet relaying his order to Pickett at Gettysburg before that fateful charge that Longstreet completely disagreed with, unable to voice the words, the order was relayed nonverbally.

The lead American tank clattered back five meters. Then another Russian tank retreated. And so on.

In an hour all the tanks were out of sight of each other, and the closest the world had come to World War III since the end of the Second World War was defused.

For the time being.

An even darker and more dangerous confrontation was rapidly approaching.

CHAPTER SEVEN
The Present

"Where are Hoover's files on Kennedy?" Burns demanded of Turnbull.

"How was Philly?" Turnbull had a clean desk. There was no sign Lucius had ever sat in the chair or died here. He'd buzzed Burns in, allowing him through the new security that was now in place inside the Anderson House. Cooperation meant concessions.

"I saw the blood your Surgeon spilled," Burns said.

"She was a bit rash," Turnbull said. "What did you learn about Kennedy and the Jupiters?"

"Evie's working on it."

"So you just came here to demand information of me?"

"If we're going to exchange information it has to start somewhere," Burns said.

"So you figured it would start here?"

"We think the key to this might be Mary Meyer's diary," Burns said. "That's some information. Kennedy confided in Meyer. He might have confided about the Jupiter missiles and this Sword of Damocles."

"Ah," Turnbull said. "Mary. I met her once. Briefly. I'd just graduated Annapolis. A long time ago, that was. She was attractive, no doubt about it, but she also had something extra, something that every man—and woman for that matter—picked up on. An allure. A combination of beauty, intelligence and insight. Very rare."

Turnbull sounded nostalgic, out of character for him.

Burns didn't allow that to sidetrack him. "I'm sure Hoover—"

"Director Hoover," Turnbull corrected.

"I'm sure Director Hoover had a thick file on Mary Meyer," Burns said. "We believe her diary might be the key to figuring out what the Sword of Damocles is."

"Apparently the Sword is some out of date missiles in northeast Turkey," Turnbull said. "And we're taking care of that problem."

"You honestly believe that's it?" Burns said.

"No." Turnbull pointed at one of the seats while glancing at the clock, calculating the time until the choppers out of Iraq reached the Jupiters. Still a while off.

"Do you have access to Hoover's files?" Burns pressed.

"They were destroyed," Turnbull said. "You know that. Every FBI agent knows that. Hoover died in 1972. Right away, Tolson, his right hand man—
"

"And lover," Burns interrupted.

Turnbull shrugged. "I don't give a shit if Hoover was fucking a goat. He was a dangerous man with his own agenda. Tolson called Hoover's secretary, Helen Gandy, told her the Director was dead, and without a 'hope you're handling this okay,' ordered her to start destroying Hoover's files. Since '57 Hoover had been keeping a set of special files at his office. Ones he didn't trust to FBI Central Filing. No one—and I mean no one—not even Gandy or Tolson, knew the extent of what was in those files."

"We know from *our* files," Burns said, "that Hoover blackmailed John F. Kennedy over an affair with Sam Giancana's mistress."

"'Our' files?"

"The APS files."

"Interesting," Turnbull said, "although everyone knew Kennedy and his brother fucked around. Trust me, *they'd* fuck a goat if it stood still long enough. Every great man has a flaw. I'm fine with it being sexual. I prefer that to incompetence. Anyway, Gandy started in on the 'D' files. Those were the ones Hoover had already targeted for destruction. Hell, I heard rumors that Gandy and Hoover had begun marking files and destroying some of them well before he died. He was sick for quite a while."

"I don't believe they were all destroyed," Burns said. "I've been around long enough to know that no one in this town gets rid of something they can use. They only get rid of it if it can be used against them."

"Slow down," Turnbull said, once more glancing at the clock. "Tolson was Acting Director for all of one day. Nixon fucking hated Hoover. Hell, every President did. He appointed Gray as director ASAP. Gray went to Hoover's office where he found Gandy hovering over the files like she owned them. He secured Hoover's inner office, but not the entire suite, and the files were in Gandy's outer office." Turnbull leaned back and put his hands behind his head, lacing his fingers. "This is where the small fuck ups can bite you in the ass, Special Agent Burns. Gray reported to Nixon that the files were secure even though she wouldn't even let him look in the boxes she had. Everyone was just so happy to be rid of Hoover that they let her take them with her to Hoover's house.

"Eventually someone wised up, and while publicly proclaiming that no files had ever been removed from headquarters, they sent people to Hoover's house to gather back what they should have never let out."

"Do you have the files or not?"

"Slow down," Turnbull said once more, checking the clock. "You mentioned Mary Meyer, and I'm trying to show how everything in this town connects, all right? They went into Hoover's house to grab the rest. Juicy stuff. Besides the dirt on the Kennedy brothers, he had the same on Joe Kennedy, their father. He had the dirt on anyone who'd ever gotten a smudge under their fingernails, which is pretty much everyone in this town."

Burns sighed.

"All right," Turnbull said. "Guess who was spotted carrying boxes of files out of Hoover's home?"

Burns thought for a second. "Same guy who grabbed Meyer's diary. Angleton."

"You are good at your job," Turnbull allowed. "Angleton claimed they were bottles of spoiled wine, which is about the worst cover story I can think of. He was—"

Turnbull paused as Burns' phone rang.

"Burns."

Evie Tolliver got to the point. "General Pegram just called me. Satellite surveillance has picked up two Iranian helicopters inbound for Ararat. They'll be on it at least thirty minutes before our people."

*****

"I've got more bad news," Haney said in response to Turnbull's message about the Iranians. His fingers were torn and bloody from ripping off the access covers on all six rockets. "There are only three warheads here. Three of the nosecones were empty. It's obvious someone opened them up after they were in place here. And not carefully."

"Did you check the lead box on the back of the truck?" Turnbull asked.

Haney was standing on the back of the truck. "I'm looking in it right now. Nothing. I've got the hatches off and the warheads are ready to be pulled. Going to take more than one man to do that, though."

The import of what Turnbull had told him was beginning to sink into Haney's reality. "Thirty minutes is a long time."

"Can you seal the hangar off?" Turnbull asked.

"I can put covering fire on the way I got in, and only one person at a time can enter that way," Haney said as he hopped off the back of the truck. He looked to the left. "But if they've got any demo, they can blow open the large doors. Going to have to open them anyway to get the bombs out."

Haney walked over to one of the flatbeds. A warhead rested in the nosecone. "I'll figure something out."

*****

Ducharme tapped Cane on the shoulder. The UH-60 was flying fast and low, the Halo behind and slightly above. They were trying to stay under Turkish radar, using the terrain to mask their movement. The Halo pilots trusted the UH-60 pilots with their night vision goggles and advanced navigation systems to keep them from crashing into the ground since they were flying blindly.

"Iranians will be on our target in five mikes."

Cane didn't seem surprised. It's a maxim of military operations that once you crossed the line of departure—line of contact (LD/LC)—all plans went to shit.

"So we're going in to a hot LZ," Cane said. "Can you get us any air support?"

"My contact is working on it," Ducharme said.

*****

The two Chinooks came to a hover, side-by-side, over the edge of the top of the hangar. Dirt blew in the air, swirling about, as the back ramps were maneuvered to a spot just above the ground. The Iranian commandoes rushed off and the two choppers lifted and moved off to land in a level spot a kilometer away to await the order to extract.

The commandoes rappelled down to the ground. While a line of five snaked into the ventilation shaft, others began prepping charges on the two large, rusting doors.

One of them had a Geiger count out, checking the level of radiation. He gave a thumbs-up to the team leader. *"Low level, but something radioactive is inside."*

*****

"Hold at all costs," Haney muttered as he used the crowbar to rip open the casing on one of the warheads.

He'd heard the faint tremble of helicopters echoing from above. There wasn't much time. A clanging noise caught his attention and he spun about, AK-47 at the ready. A rope came tumbling out of the hole in the airshaft and a second later a man in camouflage rappelled in.

He didn't make it to the ground alive as Haney stitched him with a five round burst. But the Iranians, like trained elite soldiers everywhere, kept coming. Haney took out the second and third, before running out of ammunition. As the fourth and fifth touched down, he slammed home a fresh magazine.

Tracers slashed by him and he felt the burn as a round cut across the left side of his head, cutting flesh and taking off the top of his ear. Haney tucked the stock of the AK into his shoulder and stood his ground, firing on semi-automatic and carefully. He hit the Iranian who'd wounded him in the chest, staggering the man back, but he didn't go down.

Realizing the man was wearing body armor, Haney lifted his aim and put a round into the man's head, hitting him in the jaw, blossoming bone and blood. He went down this time.

But the fifth man was now behind the last flatbed, popping up to fire, then ducking back down.

Gaining time.

Haney didn't have time. He knew once the main doors were blown open, this was over. The friendlies were still twenty minutes out.

Once more channeling his inner Chamberlain, Haney jumped up and then ran along the flatbed and leapt over to the middle one. Then to the one the Iranian was hiding behind. All before he could pop up to fire again. When he did, Haney was above him and the American fired on full auto.

Dropping the AK, Haney reversed his course and went back to the first missile and warhead. Using the crowbar, he ripped open the bomb's outer casing.

*****

The charges were in place. The Iranian commander gave the order. With a loud bang and a bright flash that slashed through the darkness, they went off. For a long moment it seemed as if nothing had happened. Then, with an accelerating fall, the one door that had been targeted fell outward and hit the ground with a solid thud.

The commander gave a hand signal for one last check as the rest of the commandoes gathered together for the final assault.

The man with the Geiger counter stepped into the opening where the door had been, shoulders hunched, expecting a burst of fire.

What he got was worse.

The Geiger counter screeched the warning and the man holding it knew he was dead, just by means other than bullet.

A voice called out of the hangar, first in Persian, then in Kurdish: *"Do not enter. You will die of radiation if you enter."*

Inside the hangar, Haney carried the core of the first warhead in gloved hands over to the truck with the lead box. He dumped it on the back, then went to the second warhead. Now that he understood how the weapon was designed, this one went faster.

He was tearing through the outer layers of the weapon to the pit, which contained the plutonium. The pit was a solid ball of plutonium shielded by a layer of beryllium. While the metal was brittle and expensive, it was also a neutron reflector. The entire thing had been built at the Rocky Flats weapons plant in Colorado. It's a testament to the toxicity of plutonium, that even in a shielded environment and under the strictest safety guidelines, that Rocky Flats, despite not having had any plutonium in the site since 1994, is still off-limits and is a game preserve for perpetuity.

By breaking the protective coating around the pit of the first bomb, Haney had made this location deadly to humans.

He was holding at all costs.

*****

"Lock and load," Cane shouted, while also giving the hand command for it. "Five minutes out!"

Muzzles pointed down, the TriOp contractors made ready for battle.

He leaned close to Ducharme. "What do you have?"

"The F-22 I came in on," Ducharme said, "is inbound. Its time on target is four minutes, and it will pave our way in."

*****

Which meant the F-22 had taken off only a few minutes ago and was flying low and fast above the Turkish countryside. It's special stealth coating and technology allowed it to proceed unseen by radar.

Stretch was doing the equivalent of driving and texting, except at high speed and with more training. He was entering the grid coordinates of the target, while also heading directly toward it.

*****

Outside the hangar, the Iranian commando leader had broken radio silence and was calling back to his headquarters for instructions on how to deal with this unforeseen development. The reading on the Geiger counter indicated that a fatal dose of radiation would be received by anyone who entered the blown door. He had his men huddled behind the one door that was still standing.

*****

By breaking radio silence, the Iranians were alerting the Turks that something was amiss in the northeastern part of their country. Alarms were ringing and flight crews were scrambling.

*****

In the Anderson House, Turnbull was on the phone with a high Cincinnatian in the State Department, outlining the current problem. The wheels of under the table diplomacy, greased by the power of the Society of Cincinnati, an organization not limited to the United States, began to turn.

Then he turned back to Burns. "I'll try to find Hoover's files...what's left of them."

"They're probably in the drawer in that desk you're sitting at," Burns said.

"Hoover had a *lot* of files," Turnbull said. "And some *were* destroyed." He pointed at Burns. "Tell you what. Have Evie—"

"She's not your friend."

"She isn't anyone's friend as far as I can tell," Turnbull said. "Have Ms. Tolliver check in the APS records for a group called the Peacekeepers. I think they're very relevant to the current situation."

*****

The bomb bay doors in the belly of the F-22 snapped open.

"Close enough," Stretch said, and he hit the fire button, then banked hard.

A GBU-39 Small Diameter Bomb was released from the bottom of the F-22. Small diamondback wings snapped out into place and the missile continued on its journey alone. Stretch had programmed in the grid coordinates for the front of the hangar and internal guidance system in the bomb had it on the correct flight path.

The GBU-39 was rated with a circular error probability of five to eight meters, which in weapons man talk meant it had a fifty percent chance of coming within that distance of the designated target.

*****

"One minute!" Cane yelled.

The Blackhawk was flying inside a canyon now, walls on either side. The Halo was up higher, above the canyon, tracking the aircraft below.

Ducharme felt a pounding in his head, the increased blood flow from the adrenaline coursing through his veins, causing spots of pain to flicker.

It was worse than ever.

*****

Stretch had one stop on his way back to Al Asad. He could see the heat signatures of the two Chinooks on his display. His M16A2 40mm cannon was in the base of his right wing. The small door covering the barrel slid open. Finger light on the trigger, Stretch made sure he had a good target, then he fired.

The cannon had 480 rounds of ammunition, which sounds like a lot to an Infantryman, but for a pilot it meant five seconds worth of firing.

Stretch used all five seconds, blasting the helicopters into scrap metal and their crews into oblivion. Then he gained altitude and speed and headed back toward Al Asad.

*****

The GBU-39 made a slight adjustment, then did as advertised, exploding six meters away from the doors of the hangar.

It was an air burst, designed for maximum damage to personnel and equipment.

It worked.

*****

Inside the hangar, Haney was working on the third core. He felt sick and had already vomited once. He was also tired, more so than he'd ever remembered. Every movement felt like he was deep underwater.

But he kept at it.

*****

The explosion ahead was a flash of lightning in Ducharme's night vision goggles.

"Let's hope that hit the target," Cane said. Over the team's net he issued orders.

The Blackhawk flew around a bend and Cane kicked his fast rope over the edge. Ducharme did the same, wrapping his arms around the thick rope and letting gravity do the rest. He half expected automatic fire to be coming his way, but there was nothing.

He hit the ground and cleared the rope and the next man was already coming down. Ducharme went to one knee and surveilled the area through his night vision goggles.

Bodies—mostly parts of bodies—littered the ground. Ducharme spotted the opening to the hangar and headed toward it, only to be grabbed by Cane.

"Hold on," Cane said. "I've got commo that indicates it's hot in there."

"Hot?"

"Radioactive."

"Shit," Ducharme muttered. "What are we going to do?"

"Switch to net three," Cane said. "The guy inside is on it."

Ducharme did as told, and he heard Cane talking to Haney.

"What's the situation?" Cane asked.

"I've got all three cores out," Haney said. "Broke the containment on one. Keep them out. To keep them out." His voice was barely above a whisper.

"How do we get the cores?" Cane asked.

The rest of the TriOp team was gathered behind Cane and Ducharme. It was pretty much impossible to take a step without a boot crunching into some vestige of a human being. They were all combat veterans, but that didn't mean they were immune to what was surrounding them.

"Give me a minute," Haney replied, not sounding like a guy who had a minute.

*****

Stretch listened to his latest set of orders and wondered in what realm of reality those in the Pentagon existed.

"I've expended all my ordnance," Stretch said, not as a protest, but as a report of the reality of the situation.

But orders were orders.

He banked away from Al Asad and headed back toward Objective Ark.

*****

Haney dropped the third core on the bed of the truck. With great difficulty, he climbed into it. Then he picked up the broken core, his hands already singed, now screaming with pain as the skin was scorched despite the gloves. He tossed it in the lead box. Then he picked up the other two cores and threw them in as well, not caring if he damaged them.

Haney slammed the door shut, leaving pieces of skin on the metal.

He fell to his knees and vomited, but there was nothing left in his stomach except the dead skin sloughing off inside, so he produced a pile of blood and inner stomach.

He practically fell off the back of the truck. Keeping one hand on the side, he made his way around to the front. He grabbed the hook on the end of a steel tow cable looped around poles on the front of the truck.

Looking up, he saw how far away the blown door was and felt despair as sharp as the pain that was wracking his body.

He thought of his mother and her sacrifice for her country. And all his ancestors, all who'd served, back to the man who'd died in that prisoner of war ship in New York Harbor during the Revolutionary War.

He held the hook in both hands and moved forward. One step. One step. One step.

*****

The news over the radio wasn't good. Turkish jets were scrambling. Satellite imagery had picked up a large group of Kurds just a kilometer and a half away, but they were on foot.

"Haney?" Ducharme said over the radio.

All they could hear was heavy breathing.

"Haney?" Ducharme repeated. He looked at Cane. "I'm going in after him."

"You go in there, you die," Cane said.

"Sir!" the man with the Geiger counter called out. "Readings dropped down. Way down. Gone in fact. He must have shielded whatever it was."

Ducharme didn't wait to hear more. He ran into the hangar.

Haney was crawling on his back, scooting his feet, hands in a death grip around the hook. Ducharme knelt next to him, taking the hook. "I've got it."

Haney looked up. "The cores are in the vault."

"Roger that." Ducharme stood, cable in hand. "You did good, soldier."

Hany reached up and Ducharme took his hand, feeling the blood and goo rubbing against his palm.

"Please?" Haney asked. "Mercy."

"My honor, sir," Ducharme said, and he fired a round through Haney's head.

Ducharme shook off the death and the pain inside his own head and pulled the cable toward the entrance. Just as all the TriOp men ran in and joined him. They pulled the cable out the blown door, into the open.

"Haul!" Cane ordered.

In unison, they began pulling. With a screech of rusted brake pads and wheel rims with the rubber rotted off them, the truck with the lead box began slowly rolling toward the doors.

"Halo, this is Six," Cane said over the radio. "Give me a heavy lift cable and get to my location ASAP."

As they did that, Ducharme tossed a couple of flares and did a quick search of the hangar. He found Jonah's body and patted him down, discovering his passport. And a coin in his pocket: a silver dollar. He saw the row of desiccated bodies and didn't have to use his imagination to know what had happened to them.

He did a quick check of all six missiles, making sure they weren't leaving any warheads behind, then joined the line of mercenaries pulling the truck out of the hangar.

The nose of the truck passed through the hangar door. They pulled it out and clear.

The Halo appeared overhead, blasting sand and dirt all around. A cable snaked down to the ground. Ducharme and Cane grabbed it, and then jumped up onto the cargo bed.

14 October 1962

In August 1962 an Air Force U-2 'mistakenly' flew over Sakhalin Island in the Soviet Far East. The next month, in early September, a U-2, purportedly operated by the Taiwanese, was lost over Western China. The official story was that the cause of the loss was unknown, but among those in the know it was widely accepted a Chinese surface-to-air-missile (SAM) had shot down the plane.

Given that back in 1960, a U-2 operated by the CIA was shot down over Russia, and the pilot, Gary Powers, was captured, effectively destroying any chance President Eisenhower had of making headway in his subsequent summit with Khrushchev, President Kennedy had his doubts about continuing U-2 missions over areas where they could be shot down.

The problem, of course, is that usually those were the exact places where an over-flight was needed.

In September 1962, analysts at the Defense Intelligence Agency discovered from satellite imagery that Cuban SAM sites were being arranged in a pattern similar to what the Soviets used to encircle their own ICBM bases. It didn't take the greatest leap of logic to imagine what that portended. The DIA immediately requested U-2 over-flights to get better imagery of what was going on in Cuba at these sites.

Kennedy, leery of being burned by the CIA as Eisenhower had been over the Gary Powers incident, where not only the plane getting shot down, but the false cover story had blown up in Ike's face, wanted nothing to do with the CIA running such an operation.

The debacle of the Bay of Pigs might also have had something to do with that decision. The gap between the President and his intelligence agency was wide and strained. Pressed by the DIA, the CIA and the Pentagon, Kennedy finally authorized over-flights of Cuba with the caveat that they be flown by the Air Force, not the CIA. A case might be made that an Air Force plane shot down was an act of war, while a CIA plane was an act of espionage. Splitting hairs, but in politics and public relations, such hairs were crucial.

After some weather delays, the first flight occurred on 14 October, with a U-2 taking 928 photographs while racing over Cuba at 70,000 feet.

The film was analyzed on 15 October.

By that evening the analysts were certain they were looking at medium range ballistic missile bases being prepared.

The National Security Adviser decided to wait until the following morning to inform the President, as if time would somehow soften the bad news.

It didn't.

*****

"The sons-a-bitches didn't have a damn plan in place," Kennedy said.

"No escape hatch," Mary Meyer murmured, unheard by the President in his anger as he continued.

"They never considered the possibility the Russians would put missiles in Cuba. We've put missiles into Europe, but it never occurred to them that the Russians might pull something similar."

Kennedy was striding back and forth in a darkened Oval Office. The world outside of the White House had little idea that today was the beginning of a crisis that would bring all of them close to nuclear annihilation. Everything up until now had been the gathering of intelligence and initial maneuverings on the chessboard of world politics and military power. But that intelligence had been brought before Kennedy. And now, as the clock struck midnight, he was alone in the Oval Office with Mary Meyer, who was seated in a high-backed chair, listening as her friend and lover ranted.

Meyer was nervous, because this was the first time she'd been in the White House alone with Jack while his wife was also in the building. Sure, Mary had been here for social occasions, but that was always in a crowd. She'd also been here to visit the First Lady, even helping Jackie with her grand plans to update the interior of the White House. But this, in the middle of the night, alone, with the First Lady upstairs, was very different.

But the situation was very different.

"I pulled a bunch of the so-called brains and experts and powers-that-be together earlier," Kennedy continued. "Get all the angles, all the bullshit. The Executive Committee of the National Security Council. EXCOMM." He laughed, as if the term were some inside joke. "I'd have a couple of them taken out and shot if I had old Khrushchev's power."

"I imagine Premier Khrushchev has his own set of problems," Meyer ventured.

Kennedy stopped in his pacing and gave her a tired grin. "I'm sure the old bear does. But this, trying to sneak missiles in to Cuba...it's underhanded."

Meyer didn't point out that he'd just said that the United States had its own missiles in Europe. "What did your committee suggest?"

"Oh, yes, the great options they presented," Kennedy said, striding toward his desk. He sat down behind it and searched through same papers.

Meyer had to smile, seeing him sit behind the old wooden desk. "Jack."

Kennedy paused, surprised she'd interrupted him. "What?"

"Take it easy." Meyer stood and walked over, perching herself on the corner of the desk. Not in a sexual way, but a more intimate gesture: of trust.

"You know this desk was made from the timbers of the HMS Resolute and donated by Queen Victoria to the United States in 1880?" She didn't wait for an answer. "We

were well on our way to our third war with Britain in 1856. One of our ships found the Resolute, *adrift after being abandoned by a British expedition trying to find the Northwest Passage. A politician who was one of the biggest proponents of a war with England strangely proposed we fix up the* Resolute *and sail her back to England as a sign of good faith. A political and publicity maneuver. It eased tensions. And when the ship was finally sent to be broken-down, a desk was made. This desk. Presented to the United States at the behest of Queen Victoria." She tapped the wood she was sitting on.*

"Your point?" Kennedy asked. "Because you always have one. You think Khrushchev is going to make a desk out of the U-2 he shot down and send it to me?"

"Sometimes the people you view as your enemy only need a small gesture in order to stop things from escalating."

Kennedy shook his head. "Not likely in this scenario."

Meyer picked up a unique paperweight. A piece of coconut encased in wood and a clear plastic cover. Etched on the surface was: NAURO ISL...COMMANDER...NATIVE KNOWS POSIT...11 ALIVE...NEED SMALL BOAT...KENNEDY

"You took a chance giving this to those natives," Meyer said. She was referring to when Kennedy carved the message on the piece of coconut and gave it to two natives after his command, PT-109, was run over by a Japanese destroyer during World War II. "They could have taken it to the Japanese."

"But they didn't," Kennedy said. "They took it to the Australian Coastwatchers."

"So you used an intermediary. And you told me about the Coastwatchers and how they put their lives on the line sending those messages that eventually got you rescued. Didn't you say during the Berlin crisis that Khrushchev sent a message via one of his spies to Bobby?" she asked, referring to his brother.

"Yes, but that fellow was recalled to Russia. And no one's approached us yet. I think Khrushchev is pushing his hand. Vienna was a mistake, as you warned me it would be."

Meyer got him back on the immediate problem. "What did the EXCOMM experts offer up as solutions to your current situation."

Kennedy twisted in the chair, trying to relieve the back pain that always seemed to get worse under stress. "They had to come up with possible solutions on the fly." He once more searched through the papers on his desk until he came up with a piece of legal paper on which he'd scrawled notes.

"Here's the collective genius. One, of course, is do nothing. The Russians having missiles in Cuba won't mean that much in the strategic picture."

"I'm sure that didn't go over well."

"Old Uncle Khrushchev would love if I did nothing, but that's McNamara's stance," he said, referring to the Secretary of Defense. "The Joint Chiefs completely disagree, of course, with LeMay being the most vocal. But McNamara does have a point." He met her eyes. "I never told you this, and it's something we have to keep a lid on, but I campaigned on the missile gap and it turns out there is one, except it isn't what the CIA and Pentagon have been putting out. We've got over five thousand warheads, and the Russians have around three hundred."

"Oh, Jack! No wonder they're sending missiles to Cuba. Can you imagine what Khrushchev and his generals must feel like with that kind of disparity? General LeMay would be birthing nukes if he were on that end of the scale."

Despite the stress and the pain in his back, Kennedy laughed. *"Mary, Mary. Always worrying about what people feel, even that old bear Khrushchev. The more important question is: how many bombs do we need to wipe each other out? When will it stop? And LeMay. He just wants to bomb something. Anything. Why have all those pretty planes and bombs if you can't use them?"*

"So the CIA and Pentagon lied to you," Meyer said.

"They've lied to me about a lot of things. They've lied to the entire country."

"So how can you listen to them now?" Meyer asked.

"Who else can I listen to?" Kennedy asked, without expecting an answer, but he got one anyway.

"I'm here to listen to you," Meyer said.

"That's why I called." Kennedy sighed. *"I've got to clear my head, Mary. I even stopped taking the pills."* Kennedy dropped the piece of paper. *"Actually, McNamara is right. Forty more warheads for the Russians isn't going to change the balance of power. Militarily. But putting them in Cuba changes things politically. Since it appears to change the balance of power and appearance contributes to reality."*

"What other options were you given?"

He glanced down at the notes. *"Diplomacy. I guess we could kindly ask Khrushchev and Castro to not emplace the missiles."* He looked up. *"By the way, that's the funny thing. The DIA boys don't even think the missiles are in place. They think they're on board a couple of Russian ships en route, and that what the imagery picked up was the preparations for them."*

"So it's not yet a true crisis," Meyer said.

"Every mile closer those ships get to Cuba, the more of a crisis it becomes." He looked back down. *"Someone suggested sending a warning to Castro, although they were rather vague about what exactly should be the threat behind the warning, except to escalate to other options. First, and probably best, would be a blockade to stop the ships carrying the missiles. The Navy likes that one since they'll be taking point on it. The Air Force of course wants to simply bomb all the missiles sites."*

"And the Army wants to invade," Meyer finished for him.

"Everyone in uniform ultimately wants to invade. The Joint Chiefs all are for it. They see it as an opportunity. They think the Russians won't go to war over Cuba."

"We were willing to go to war over Berlin," Meyer noted.

"Were we?" Kennedy said, and it was clear in his own mind that he'd never completely committed to that course of action. *"We go into Cuba, there's no doubt the Russians will roll over West Berlin and then where will it stop? The English and the French won't be thrilled if Berlin is attacked as they have people there, too. We're sitting on top of a possible World War. With a nuclear exchange more than likely."*

"The Guns of August," *Meyer said, referring to the Pulitzer prize-winning book about the road into the debacle of World War I. She'd given it to Kennedy years ago and he'd devoured it, as he did anything that contributed to his base of knowledge.*

"Exactly," Kennedy said. "The Chairman wants me to go to NATO to get them on alert and to start mobilizing. But once everyone starts mobilizing, where does it stop? Who backs down first? This isn't a handful of tanks at Checkpoint Charlie. We're talking bombers and submarines with nuclear weapons. Missiles with nuclear warheads. It's a slippery slope into what could be a freefall of Armageddon." *Kennedy got up, a look of irritation on his face, both from his back and the situation.* "Khrushchev is a damn liar. He told me he had no designs on Cuba. And the timing. He wants to keep me from getting re-elected in '64 if I back down. Americans won't stand for missiles in Cuba."

"The election is a way off," *Meyer said, but Kennedy was working himself into a rage only a few in his inner circle had experienced.*

"He's an immoral gangster. A thug. I don't give a good Goddamn if the missiles are coming from Russia or from Cuba. He's trying to blackmail me. If he gets away with this, he'll push in Berlin again and probably some place else. Maybe Southeast Asia."

"We're in Berlin, and you've sent advisers to Vietnam," *Meyer said calmly.* "And we've placed Jupiter missiles in Italy and Turkey."

"Whose damn side are you on?" *Kennedy demanded.*

"I'm on the side that wants to keep the Guns of August from turning into the Missiles of October," *Meyer said.*

*****

World War I resonated differently with Russians than it did the rest of the world, so The Guns of August *wouldn't have mattered much to Khrushchev. That First World War presaged the collapse of the Czars and the entire Russian way of life into its present incarnation of Communism.*

"They know," *Mikoyan said. They were in the Premier's office and Mikoyan was forcing himself not to fidget. It was dawn in the Soviet capitol while it was the middle of the night in Washington, DC.*

"What exactly do they know?" *Khrushchev demanded.*

"They know about the sites in Cuba," *Mikoyan said.* "A U-2 flew over Cuba on a flight path that indicates they were looking for the sites. Our people in Washington say that the Joint Chiefs and Secretary of Defense, the Secretary of State and other key people were at the White House all day."

"And Penkovsky?" *Khrushchev asked.* "What does his source tell him?"

"That Kennedy is angry. He feels you betrayed him."

"The hell with him!" *Khrushchev banged a fist on the top of his desk.* "They came into our neighborhood, our part of the world, and put missiles in Italy and Turkey. West Berlin is bad enough. Who does he think he is? Cuba has a right to protect itself from Imperialist aggression. The Americans already sponsored one invasion attempt on the island. We know they are planning another. We have a right to help our ally when they *ask for our help. The Americans believe everything in the world must align with their vision, no matter how misguided."*

"The Americans might not be the real problem," Mikoyan said.

"Castro?"

Mikoyan nodded. "I told him the Americans will just make a fuss and then accept it, just as we've accepted the missiles in Italy and Turkey. I told Che Guevara not to worry. I cannot promise them more than that. But now that the cat is out of the bag, so to speak, Castro and Che feel it is time for a showdown with the United States."

"Ha!" Khrushchev slapped the palm of his hand on the desk. "They do? Very nice of them to try to raise the ante with my military forces. Would Castro take his ragtag army and invade Florida? How far would he get?"

"Comrade, our man in Havana says Castro is talking of a beautiful death."

"What is the point of fighting the Imperialists if we die?" Khrushchev didn't expect an answer. "Tell Gromyko to meet with Kennedy. If pressed specifically on it, have him inform the American President that the missiles are only for defensive purposes, especially given the Bay of Pigs. Surely he can understand that. We have no designs on attacking the United States. But he is not to mention the missiles if Kennedy doesn't. Let us see what kind of player the American really is."

Mikoyan stood. "Yes, Premier." He headed for the door.

"And Comrade," Khrushchev halted him in his tracks. "Tell Penkovsky to make an initial feeler to the Americans for a back door."

Mikoyan turned. "What kind of back door, Premier?"

"You need not concern yourself with that," Khrushchev said. "He'll know what I mean."

A look of irritation that couldn't be controlled flashed across Mikoyan's face, but he nodded. "As you wish, Comrade."

He left and Khrushchev opened his center desk drawer. A dog-eared paperback was resting on top of a pile of folders stamped TOP SECRET.

He leaned back in his seat and continued reading Fail Safe.

CHAPTER EIGHT
The Present

Evie gave up on McBride's notes and the electronic archives of the APS for the time being. Burns' call with Turnbull's tidbit about the Peacekeepers drove her to the stacks. A climate-controlled room at the back of the second floor filled with rows and rows off books and papers, carefully indexed on three-by-five cards in several drawers.

It was archaic, but effective for two reasons: even though the computer system here was shielded and cut off from the outside world, no one in the covert world trusted electronic records. Not only could they be hacked into, they could also be destroyed by EMP. More important, the original documents were here, which meant they hadn't been altered; electronic records could never be trusted.

The problem with the index cards though, was that they weren't exactly Google. Without Turnbull's tip, why would she ever have looked for the term 'Peacekeeper?' And even if she had stumbled across the card, what importance would it have had?

She found the card easily enough in the alphabetical order.

Following the stack, row and order number, Evie found a folder sandwiched between two leather-bound books. As she pulled it off the shelf, a paperback fell out and hit the floor.

Evie picked it up. *Fail Safe*. A classic, both in print and film.

Suddenly, Evie remembered that there was a world outside of this Archive. She looked at her watch. The Turkish warplanes must be close to an interception with Ducharme and the plutonium cores.

But there was nothing she could do about it from here except continue to do her duty.

She carried the book and the file over to a standing desk in a corner of the Archives. She opened the file up and was rewarded with a single page of yellow legal pad on which some notes were scrawled:

Peacekeepers—New York City—initial roster two: code names Aaron and Bathsheba—contact: Groves

Evie's eyes became unfocused as she processed the scant information, adding in the copy of *Fail Safe*. And the Jupiter missiles in Turkey and three missing warheads.

This was not good.

*****

"We've got Turkish F-16s inbound," Stretch reported over the radio. "I've got 'em on my scope and they'll be on top of you in about two minutes."

Ducharme heard the report. He was busy with Cane and the TriOp's men, hooking the lift cable from the Halo to the attaching point on top of the lead safe, while others were trying to unhook the chains that held the box to the bed of the track.

The latter was proving to be difficult after half a century of rust.

"Hold on, attaching the cable," Cane finally ordered, just as they were about to snap it in place. Tethering the huge helicopter to the chained vault wasn't the smartest idea.

"How about lifting truck and box?" Ducharme shouted, trying to be heard above the roar of the blades over their head. "We don't have time to dick around."

Cane was decisive, if anything. "Stop!" he ordered the men trying to cut the chains. "Halo, this is Six. We're hooking you to the box in the cargo bed of the truck. The box is attached to the truck by chains. You're taking the whole thing. If the truck gets loose from the box during flight, that's fine. Over."

There was a moment of silence, then a voice with an Eastern European accent responded. "Roger. But that is going to be an unstable load. It gets us out of balance, I punch it."

"We're doing it."

Cane and Ducharme grabbed the large hook and stuck it through the attaching point, latching it shut and then securing it with a safety.

"Get off!" Cane shouted to his men. "Lift," he ordered the Halo pilot.

Ducharme ran to the end of the tailgate and jumped off, tumbling on the ground, into a mix of dirt, rock and viscera. The roar of the Halo's engines increased and the truck slowly lifted off the ground.

It floated away to the south. As soon as it was clear, Cane called in the Blackhawk. The chopper came in fast, touching down fifty meters away from the hangar. Ducharme ran with the rest of the TriOp men to it and slid on board. It was airborne as the last set of boots left the ground.

Ducharme grabbed a headset. The Blackhawk was faster, and not carrying a truck with a lead safe, so it quickly took a position above and behind the Halo. The time for stealth was over. Both choppers gained enough altitude so they would clear any obstacles and headed south.

The radio crackled and Ducharme recognized Turnbull's voice. "Cane. I've got someone at the Embassy working on calling off the Turks, but they haven't gotten through yet. Over."

Cane glanced at Ducharme in the dim light of the cargo bay. "Roger that. We've got a fighter that's going to give us some cover." The fact the fighter had no ordnance was an irritating and significant one if the Turks decided to escalate the situation. Ducharme's hope was that they wouldn't fire on the American aircraft. The two unmarked helicopters were a different story.

"Thirty seconds out," Stretch said. "I've pinged them with my radar. Trying to raise them on the radio. Anything you want me to tell them other than not to shoot you down?"

"Tell them we're recovering equipment from Operation Provide Comfort," Ducharme said, a weak cover story at best, but as his first company commander in the Army had always said, any plan was better than having Rommel shoving it up your rear on the drop zone.

He'd never been quite sure exactly what his commander had meant by that.

Provide Comfort had been a humanitarian mission run by the United States to help the Kurds after the First Gulf War.

The two fighters roared by, an inspection pass. Dawn was just beginning to tinge the sky in the east, and Ducharme could make out the silhouettes of the pilots' heads in their cockpits. They were F-16Cs with the large bubble cockpit; an American fighter built in Turkey under a licensing agreement. The eclectic nature of the armaments of the world indicated that corporations cared little for political borders or alliances. It was not uncommon in modern warfare for the same model of aircraft or tank or ship to be battling its mirror image on the other side.

"They're looping back," Stretch said. "Not responding to my hails. I'm picking up targeting radar from them."

"Who are they targeting?" Cane asked.

"Not me," Stretch said. "They're going weapons hot," he added. "I can try to get between you and the missiles when they launch and draw them off."

He didn't sound very optimistic, and Cane surprised Ducharme with his response.

"Negative. This is our play. We're unsanctioned. You're official US government."

"I can put the fear of God in them, at least," Stretch said.

Ducharme and Cane watched as the F-22 banked hard and headed toward the F-16s that were closing.

"You know how to win a game of chicken with two cars heading toward each other?" Stretch asked, not waiting for an answer. "You throw your steering wheel out the window."

Stretch won as the Turkish jets blinked, avoiding an air-to-air collision by breaking off their run.

This gained them about a minute and a half. The Iraqi border was a good fifteen minutes away.

"They're splitting up," Stretch said. "One of them at least is going to make a solid run on you this time."

"Our turn to run that one off," Cane said.

"I'm taking the one from the north," Stretch said. "You've got the one from the west."

He leaned forward and tapped the pilot on the shoulder. The Blackhawk arced around toward the second Turkish jet.

The distance closed rapidly. Ducharme was shoulder to shoulder with Cane in the cargo bay, staring at the oncoming F-16. But before it got within dangerous distance it broke off. So did the other one. The two rapidly gained altitude and took up a racetrack five thousand feet overhead.

"Cane?" Turnbull's voice came through the radio. "Our man got hold of the right person in the Turkish government. You are clear to the border."

*****

Baths stood in front of Arlington House in the darkness. The cemetery was so large, it was easy to infiltrate at night. She knew the history of the place and the land. Arlington House had been the Custer-Lee House, owned by Robert E. Lee's wife. He'd become the owner of it and the slaves tied to it when he married. During the Civil War, the Union seized the house and lands to serve a specific purpose: a cemetery for the thousands of Union dead.

Perhaps the very definition of irony.

Looking to the east, Baths could see the Lincoln and Washington Memorials, well lit on this chilly night. At the base of the hill the house was on, a small flame flickered, fighting bravely against the darkness and the cold. It marked the gravesite of John F. Kennedy, his wife and his two children (one who'd died in childbirth and the other slightly after).

Turning to the right, she could now see the Pentagon, many of the windows lit, as running the military was a twenty-four hours a day operation.

"We keep the peace," Baths said and began to make her way down the hill to do her checks.

18 October 1962

"The missiles have a range of one thousand, one hundred and seventy-four miles," the CIA analyst informed President Kennedy and the rest of the EXCOMM staff. He slapped a pointer on a map and ran it along a circle outlined in red. "Washington, DC is within range, and if the missiles are launched, could reach here in thirteen minutes."

"Tell me something I don't already know," Kennedy said, shifting irritably in his seat.

Robert Kennedy, the Attorney General, spoke up. "You fellows asked for this briefing. Why?" Robert also knew something no one else in the room did: everything was being recorded by his brother. If it came down to the Missiles of October, the President wanted the record to be clear, even though there was a good chance no one would be around to listen to the recordings.

The CIA analyst glanced at his boss, Director McCone, who gave a slight nod. They were in the Cabinet Room in the West Wing of the White House. It was a beautiful fall day outside, belying the tenseness inside the room.

"Sir, we can't make an estimate on when the missiles will be ready for launching. It really depends on how soon the nuclear warheads can be attached."

"Wait a second," the President said. "I was told the missiles and warheads were on ships still at sea."

"We believe the R-12 Dvina ballistic missiles are on those ships, sir," the analyst said. "Most likely along with their warheads. However, there is some intelligence indicating that some nuclear warheads are already in Cuba, capable of being delivered either by Soviet artillery or aircraft."

"'Some intelligence?'" the President repeated.

Director McCone stepped into the breach. "Unsubstantiated reports from agents on the island, sir. The accuracy of the reports and the reliability of the agents are both suspect. But I felt it best that you are aware of all possibilities. It is also possible some missiles are on the island, we just haven't picked them up yet with imagery."

An argument immediately broke out, splitting along the lines of those who wanted a pre-emptive strike on Cuba, those who wanted not only that but also an invasion, and those who wanted a more peaceful resolution.

The whole point of forming EXCOMM was to avoid the group-think that had led to the Bay of Pigs. The argument raging now indicated that the goal had been achieved, perhaps too well.

"Enough," Kennedy finally said in a low voice, but one that cut through all the cross-chatter. "Secretary McNamara. Give us the latest status of our armed forces."

"Yes, sir." McNamara glanced down at his notes. "The entire military is on high alert. The First Armored Division has been deployed to Fort Stewart in Georgia, where it can move to Savannah Harbor and take ship for an invasion. Five more divisions have been alerted for combat operations. The Air Force has extra B-52s airborne around the clock. B-47 Stratojet medium range bombers have been dispersed to civilian airports as per their war plan. The Navy is positioning ships for both a blockade or invasion."

"Or both," Robert Kennedy said.

"Or both," McNamara quickly covered his gaffe.

"Or neither," the President said.

McNamara flushed. "Yes, sir, but I must relay the advice of the Joint Chiefs. They believe unanimously and strongly that an air strike should be launched against the missile sites before they are completed. The sooner the better."

"Thank you for your input." President Kennedy leaned forward in his seat. "I have a meeting with the Soviet Minister of Foreign Affairs in a few minutes. I'm going to put his feet to the fire and get some answers on what's going on. I'm not going to let him know we have a good idea of the build up in Cuba, but push him enough to worry him."

The President stood. "Gentlemen, we'll meet again in six hours."

Everyone filed out of the room except for Robert Kennedy.

The President jumped right into it with his brother. "I'm going to have to take out those missiles."

"You can't pre-empt," Robert said. He slapped a hand on the conference table. "You launch a surprise air attack on Cuba, you'll go down in history like Tojo and Pearl Harbor."

"Now, that's a bit much, Bobby," the President protested. "Pearl Harbor was a long way from Japan, and the fleet had been there for decades. The Japanese were offensive in that attack. We're on the defensive."

"Sabotage," the younger Kennedy advised. "Blow up a ship near Guantanamo and blame it on Fidel. Then you have free reign to do what you want. Bomb them. Invade. Whatever."

"'Remember the Maine,'" the President said. "No one knows what happened there. We've invaded Cuba before, although not many remember." He walked over to his brother and slapped him reassuringly on the shoulder. "Let me talk to Gromyko and see what he has to say." Kennedy reached under the desk and turned off the recorders. "Bobby, contact Penkovsky. Tell him I need to get a direct line to Khrushchev. We're walking a tight line here."

Kennedy left the conference room and walked through the White House. Everyone in the building knew something was up, but outside of EXCOMM and those directly in the intelligence and military lines of communication, no one knew exactly what it was. Kennedy was keeping this close to the vest, hoping to resolve the crisis before public opinion skewed the reaction.

Kennedy sat behind his desk. He made sure the recorder in here was off.

When Gromyko entered Kennedy stood, but everyone else left. There were no photographers to take photos for the next day's papers. No staff. No aides.

The Russian moved forward warily, toward the chair in front of the President's desk.

"May I sit, Mister President?"

"Certainly," Kennedy said. As the Russian sat down, Kennedy began speaking. *"So. All is quiet in Berlin."*

"It is."

"Will it stay quiet, Minister Gromyko?"

"There is no reason it shouldn't, Mister President."

"I assume Premier Khrushchev knows I misspoke in Vienna. I consider West Berlin as vital to my country's interests as, let us say, Florida."

Gromyko raised a bushy eyebrow. "I do not know what Comrade Khrushchev knows. Why would you mention Florida?"

"Because it's close to Cuba."

"I believe Cuba has more to fear from the United States than the opposite. You have, after all, attempted to invade its sovereign territory."

"Some exiles attempted a coup," Kennedy said. "We have no intention of invading Cuba. If we had, wouldn't we have given at least air and naval support to those exiles? I can tell you this, though. We will not tolerate any offensive weapons being placed in Cuba by your country."

"We have advisers in Cuba," Gromyko allowed. "Much like you have advisers in South Vietnam. You have many troops stationed overseas. Throughout Europe. In South Korea. We have made no protest about that."

"My advisers in Vietnam are to help a democratically elected government stay in power."

"Our advisers in Cuba are there to help train the Cubans on defensive armaments only. They are by no means offensive. Even if requested, the Soviet government would never become involved in rendering such assistance."

Kennedy stared at the Foreign Minister who returned the gaze without blinking. They remained like that for almost a minute, then Kennedy nodded. "So be it. It's good we have an understanding." He stood and Gromyko lumbered to his feet.

Kennedy walked Gromyko to the door and saw him off. As soon as he was gone, Robert Kennedy came in from another door.

"That lying bastard," the President said.

"Why didn't you tell him we know about the emplacements being built for the missiles?"

"That's my hold card," Kennedy said. "There is no way those missiles are being emplaced to defend Cuba. If, God forbid, the Russians already have nuclear warheads in Cuba, they can deliver them defensively via aircraft and artillery. They don't need missiles with the range to hit here. There's only one reason Khrushchev would be putting missiles into Cuba and that's for offensive reasons. I have no doubt he wants to use them as leverage to get us to give up West Berlin."

"LeMay just phoned me while you were Gromyko," Robert Kennedy said. "He feels, and I quote, 'a naval blockade is the equivalent of appeasement at Munich.'"

The President slammed a fist onto his desk. "Who does that son-of-a-bitch think he is? That he can talk to you like that, knowing you'd bring it to me? He's been itching to use his planes and drop nuclear bombs as long as I've known him." Kennedy shook his head. "Isn't he afraid of a nuclear conflagration?"

"I don't think he's afraid of anything," Robert Kennedy said.

"We go with the blockade," Kennedy said. "We keep those missiles on those ships from making it to Cuba."

"And if the Russians don't honor the blockade?"
"I'll deal with that when we get to it."

CHAPTER NINE
The Present

The men Ramsay hired were the best private detectives in New York. He'd used them before on various missions, usually corporate espionage. He'd also used them on and off over the years to look into the Peacekeepers, but they'd always drawn a blank.

But now that they had a name, Joseph Penkovsky—a name that existed in various databases because Jonah had needed a passport and money to travel overseas—they were able to do more in two hours than in the past decade.

It turned out that Penkovsky had been preparing to leave the Peacekeepers for a while. His name change from Pensky had occurred five years ago. The passport under the new name had been applied for two years ago. He'd withdrawn money from an ATM just this past week prior to leaving the country.

It was this last tidbit that allowed them to zero in on his trail. They found his bank account, his account number and the last ATM he'd used. Then they examined the ATM's camera and uncovered his image. Using his image, they were able to access New York's fledgling, but growing, system of surveillance cameras that dotted Manhattan, and using facial recognition technology they searched the databases.

They were rewarded with over a dozen positive hits. Using those hits, they tracked Penkovsky from the ATM along the streets of lower Manhattan until he went down into the Fulton Street Subway station.

Then it became interesting. Surveillance inside the station showed that he didn't board a train. Rather, he waited until a train had just pulled out and the platform was clear of people before he slipped off the platform and disappeared into the dark tunnel.

Finally, Ramsay had good news to call in to Turnbull.

*****

The Blackhawk hovered nearby as the Halo slowly lowered the truck to the tarmac at Al Asad. The F-22 had already landed and was now parked near the hangar where they'd staged out.

Sure the truck was safely down, Cane had the Blackhawk land. As the engine powered down, Ducharme got off the chopper, Cane at his shoulder.

"That was fun," Cane said.

"Fun?'" Ducharme said.

"I know you think I do it for the money, but I'd do it if they didn't pay me," Cane said. "For a lot of my boys, the regular army is too boring."

"But they take the extra pay," Ducharme said.

"Yeah, we take it." Cane halted and put an arm out. "See my team sergeant over there?" he pointed at the man directing the TriOp men offloading the chopper.

"Yes."

"He donates almost all this money to a cancer research facility. Where his wife died. He has nothing to go back to. A lot of us have nothing. Some who do have something know better than to go back. You got what, ten, twenty vets killing themselves every day back in the States, right?"

Ducharme didn't say anything.

"Ever occur to you that maybe some of us want to do something useful at least? We hold the true front lines in the war on terror."

"And fight for the corporations," Ducharme added.

Cane dropped his arm and gave a conciliatory smile. "Yeah. That too." They began walking toward the truck as the Halo punched the cable and moved a hundred meters away to land. "But what makes you think the US Army isn't ultimately fighting for the corporations, too?"

Ducharme acknowledged that with a nod. "You should talk to my friend Evie. She'd give you the entire history of all the banana wars, the wars for oil, for empire. All of it. I know the history and it isn't pretty."

"But today," Cane said as they reached the truck, "we did something good. If the Iranians had gotten hold of this plutonium, God knows what they would have done with it."

Ducharme nodded once more. "Your men did a good job." He grabbed the door handle and gave it a tug. With a screech of protesting rust, the driver's door came open. Ducharme climbed in. He looked around the cab. An old thermos rested on the passenger seat, awaiting an owner who'd died more than five decades ago.

Ducharme flipped down the visor and a yellowing piece of map fell out.

It was a map of Moscow.

Ducharme turned the paper over and an eight-digit grid coordinate was scrawled in pencil, the numbers so faded as to be almost illegible.

Almost, but not quite.

"I need—" Ducharme turned to face the muzzle of Cane's pistol. "You gotta be kidding me."

"You weren't supposed to make it out of Turkey alive," Cane said. He had the gun just out of arm's reach. A professional. "A casualty of the mission."

"So why am I here?" Ducharme asked.

Cane sighed and lowered the pistol and holstered it. "Because we did do good and you were part of it. This part, killing you, is politics. I'm not playing."

"Won't you lose your Christmas bonus or something?"

"Funny guy," Cane said. "There's a good chance they'll send someone after me. But I like to think I'm too valuable. Of course no one is too valuable." He nodded at the piece of paper. "Find something?"

"Grid coordinates. I think they're in Moscow."

"The missing bombs?"

"A good chance that it is. I need a Satcom link to Turnbull. I'll also mention that I overpowered you."

"You wish," Cane said. He hopped off the running board of the truck. "Come on." He led the way toward the Forward Operating Base in the hangar. "You also need to call your people and get some official US Military here to take control of that box. This is as far as we're taking it."

*****

"Here you go," Turnbull said. He'd just spun the combination on a large steel door deep in the bowels of the Anderson House. There was a loud click and Turnbull turned the metal wheel and then pulled open the door. "What we have of Hoover's files."

The vault beyond was jammed full of cardboard filing boxes.

"You don't have them inventoried?" Burns asked.

"They're stacked exactly the way Hoover had them stacked in his outer office," Turnbull said. "The information is too valuable to allow just anybody to know what's contained in these files. Lucius knew exactly what was in here and where it was, but unfortunately, your friend Ducharme took that knowledge away when he took Lucius's life. The new Head of the Society will have to spend several months in here going through everything. His brain will be the inventory."

"Not very efficient," Burns said.

"Lucius was Head for decades," Turnbull said. "It might not be efficient but it's very secure. And you can have the best inventory in the world, but someone still has to know exactly what it's an inventory of. Information that can't be accessed is useless."

"You expect me to dig through all this?" Burns asked.

"No," Turnbull said, walking down the narrow space between the stacks of boxes. He reached up and pulled one off a shelf. "I believe this is what you want." He took off the lid and extracted a leather-bound journal. "Mary Meyer's diary."

His Satphone buzzed.

Turnbull pulled it out of his pocket. "Yes?"

"It's Ducharme. I don't appreciate you trying to have me killed."

Turnbull sighed. "It didn't take so let's let bygones be bygones. How is Cane?"

"He'll live."

"What do you have for me? I assume this isn't just to bitch about the realities of our business?"

"You prepared to copy?"

Turnbull extracted a pen and pad from his breast pocket. "Go."

Ducharme rattled off eight numbers.

"This is a grid for...?" Turnbull asked.

"I think it's where our three missing nukes are."

"Any idea where this is?"

"I'd say somewhere in Moscow, probably close to the Kremlin. You might want to let your Russian friends know."

"That I will do."

"I'm coming back," Ducharme said. "I'll see you soon."

"Have a safe trip."

The line went dead.

*****

Evie was back in the main office of the APS with the folder and the book. The phone on the desk rang and she picked it up. "Yes?"

"Evie, you need to get General Dunning to send some forces to Al Asad to secure this plutonium."

"Will do. I just got a text from Burns. He's got Mary Meyer's diary, so I'm going to head to DC. I have a feeling it isn't as easy as this."

"It never is. Turnbull tried to have me killed in Turkey after we recovered the nukes. So be careful."

"I will."

There was a pause. "Are you happy I'm still alive?" Ducharme finally asked.

"Of course!"

"I can't read your mind, Evie."

"I'm sorry."

Ducharme's sigh echoed through the phone from the other side of the world. "And I found a map of Moscow and some grid coordinates. I have a feeling that's where the other three are."

"*Fail Safe*," Evie said.

"What?"

"I found something in the Archives here. A piece of paper mentioning Peacekeepers in New York City. All it said was quote: *Peacekeepers—New York City—initial roster two: code names Aaron and Bathsheba—contact: Groves*. End quote. But there was also a copy of *Fail Safe*. At the end of *Fail Safe*, after an American bomber gets through to Moscow and destroys it, the President has another American bomber destroy New York City. I think Kennedy and Khrushchev put bombs in both cities as their own form of Fail Safe."

"The Sword of Damocles," Ducharme said.

"Yes," Evie said.

"I relayed the info about the Moscow location to Turnbull. I think we let the Cincinnatians take care of that. They've got contacts there."

"And New York City?"

"I imagine Turnbull is on that, too. But you need to sit on him. Let Burns know he's got to be on alert and to cover your back."

"I don't think it's this simple," Evie said. "I think there has to be more to this."

"Isn't hidden nukes in Moscow and New York enough?"

"I just have this feeling we're missing something."

"Let's deal with what we have. I'm going to take the F-22 and fly back. I'll meet you in DC."

*****

Burns was seated in a corner of the office, leafing through Meyer's diary searching for something—anything—that would shed some light on the current situation. Turnbull was back at his desk, listening to Ramsay's report. When his New York agent was done, Turnbull issued his orders: "Get the NYPD to provide a perimeter. I'm sending in a special team to go into that tunnel and track down the Peacekeepers."

"Going to be hard to keep a lid on that," Ramsay said.

"You're wrong," Turnbull said. "It's going to be very easy. The Peacekeepers are deep underground, some place where no one has found them in decades. So taking them out will go unnoticed. And the police will be more than happy that we're most likely removing nuclear weapons from underneath the city. A win-win all around. Clear?"

"Clear, sir."

"Pull in some markers. There's plenty of people high in New York who owe us."

"Yes, sir."

Turnbull turned the phone off and looked up to see Burns standing in front of his desk, his pistol in his hand, although the hand was hanging at his side.

"You tried to kill Ducharme?"

"It was a thought," Turnbull said. "He's a very dangerous man, and he did kill my boss. I have some allegiance to those I serve with. Just as you do."

"So how about I shoot *you* right now?"

"How about we do what we set out to do? This is bigger than you or me." He tapped a folder he'd taken from the vault while Burns took the diary. "There's a record here of a team from the Philosophers, some of the Green Berets who stood in the honor guard for Kennedy's body, killing three of the Society's agents right here in DC."

"When?"

He opened the folder. "The twenty-fourth of November, 1963. Our agents intercepted the Soviet Ambassador, Mikoyan, as he was leaving Kennedy's lying in state at the Rotunda. Mrs. Kennedy had passed something to him. A piece of paper. We believe it was part of this Sword of Damocles. We tried to get it, but your people intercepted our interception. Killed our agents. So you can get down off your high horse, Burns. This is a bloody business we're in. And remember, you're inside *my* house right now. I could make you disappear and no one would be the wiser."

"Evie would."

"That's true," Turnbull said. "And that's part of the reason I'm letting you live."

"What's the other part?"

"I don't think we have all the pieces of the Sword yet."

"And when we get them?"

"Let's cross that wall when we get to it."

"What was on the paper?" Burns asked.

"That's a good question," Turnbull said. "Too bad our men were killed before they could get it."

"I'll ask Evie if she has any record of this."

*****

Ducharme took off in the F-22 as soon as the Air Force transport landed at Al Asad and two teams of Special Forces exited, taking over security for the lead box from Cane's men. He didn't swap spit with Cane upon departing, but he did shake the man's hand.

"Thanks for not killing me."

Cane laughed. "Actually, I think Turnbull knew I wouldn't. It was as much a test of me as it was a mission."

"So you failed?"

"Actually, I think I passed." He held out a Fairbairn commando knife. "Noticed you don't have a knife. Take one of ours."

Ducharme then got in the back seat of the fighter and they were airborne in seconds, gaining altitude as fast as the powerful engines could get them. The classic knife, with a TriOp crest on the handle, was now on Ducharme's belt.

"You good to make this trip?" Ducharme asked Stretch over the intercom.

"We don't do crew rest like the airliners," Stretch said. "I took a happy pill and will take another about halfway back. I'll get you back to the States. Then I'm going to sleep for a couple of days."

"Sounds like a good plan," Ducharme said, rubbing his forehead.

"Those were nukes you recovered?" Stretch asked.

"Yep."

"Fuck. That's not good."

"No, it's not."

"This over?"

"Nope."

22 October 1962

Go here: http://youtu.be/WYVPx3x3oCg view JFK Cuban Missile Crisis Speech

Mary Meyer was alone to watch this Presidential news conference. She was often alone. Despite her reputation, both real and rumor-earned, she valued the privacy of her home. With her insider knowledge, she wanted to see how much Jack leveled with the American people as her TV set flickered and then the picture resolved to show the newscast.

"Good evening, my fellow citizens." Kennedy sat behind a table, a small podium with two microphones set in front of him. He was in the Oval Office, facing an array of cameras.

"This Government, as promised, has maintained the closest surveillance of the Soviet military buildup on the island of Cuba. Within the past week, unmistakable evidence has established the fact that a series of offensive missile sites is now in preparation on that imprisoned island. The purpose of these bases can be none other than to provide a nuclear strike capability against the Western Hemisphere.

"Upon receiving the first preliminary hard information of this nature last Tuesday morning at nine A.M., I directed that our surveillance be stepped up. And having now confirmed and completed our evaluation of the evidence and our decision on a course of action, this Government feels obliged to report this new crisis to you in fullest detail.

"The characteristics of these new missile sites indicate two distinct types of installations. Several of them include medium range ballistic missiles, capable of carrying a nuclear warhead for a distance of more than one thousand nautical miles. Each of these missiles, in short, is capable of striking Washington, D. C., the Panama Canal, Cape Canaveral, Mexico City, or any other city in the southeastern part of the United States, in Central America, or in the Caribbean area.

"Additional sites not yet completed appear to be designed for intermediate range ballistic missiles—capable of traveling more than twice as far—and thus capable of striking most of the major cities in the Western Hemisphere, ranging as far north as Hudson Bay, Canada, and as far south as Lima, Peru. In addition, jet bombers, capable of carrying nuclear weapons, are now being uncrated and assembled in Cuba, while the necessary air bases are being prepared.

"This urgent transformation of Cuba into an important strategic base—by the presence of these large, long-range, and clearly offensive weapons of sudden mass destruction—constitutes an explicit threat to the peace and security of all the Americas, in flagrant and deliberate defiance of the Rio Pact of 1947, the traditions of this Nation and hemisphere, the joint resolution of the 87th Congress, the Charter of the United Nations, and my own public warnings to the Soviets on September fourth and thirteenth. This action also contradicts the repeated assurances of Soviet spokesmen, both publicly and privately delivered, that the arms buildup in Cuba would retain its original defensive character, and that the Soviet Union had no need or desire to station strategic missiles on the territory of any other nation.

"The size of this undertaking makes clear that it has been planned for some months. Yet only last month, after I had made clear the distinction between any introduction of ground-to-ground missiles and the existence of defensive antiaircraft missiles, the Soviet Government publicly stated on September eleventh that, and I quote, 'the armaments and military equipment sent to Cuba are designed exclusively for defensive purposes,' that, and I quote the Soviet Government, 'there is no need for the Soviet Government to shift its weapons for a retaliatory blow to any other country, for instance Cuba,' and that, and I quote their government, 'the Soviet Union has rockets powerful enough to carry these nuclear warheads that there is no need to search for sites for them beyond the boundaries of the Soviet Union.' That statement was false.

"Only last Thursday, as evidence of this rapid offensive buildup was already in my hand, Soviet Foreign Minister Gromyko told me in my office that he was instructed to make it clear once again, as he said his government had already done, that Soviet assistance to Cuba, and I quote, 'pursued solely the purpose of contributing to the defense capabilities of Cuba,' that, and I quote him, 'training by Soviet specialists of Cuban nationals in handling defensive armaments was by no means offensive, and if it were otherwise,' Mr. Gromyko went on, 'the Soviet Government would never become involved in rendering such assistance.' That statement also was false.

"Neither the United States of America nor the world community of nations can tolerate deliberate deception and offensive threats on the part of any nation, large or small. We no longer live in a world where only the actual firing of weapons represents a sufficient challenge *to a nation's security to constitute maximum peril. Nuclear weapons are so destructive and ballistic missiles are so swift, that any substantially increased possibility of their use or any sudden change in their deployment may well be regarded as a definite threat to peace.*

"For many years, both the Soviet Union and the United States, recognizing this fact, have deployed strategic nuclear weapons with great care, never upsetting the precarious status quo which insured that these weapons would not be used in the absence of some vital challenge. Our own strategic missiles have never been transferred to the territory of any other nation under a cloak of secrecy and deception; and our history—unlike that of the Soviets since the end of World War II—demonstrates that we have no desire to dominate or conquer any other nation or impose our system upon its people. Nevertheless, American citizens have become adjusted to living daily on the bull's-eye of Soviet missiles located inside the U.S.S.R. or in submarines.

"In that sense, missiles in Cuba add to an already clear and present danger . . ."

Kennedy continued on, laying out the background to the missiles, then moving forward to the current situation, connecting naturally, to the concept of appeasement, on which Meyer knew he'd written his thesis and was very sensitive about.

"The 1930s taught us a clear lesson: aggressive conduct, if allowed to go unchecked, ultimately leads to war. This nation is opposed to war. We are also true to our word. Our unswerving objective, therefore, must be to prevent the use of these missiles against this or any other country, and to secure their withdrawal or elimination from the Western Hemisphere.

"Our policy has been one of patience and restraint, as befits a peaceful and powerful nation, which leads a worldwide alliance. We have been determined not to be diverted from our central concerns by mere irritants and fanatics. But now further action is required—and it is under way; and these actions may only be the beginning. We will not prematurely or unnecessarily risk the costs of worldwide nuclear war in which even the fruits of victory would be ashes in our mouth-but neither will we shrink from that risk at any time it must be faced.

"Acting, therefore, in the defense of our own security and of the entire Western Hemisphere, and under the authority entrusted to me by the Constitution as endorsed by the Resolution of the Congress, I have directed that the following initial steps be taken immediately."

Meyer nodded as Kennedy laid out seven steps, the first of which was the blockade, addressing Khrushchev as much as he was addressing the American people. She'd been with him when he'd sketched this speech, but she was impressed how much better he'd made it in the time since she last saw him. The third step linked any launch from Cuba as an attack by the Soviet Union, in essence making Cuba a match point that would start an all out nuclear exchange between the two super-powers. In essence, another West Berlin, as if the world needed another such hot spot.

The seventh and final step was a direct appeal to Khrushchev to resolve the issues. Meyer knew Kennedy already had a copy of the speech delivered to Gromyko, who would have transmitted a copy to Moscow. By the time Kennedy was on the air, Khrushchev would have already read the speech and most likely ordered a heightened state of readiness for Soviet Forces.

Then the President wrapped up the speech, addressing once more, the American people:

"My fellow citizens: let no one doubt that this is a difficult and dangerous effort on which we have set out. No one can foresee precisely what course it will take or what costs or casualties will be incurred. Many months of sacrifice and self-discipline lie ahead—months in which both our patience and our will will be tested—months in which many threats and denunciations will keep us aware of our dangers. But the greatest danger of all would be to do nothing.

"The path we have chosen for the present is full of hazards, as all paths are—but it is the one most consistent with our character and courage as a nation and our commitments around the world. The cost of freedom is always high—but Americans have always paid it. And one path we shall never choose, and that is the path of surrender or submission.

"Our goal is not the victory of might, but the vindication of right—not peace at the expense of freedom, but both peace and freedom, here in this hemisphere, and, we hope, around the world. God willing, that goal will be achieved.

"Thank you and good night."

Meyer turned off the TV. She placed a hand on it, feeling the warmth generated by the tubes inside. "Good night, Jack. I hope you get some sleep. You're going to need it."

CHAPTER TEN
The Present

The Russian assault teams were in three unmarked vans. It was morning in Moscow, with millions of people at work and home, unaware that a relic of the Cold War threatened their very existence. The three vans wove through the streets toward the Kremlin. The team leader, Major Koransky, took off his red beret and stuffed it in a pocket. His Spetsnatz team was from the Ministry of Internal Affairs (MVD), the 33rd OSN (special purpose detachment) stationed in Moscow. The red beret was worn only by those Spetsnatz soldiers who were the 'most professional, physically and morally fit' soldiers. To earn one required passing a series of tests including a 12 kilometer cross-country run in full combat gear, an urban assault exercise, and a 12 minute freestyle sparring, no holds barred, against three opponents. The success rate was less than 10%, and once in a while, during the sparring, a candidate died.

Such was the price of the red beret.

"Stop," Koransky ordered, checking their position on the GPS. He also had an old map open in his lap, something he'd had couriered to him from the Kremlin Archives: a map of the old World War II tunnel system underneath the capitol. Stalin, and those that followed him into the Cold War, had built an extensive tunnel system under the Russian capitol. First as protection against Nazi bombers, then in an attempt to make a nuclear strike survivable. At least for the power elite.

Koransky put a small earpiece in and wrapped a mike around his throat. He did a comm check and his team leaders responded promptly.

Koransky and his soldiers wore unmarked black fatigues, over which they had black Kevlar body armor, and on top of that was a combat vest. He had an AK-74, the upgrade of the venerable AK-47, chambered with a higher velocity, smaller 5.45 mm round, for his primary weapon.

"Let's go."

Koransky led the way, out the side door of the van. Four of his men moved up the slope toward the wall of the Kremlin, spreading out, weapons at the ready as police cars took positions in front of and behind the vans, blocking all traffic and covering their movement. Two more men covered each flank, and the last four covered the rear.

They arrived at a portal in the red brick wall surrounding the Kremlin. It was blocked by a steel gate. Koransky produced a plastic card that he pushed into the electronic lock. He entered a sequence of numbers. The light went from red to green, and the gate slid open.

Koransky entered a small alcove, to be faced by another door. He used a different card and a different code on its lock, and the door rumbled open, revealing a descending stairway into the bowels of the system underneath the Kremlin. Koransky slid down a set of night-vision goggles. The rest of his team did the same. Then he signaled with two fingers and gestured down. Two of his men descended into the darkness.

"Clear to another door," his lead scout reported. "It's sealed with a retinal scanner to one side."

Koransky moved forward, the rest of the team following. He considered the scanner. It was covered in dust. He knew they could blow the door, but that would lose them the advantage of surprise. He signaled for his electronics expert to come forward. The man pulled out some tools and worked on the scanner.

He paused and looked at Koransky. "It's dead. Not functioning. I will bypass and open the lock."

After a few second there was a click and the man pulled the steel door open, revealing a corridor. The floor was gray and the walls were painted the same flat color. Koransky pulled up the night-vision goggles since recessed lighting dimly lit the corridor.

Koransky detailed a pair of his men to stand guard, then looked ahead. The corridor was straight as far as he could see. From the briefing he'd received as they'd rapidly prepared this operation, he'd learned that the first tunnel built under the Kremlin had been finished during the time of the tsars as an escape route in times of extreme trouble. *Obviously it had not been used when they really needed it*, Koransky thought as he gestured for his two point men to move ahead. He followed right behind.

During World War II, Stalin had begun by building a large bomb shelter directly under the Kremlin as the Nazis approached Moscow. He'd also had bunkers dug under other government buildings and connecting tunnels bored out. However, the rudimentary bunkers, designed to provide survival against Stuka dive-bombers, were obviously inadequate against nuclear weapons. So the government dug deeper and deeper, burrowing into the earth below Moscow in the foolish hope that perhaps the leadership could survive a direct nuclear attack. That there would be nothing on the surface to govern had not seemed to occur to anyone.

Koransky thought it the height of irony that nuclear bombs would be secreted here as a threat against the government that thought it could survive nuclear bombs down here.

The point man opened another door. The tunnel beyond was older and smaller. Beads of moisture glistened, illuminated by naked lightbulbs attached to an electric cord bolted to the ceiling. Most of the bulbs were burnt out, with just a few still providing lonely pools of light. There was graffiti on the walls. Koransky spared it a glance and noted that someone had posted rude references to 'Keepers of the Peace.'

They moved about one hundred meters before reaching another door. Unlike the previous ones, though, this door was wooden, with metal bands across it. It had an ancient lock that Koransky's men made short work of. They swung the door open. A tunnel paved with brick beckoned, curving downward. Koransky no longer had a GPS signal, but he'd been keeping a pace count and staying oriented. He checked his map. They were off the mapped portion of the tunnels, entering unmarked territory.

They moved forward, going ever deeper underneath the Kremlin.

After five minutes they came to another door—this one steel, more modern than the tunnel, but still aged. Koransky cursed as he noted that the edge of the door was spot-welded shut to the frame. Koransky snapped an order and one of his men ran up. He tossed off his backpack, pulled out a welding torch and fired it up.

Koransky checked his watch but displayed no sense of impatience, knowing it would do no good. The man was working as fast as he could. The flame went out and the welder stood. "It's clear to open."

Two mercenaries began unscrewing the door, which seemed to consist of a single large threaded metal disk, about five feet in diameter. It moved easily and they had it unscrewed in less than fifteen seconds. It slowly rotated away from the entrance on hydraulic arms.

It was dark inside. Koransky pulled down his night-vision goggles and turned them on. He waited until the green glow came alive, then poked his head in the opening. He saw a large chamber, the far end of which wasn't visible in the goggles.

There was a glow in the distance, about sixty meters away, and Koransky saw movement.

The time for discretion was over.

"Flash bangs," Koransky hissed as he pulled up the night-vision goggles, put a hand over his eyes and averted his face.

Two of his men fired flash bang rounds from their grenade launchers, directly at the light. The grenades went off as advertised: with an ear numbing bang and a blinding flash.

Koransky led the charge as the two grenade men fired flares, lighting up the cavern.

Koransky had a series of images as he brought the AK-74 to his shoulder to fire: a cluster of three people, dressed in rags, gathered around warheads set on a low pedestal. Someone off to the right was screaming something into a phone.

Then Koransky and his men began firing.

They had gotten a good burst off when there was a blinding flash from the warheads, and the wave of a blast threw Koransky backward. He lay on his back stunned for a moment, wondering how he'd survived a nuclear blast.

Blinded, he got to his feet. All he could hear was ringing in his ears.

*****

Aaron heard the firing, then the red phone went dead. "Caleb!" he called out.

The large man came running. "Yes?"

"Moscow is down. They were attacked."

Caleb nodded. "We need to prepare our final defense and activate the Sword."

*****

Koransky called out for his men and was rewarded by a scattered response, which he could barely hear above the ringing. The flashes in his retinas were slowly fading out and darkness was taking over.

For a moment, Koransky panicked, afraid he'd been blinded. But when he pulled down his night-vision goggles and turned them on, a flickering green image appeared. Blinking hard, Koransky's vision slowly returned.

The people who'd been at the bombs were now scattered bits and pieces of humans, blown to bits. Koransky now understood what had happened: they'd detonated the bomb's initiator, but it had failed to ignite the plutonium core.

The realization was immediately followed by another one, chilling in the utmost. "Gregor?" Koransky called out.

"Sir?"

"Reading, please."

There was a long pause, then his engineer reported what the display of his Geiger counter indicated. "We're dead men, sir."

*****

Aaron walked down the corridor he'd passed through every day for the past half a century, knowing this was the last time. Fourteen paces. Left turn. He put his right hand-his only hand-on the flat screen next to the door. The screen flashed green and the optical scanner swung down. Aaron placed his face against it.

The door rumbled open.

Aaron paused before entering, looking at the guard standing to the right. "Join with Caleb. We're in final defense."

Despite having prepared for this for years and training for it constantly, the man's face showed his surprise. But he pulled himself together. "Yes, Aaron." And then he ran off.

Aaron entered and turned to the woman in the bulletproof booth. "It is time. Switch control of the gas to remote. Then go join the others."

"Yes, Aaron." The woman kept one hand on the dead man's switch while she did as he instructed.

Aaron went to the last steel door. He reached inside his shirt and produced a skeleton key on a chain. There was also a second, more intricate tube key. He inserted the skeleton key in the opening and turned it. With a loud click, the door unlocked and he opened it. The two guards had their weapons at the ready, but recognized Aaron.

"It is time for the Sword," Aaron said.

He heard a noise behind him and Caleb walked into the vault and joined him as the two guards left. In the center of the room was a large metal box, ten feet square and four feet high. On top, facing them, was a monitor and a keyboard. On each corner of the top of the metal box was a small cube with a single keyhole.

Aaron looked at Caleb. "Ready?"

Caleb nodded. "I've been ready for years."

They each went to one corner. Both produced the tube key on the chain around their neck and inserted it into their respective cubes.

"On three," Aaron said. "One. Two. Three."

They both turned at the same time. The screen on the monitor came alive. Leaving the keys in place, they met at the monitor. Aaron extended his hand. "Would you do the honors?" he said to Caleb.

Caleb began typing, then paused. "What delay?"

Aaron checked his watch. "Two hours."

Caleb typed in the command. He stepped back and Aaron took his place.

"We keep the peace," Aaron said and hit the enter key.

The screen flashed and then numbers in red appeared.

Counting down.

2:00:00

1:59:59

23 October 1962

The sun had not yet risen, but President Kennedy had not slept a wink since delivering his speech the previous evening. He'd prepared a 'Presidential Proclamation for Interdiction of the Delivery of Offensive Weapons to Cuba' and signed it, an escalation of tensions in an already tense situation.

The door to the Oval Office creaked open and his brother stuck his head in, hoping to see the President asleep at his desk.

"It's fine, Bobby," the President said.

His brother stepped into the office. "I've got him."

"Where?"

"The pool. It's the safest place." If the situation had been less tense, that might have been a little humorous. The White House pool was the place where the President, often accompanied by his brother, met young women, usually escorted to the White House by his special aide, Dave Powers. The Secret Service had long ago been instructed to steer clear of that section of the White House while the President 'exercised.'

The President got up, carefully stretched his back, then followed his brother. The White House, despite the crisis, was deceptively still and quiet this early in the morning. Guards snapped to attention as the President and his brother walked by. A pair of Secret Service agents followed at a discreet distance, then halted at the start of the corridor leading to the pool.

The two men entered the indoor pool area. Standing in a corner, anxiously smoking a cigarette, waited a man dressed in a cheap suit. He stubbed out the cigarette upon their entry.

"Jack," Bobby Kennedy said, "this is Oleg Penkovsky."

Penkovsky snapped to attention and visibly fought back an urge to salute.

Surprisingly, the President stuck out his hand. "All right if I call you 'Oleg?'"

"Yes, Mister President. It is fine, I mean."

They shook hands.

"I need to sit," the President said, heading over to a lounge chair and sinking down into it. He wedged a folded towel behind his back. "So, Oleg. What does my friend Premier Khrushchev have to say to me in private that he can't say in public or via his ambassador, Gromyko?"

Penkovsky reached into his pocket and pulled out a piece of paper. "Premier Khrushchev will be sending you a telegram tomorrow which will be made public."

"Guess I'll read it tomorrow then," Kennedy said. "Give me the gist."

Penkovsky shoved the paper back into his pocket. "You know, Mister President, that according to international law a blockade is considered an act of war."

"I know that's the letter of the law. I don't look at it that way. I see it as a way of defending my country. And eighty percent of my countrymen agree with me."

"Yes, Mister President, but you want to be allowed a concept of defense that you are not extending to either Cuba or the Soviet Union."

Kennedy looked amused. *"Go on. I assume you know Khrushchev's mind and are speaking for him."*

"He has spoken to me at length about this," Penkovsky said. *"I believe I am relaying his intent and his intentions."*

"Very good," Kennedy said. *"How am I not extending the concept of defense? Don't tell me the missiles are for defensive purposes only. I've already heard that bullshit to my face by Gromyko."*

"Publicly, Premier Khrushchev will call the blockade an act of outright piracy that will lead to war. He will call it an act of aggression."

"And privately?" the President asked.

"The Premier feels that we have danced ourselves into a corner that will be difficult to dance out of."

"I can't picture the Premier dancing," Bobby Kennedy said.

"The Premier is an excellent dancer in politics and power," Penkovsky said. *"He survived Stalin."*

"I'll grant him that," the President said.

"The problem is three-fold, Mister President."

Jack Kennedy chuckled. *"Two-fold is bad enough. Three is much worse."*

Penkovsky soldiered on. *"First is public opinion. Neither side can afford to completely lose face. Second is the opinion of the generals. On either side they will not accept a complete capitulation. Third is the threat of nuclear annihilation.*

"For the first, the Premier suggests we do as was done in Berlin. Both sides back off, step by step, and the Premier is asking that you make the first step this time, Mister President. The missiles in Turkey, Mister President. If you agree to withdraw those, we will withdraw our weapons from Cuba and turn the ships around."

"Which will piss off number two," the President said. *"The generals."*

"For that, Comrade Khrushchev suggests while it is publicly announced that all the missiles will be removed, they will not all be removed. To appease the Generals, we leave a token force of missiles in both Turkey and Cuba. Without letting the Generals know the other side is doing the same. Thus each side's generals will think that they are pulling, how do you say, a fast one *on the other side."*

Kennedy nodded. *"I like that."* He glanced at his brother. *"That might even make LeMay smile."*

"I don't think anything can make that sonofabitch smile," Bobby said.

"And number three?" the President asked.

"That is the most difficult part," Penkovsky said. *"Have you read* Fail Safe, *Mister President?"*

"I have."

"Comrade Khrushchev proposes secretly setting up a fail safe before a Fail Safe *type scenario occurs."*

"Meaning?" Jack Kennedy asked.

"No matter where our hearts are, there is always the chance the generals can push too hard. The danger of allowing them to think they won the standoff and have missiles in place that the other side doesn't know about is that they will be tempted to use them. So Comrade Khrushchev suggests keeping the peace with a heavy hand."

"How exactly do we do that?" the President asked.

"That is the most difficult part of this endeavor, Mister President. Let me explain what Premier Khrushchev envisions."

CHAPTER ELEVEN
The Present

"The Russians found the three missing warheads at the grid coordinates Ducharme sent," Turnbull informed Evie and Burns.

"They were from the Jupiters?" Evie asked.

"Yes."

"And there were people with them?" she asked.

"Yes," Turnbull said. "Four. They were in pretty bad shape. Apparently they've been isolated down there for years. And they were trying to arm one of the warheads when the Russian Spetsnatz assaulted them. They'd cannibalized the other two to maintain one as functional." Turnbull sighed. "They detonated one warhead."

Evie was startled. "There have been no news reports of a nuclear explosion under Moscow."

"That's because there wasn't," Turnbull said. "The initiator went off but the core didn't go critical. Apparently, despite their efforts and using the other two warheads, they couldn't maintain the integrity of the warhead after so many years and being so isolated."

"Thank God," Evie said.

"Tell that to the Russian Spetsnatz who are trapped down there. They all received a fatal dose of radiation. The entire site has been sealed off and will probably remain that way forever. And that's not the worst part. The team leader reports that just before the blast, he saw one on a 'hotline.'"

"To?"

"We assume the Peacekeepers in New York City. The line is dead now."

"Fail Safe," Evie said.

"Exactly," Turnbull agreed.

"Then there's a bomb, or more than one given there were three under Moscow, in New York, primed to go off," Evie said.

"Most likely," Turnbull said. "And I have a feeling the bombs here will be in better shape." He held up a hand before she could say any more. "Luckily, I've got a line on the location underneath the city. I've got teams moving in now."

Evie turned to Burns. "Contact Duke. Tell him to divert to New York."

"You don't trust my men?" Turnbull asked.

"A stupid question," Evie said. "It seems as if Kennedy and Khrushchev worked out a covert form of mutually assured destruction, at least for the two most important cities in their respective countries."

Turnbull nodded. "We knew they'd done something like this fifty years ago. Kennedy threatened the Joint Chiefs after the Crisis. That's why our agents were trying to find the location of the bombs." He then told her about the encounter with Mikoyan and the death of the SOC agents at the hands of the Philosophers.

"What was on the paper?"

Turnbull shrugged. "That's what we were trying to find out."

"I found no record of this in the APS," Evie said.

"I was hoping there might be a mention of it in here," Burns said, holding up Meyer's diary. "I've been going through it. Some titillating stuff, but nothing of significance so far."

"That's strange," Evie said. "Meyer was with Kennedy a lot during the crisis and he confided in her." Her eyes got that distant look, then she refocused. "Go to March twenty-second 1962," Evie ordered Burns.

He thumbed through. "Just a short entry. She went for a walk. Ate dinner at home. Nothing exciting."

"It's a fake diary," Evie said. "A diversion."

"How do you know?" Turnbull demanded.

"Because we know from our records that on March twenty-second 1962 she went to Kennedy and relayed a threat from the Philosophers to back off," Evie said. "That's a rather significant thing, and if she didn't record that in that diary, then it's a fake diary. One she wanted people to find so they wouldn't look for her real diary."

"So where is her real diary?" Turnbull said.

"I don't know," Evie said. "But I'll figure it out."

*****

As Aaron left the cube with the countdown displayed, he glanced at the security monitors. He saw the police cordon around the Fulton Street Subway entrance. Several unmarked white panel trucks were pulling up and armed men were disembarking. They had several dogs with them.

"They'll find us," Caleb said.

"Yes. They will. But we can give them a good fight."

"We can." Caleb slapped his old friend on the shoulder. "I'll get our people ready."

*****

Ducharme absorbed the news from Burns about the bomb going off under Moscow and the expedition that was getting ready to hit the tunnels under New York while the F-22B was 40,000 feet above the Atlantic Ocean, having regained optimum altitude after dropping down for a refueling.

"If they were on a hot line to New York," Ducharme said, "then these Peacekeepers know Moscow has been compromised."

"Correct," Burns said.

Ducharme was trying to sort through this fifty-year-old plan. "Then the Fail Safe isn't a fail safe any more. What about missiles in Cuba? If we left some Jupiters in Turkey it's likely that the Russian left some in Cuba."

"I'll check on that," Burns said. "Turnbull hasn't mentioned it."

"There's a lot Turnbull isn't mentioning," Ducharme said. "Tell Evie to focus on Groves. He's the one who was the connection from the Philosophers to the Peacekeepers. He's also the point of contact for Penkovsky."

"Will do. But Evie's trying to find Mary Meyer's real diary. She says the one Angleton took is a fake."

"If anyone can find the real one after all these years, it's her."

"When do you land in New York?" Burns asked.

"ETA?" Ducharme asked Stretch.

"Twenty-two minutes," the pilot replied.

"I'll have an FBI chopper waiting for you to take you to Manhattan," Burns said.

"Let's hope there's still a Manhattan for me to go to," Ducharme said.

27 October 1962

The Russian ships turned around on the 24th of October 1962, causing premature celebration among most of the members of EXCOMM. Secretary of State Dean Rusk felt it had been a case of an eyeball-to-eyeball standoff with the Russians and they'd blinked first.

Blinking isn't surrendering.

A U-2 spy plane had flown off course over Soviet land just west of Alaska, leading both sides to scramble jets armed with nuclear tipped air to air missiles. McNamara had almost lost it, yelling it meant war with the Soviet Union, but the U-2 turned around and escaped before any shots were fired.

There was also the issue of the weapons that might still be in Cuba.

On the 26th, Kennedy held a meeting of the senior military focused on that issue. He invited some of the strongest opponents to his course of action, desiring to get a wide range of opinions.

He might have gotten more than he bargained for.

"Khrushchev's letter is a load of bullshit," General LeMay thundered. "He must think we're a bunch of dumb shits, if we swallow that syrup he's pushing."

Bobby Kennedy leaned close and whispered to his brother. "Some day he'll tell us what he really thinks."

"Not sure he's thinking," the President replied in a low voice. Khrushchev's second letter during the crisis, delivered to the US Embassy in Moscow, had been long and a mixture of offers of compromise while maintaining some of the same lies, particularly the one about the weapons only being defensive.

Congress was starting to side with the military men like LeMay, banging the war drum. Everyone seemed to think the military could roll right over Cuba and take the island in a day or two.

The President spoke up. "Well now, gentlemen. The quarantine, while it has turned the ships around, won't remove any weapons that are already there. So we have only two ways of removing those. One is to negotiate them out, in other words trade them out."

LeMay snorted. Kennedy remembered meeting the Joint Chiefs for the first time. They were an intimidating group, their uniforms bedecked with stars and ribbons and badges. All older; all with decades of military experience. As he spent more time in office and met with them more often, Kennedy was less intimidated and better able to gauge the man behind the uniform. He had little use for LeMay, but he was a political hot potato. General Maxwell Taylor, who Kennedy had recalled back to active duty and just made the Chairman of the Joint Chiefs, was one whose wisdom he trusted.

The President continued. "The other is to go in and take them out. I don't see any other way we're going to get whatever weapons they've snuck in there out."

"Mister President," Taylor said, "if the Russians already have nuclear warheads in Cuba, an invasion could be disastrous."

"Khrushchev wouldn't dare use them," LeMay said.

Taylor looked at the Air Force officer. "Are you willing to risk the lives of tens of thousands of American soldiers on that?"

"If they nuke our assault forces," LeMay said, "we level Moscow."

"What if we trade Turkey for Cuba," President Kennedy said. He wasn't recording this meeting, setting the stage for possible future actions that could never be recorded in history.

That comment brought a moment of silence, then, as expected, LeMay exploded. "Mister President, our missiles in Turkey are there legitimately. We are there at the request of the Turkish government."

"Let's not stretch the truth, General," Kennedy responded. *"We did some major arm twisting to get those missiles in Turkey. I don't think they'd be shedding big tears if we pulled them out."*

"We'd look weak, sir!" LeMay protested.

"Are we weak?" Kennedy said. *LeMay blinked at him and Kennedy pressed home his point.* *"We don't need Turkey. And frankly, Khrushchev doesn't need Cuba. He's got missiles on subs right out there,"* Kennedy pointed to the east, *"that can hit us in a couple of minutes. Cuba is smoke and mirrors. So is Turkey. Those missiles are almost obsolete already."*

"It would weaken us in the eyes of NATO," the President's National Security Adviser, McGeorge Bundy argued.

"That's not really a priority concern for me at the moment," the President said. He picked up a copy of the letter transmitted from Moscow. *"Khrushchev is correct in predicting catastrophe if we have a nuclear exchange."*

As LeMay began to protest, Kennedy waved him to silence. *"Gentlemen, it's not for me or you or our peers that I am concerned. It's for the children. Do we give them a future? What are we willing to do to ensure their future?"*

Before anyone could respond to that, a door swung open and an aide hustled to General Taylor's side, leaned over whispered something to him. The General closed his eyes and a ripple of irritation crossed his face. He turned to the President. *"Sir. We just lost a U-2 over Cuba. Shot down by a Soviet missile."*

"The pilot?" Kennedy asked.

"We presume he is dead."

"We have no choice now," LeMay said. *"We must retaliate. If we don't do something it won't just be Cuba, they're going to push us on Berlin, and push hard because they think they have us on the run. We launch air attacks immediately and we can start the invasion in seven days."*

The President raised a hand. *"I'd like the room cleared of everyone except the Joint Chiefs."*

That took a minute and then it was just a small circle. Kennedy leaned forward. *"Gentlemen, here is the deal: we pull our missiles out of Turkey and the Russians will pull their missiles and nuclear weapons out of Cuba. I've got Khrushchev's personal assurance on that."*

LeMay's snort of derision indicated what he through of the Soviet's 'personal assurance.'

The Commandant of the Marine Corps spoke up. *"Sir, with all due respect, Khrushchev, like all the other communists, is a slavish follower of Sun Tzu. One of Sun Tzu's tenets is to pretend accommodation of the enemy while secretly preparing for attack."*

"Sun Tzu was Chinese," Bobby Kennedy observed. *"Not Russian. And not a communist."*

"It's like Berlin," Kennedy said. *"I got Khrushchev's word there that he'd back up his tank first and he did."*

As LeMay opened his mouth to protest, Kennedy held his hand up, palm out, stopping him. *"Listen to me. This stays in this room, gentlemen. I will gut any one of you that breathes a word to anyone except your successor. This stays here in the White House and with the Joint Chiefs from here on out.*

"First, while we publicly announced we're withdrawing all the missiles in Turkey, we're not pulling all our missiles out. We're going to leave some in place."

"Now you're talking, sir," Le May said.

"Please listen and let me finish," Kennedy said. "I've listened to you gentlemen and I've considered all you've had to say. I appreciate your patriotism and your service and your expertise. But this is my decision and this is the way it's going to be. Not only are some of our missiles staying in Turkey, three of the nuclear warheads are going to be secretly transported into Russia and emplaced underneath the Kremlin."

An electric silence filled the conference room at this unexpected turn of events.

"It does not stop there, though. Some of the Soviet's missiles will stay in Cuba. Three of their nuclear warheads will be brought here to the United States. They will be emplaced underneath New York City. The people responsible for both sets of warheads, from the respective host countries, will establish a hot line directly between them. This hot line will not run through the White House, nor will it run through the Pentagon. Once these two groups are established, they will have no further contact with anyone except each other. If either country attacks the other with nuclear weapons, these two groups will detonate their weapons and Moscow and New York will be no more. This is not a quid pro quo that can adjusted or negotiated. It is a fail safe type scenario that will be a reality."

There was a stunned silence in the conference room. LeMay opened his mouth to say something.

"No, General," Kennedy said. "You've had your say. I'm doing this for the children. My brother will leave this meeting and go the Soviet Ambassador and tell him we agree to the proposal publicly. We will not attack or invade Cuba. We will publicly declare we are removing our missiles in Turkey. And that, gentlemen, is the reality."

*****

Bobby Kennedy had just come back from talking with the Russian ambassador and relaying his brother's public reply to Khrushchev's public letter. He walked into the private residence, where a handful of people who were personally close to the President were eating dinner. Jackie and the kids were at Glen Ora in Virginia, out of the capitol.

Bobby was glum, not happy about the meeting with the Russian ambassador. David Powers, the man the President counted as his right hand man for personal matters, was also there. The two Kennedy brothers were talking about whether Khrushchev could really be trusted. About the letters. About the missiles. And in the midst of that, the President looked over at Powers: "Dave, you're eating the chicken and drinking the wine like it's your last supper."

Powers put down his fork. "Mister President, after listening to you and Bobby, I'm not so sure it isn't."

The President laughed, but it was a forced laugh. "Dave, I think we've got this worked out. I hope we've got this worked out. But I've got a feeling the working out part is going to come back to haunt me after this is all over."

And then he went back to talking to his brother.

A couple of hours later in the White House theater, they all watched Roman Holiday *starring Gregory Peck and Audrey Hepburn. Some time during the film, the President nodded off and no one dared move, for fear of waking him. Finally, though, the movie was over and it was time to get the President to bed. Dave Powers was the one who was close enough to the President to do that. He walked over and tapped the President on the shoulder.*

"It's all over, Mister President."

Kennedy blinked awake. "No, it isn't."

And then Powers realized he wasn't talking about the movie.

******

Unknown to anyone in the White House or the Kremlin, the most dangerous episode of the entire Cuban Missile Crisis was being played out on the high seas. The USS Beale, a destroyer escort, had tracked a Soviet submarine near the picket line for the blockade. Few on land realized the high stakes games played out by the American and Soviet Navys throughout the Cold War.

In an attempt to get the Russian submarine to service and be identified, the Beale began to drop signaling depth charges on the B-59 Foxtrot class submarine. The signaling depth charge had the blast of a hand grenade, not enough to damage a submarine, but enough to rattle the crew and make them think they might be getting attacked.

What the American commander of the Beale didn't know was that the Russian submarine was armed with a 15-kiloton nuclear torpedo.

The Beale kept the pressure up, tracking the sub and dropping charge.

Below the American ship, things began to get a bit desperate. Even though the charges couldn't sink the sub, it was like they were sitting in a metal barrel while someone was slamming on it with a sledgehammer. The temperature inside the submarine rose to 120 degrees. Oxygen began to run short. Out of radio communications with their own fleet, the crew had no way of knowing if the charges were a sign that war had begun.

Between the heat and the lack of oxygen, sailors began to collapse at their duty stations.

The captain of the B-59 ordered his weapons officer to prepare the nuclear torpedo for launch.

Fortunately for the world, the second officer, Captain Arkhipov, interceded, arguing forcefully and successfully against a launch.

The B-59 surfaced and the Americans stood to, simply watching, confirming that the two countries were not at war.

But they had just come ever so close to it. Only one Russian second in command officer away.

Penkovsky and Arkhipov.

CHAPTER TWELVE
The Present

Ducharme arrived as the first assault teams descended into the Fulton Subway station, led by two tracking dogs. He wasn't surprised to find they were TriOp, the mercenaries of choice of the Society of Cincinnati. He was a bit surprised by how quickly the NYPD ceded the operation over to the mercenaries. It made him wonder how often the two organizations had worked together before, and confirmed that in terms of power, SOC trumped NYC.

Ducharme took a position behind the point element, which consisted of the two dogs and their handlers, and a six-man assault team. Two more assault teams of six men followed. The team leader must have talked to Cane, because while he acquiesced to Ducharme's presence, he told him he was to stay back once contact was made.

A quarter mile away from the station, they left the subway tunnel and went into a service tunnel that appeared long out of use.

But the dogs indicated someone was using it.

As far as what it had serviced, as near as Ducharme could tell, it appeared to be coal, back when that was the fuel of choice for heating buildings.

The pain in his head increased the further the assault teams wove their way into the warren of tunnels. Stress, yes, he accepted that, but he also knew it was part of his combat experience ticking, warning him.

They were in enemy territory. If the Peacekeepers had been down here for fifty-odd years, they were intimately familiar with them. There wasn't a place in the world that Ducharme had infiltrated where the locals-the inhabitants-hadn't known he was there, no matter how stealthy he was.

They were being drawn in. Ducharme was sure of it.

They were now in a concrete tunnel, the walls lined with cracks and chips, indicating it was old and not maintained. A train was rattling by, how close, Ducharme had no way of knowing, but it wasn't far away.

Was the trap being set by the Peacekeepers in the form of an ambush, or in the form of the nuclear weapons they might be approaching that were going to be detonated?

The ambush happened first as a series of distinctive blasts, which Ducharme recognized, echoed down the tunnel, indicating the lead element had been decimated by claymore mines.

*****

Mary Meyer was a woman who had never gone out of her way to hide her lifestyle. Evie found that interesting as she read up on Meyer, seated on the far side of the room from Turnbull in the Anderson House. Certainly Meyer had kept some things secret, such as her affair with the President, but it was a secret hidden inside a flamboyant lifestyle of sex, drugs and art.

In Evie's opinion, people weren't that difficult to understand. Ninety-nine percent of what people did was habit. While most people connected profilers with serial killers, the reality was that anyone could be profiled. When she was in the CIA one of her jobs had been profiling potential threats to the United States. What did they have in common? What was similar in their upbringing? What was similar in the way they acted out?

Evie sat back in the chair, aware that Turnbull's eyes were on her. He was a dangerous man but also predictable in his own way. As long as he needed someone, he was not a threat. If he needed someone but they were becoming a threat, he had a tipping point. Obviously one he'd reached with Ducharme in Turkey. Ducharme had become a larger threat than asset.

Evie shook her head, wondering why her mind had wandered to the conflict between Ducharme and Turnbull when the issue was Mary Meyer. A woman who'd been killed less than a year after Kennedy's assassination, shot in the heart and head while taking a walk on the Chesapeake and Ohio Canal Towpath.

A black man had been arrested for her murder, but acquitted. A strange turn of events given the racial tensions at the time. Especially since the judge had ruled that nothing about Mary Meyer's personal life could be admitted in court. The man's lawyer had said that it was as if the only existence Mary Meyer had in the trial had been that moment on the towpath when she died.

Sex, drugs and art.

Two were ephemeral. Passing. But art. Art lasted.

Meyer had to know that she was under surveillance. During her sting with the CIA, Evie had gotten a glimpse of the surveillance state that the United States had been and is. She had no doubt that the FBI, the CIA, the NSA and others had kept Mary Meyer under deep surveillance. A woman who was with the President during the darkest hours of his life, whether it be the Cuban Missile Crisis, the death of Marilyn Monroe or the death of his child, was a woman they'd want to keep tabs on.

Having been married to Cord Meyer, a CIA agent, Meyer had to know she'd been under surveillance. She'd had to know that no matter what plan she set up, others would act quickly if something happened to her.

Thus the fake diary.

Evie closed her eyes. Think like the other person.

Art lasted.

Evie opened her eyes and began to type, expanding her search while narrowing it.

*****

Inside the vault, the digital countdown clicked below one hour.

00:59:59

*****

It was turning into a clusterfuck. Ducharme was riding this out so far, staying back from the front edges of the fire fight as more TriOp personnel assaulted down the tunnel, channeled into a narrow space already filled with their dead and wounded. The Peacekeepers were anything but as they fought back against the assault. Ducharme wondered how long the mercenaries would keep up their assault given their losses, but he had to grant Cane something— they were fighting as hard as any soldiers Ducharme had ever served with. They knew what was at stake here, most likely the city itself, and they fought furiously.

Inch by inch, body by body, the mercenaries pressed the attack forward.

Ducharme had graduated Ranger School many years ago. Where it was drilled into the Ranger Candidate's head that the only way to break an ambush was to assault directly into it.

That was the school solution and what the TriOp men were doing.

Sometimes the school solution didn't fit.

Ducharme backed up, searching for another tunnel. He found one: a three-foot high tube that was crowded with fiber optic cables. It was pitch black and extended as far as his flashlight could reach. He turned the light off and turned on his night-vision goggles, slipping them down over his eyes.

One thought truly disturbed him. Since the Peacekeepers knew the tunnels so well, they could have easily escaped. They'd chosen to fight. That meant they were trying to gain something, and the only thing Ducharme could figure that was, was time. They were fighting a delaying action.

Which meant they were waiting for something to happen, and that thought chilled him.

He slid into the tunnel and began crawling, hoping it would lead him in the right direction.

*****

Baths sat on a park bench, apparently oblivious of the cold. She was staring at her small notepad, re-reading the text message that she had just laboriously decrypted by hand.

The countdown had begun. Less than an hour before the Peace was finally kept by the Sword.

*****

"Half Light," Evie said, not even aware she was speaking out loud.

"Excuse me," Burns said, looking up from a folder on Admiral Groves that he'd been perusing.

"Proto-hard-edge-style minimalism," Evie said. "Painted in 1964 by Mary Meyer. Not long before she was killed. After Kennedy was killed. After the Peacemakers were in place. After Jackie Kennedy gave Mikoyan that piece of paper."

"English please," Burns said.

Evie glanced over at Turnbull, who was now pretending to be engrossed in whatever was on his computer screen.

"Like the purloined letter," Evie said.

"Hidden in plain sight," Burns said.

"Exactly." Evie stood, throwing on her coat. "Let's go."

Burns paused. He turned to Turnbull. "How are things in New York?"

Turnbull looked up from his computer. "Hot. Very hot. I'm allocating more assets. What are you two up to?"

"We're going to the Smithsonian," Evie said. Then she strode away, Burns behind her.

Turnbull waited until they were gone from the room, then he began making calls.

*****

Ducharme fell out of the tube into a sewage tunnel. He'd smelled it long before he fell into it, so he thought he was ready.

He wasn't.

He threw up as he got to his feet, the smell overwhelming. It was so bad; it made him forget about the pain in his head for the moment, which made it almost worth it.

Almost.

The sound of the firefight was a distant echo, but one that oriented Ducharme. He turned to the right and moved to the sound of the guns, a maxim of combat since gunpowder was invented.

*****

At Al Asad, the lead contained box was secured inside an Air Force C-5 transport. A pair of F-16 fighters were circling overhead to escort the C-5 back to the United States.

The last of the Jupiter warheads were coming home, fifty years late.

*****

Ducharme waded through the waist-deep sludge, barely breathing. He was getting closer to the firefight.

At least he hoped he was. The echo of sound off the walls of the tunnel was disorienting. There was another sound that was growing louder, a mechanical, rhythmic thump. Ducharme bumped into something and he looked down.

In the green glow of the night-vision goggles it was hard to make it out at first. Then he realized he was looking at a severed hand. Not decomposed. Which meant the death was fresh. Which indicated to Ducharme that he was heading in the right direction. It was a small hand, a woman's hand to judge by the fingernail polish, the size, and the rings.

Ducharme brought his automatic rifle up to firing position, tucking the stock tight into his shoulder. Since he was using the night-vision goggles and didn't have a night sight for the weapon, he would have to aim as best he could.

With his training, that was pretty damn good.

*****

Caleb fired a sustained burst from the M-60 machinegun. Twelve to fifteen rounds exactly as he'd been taught on the firing range at Parris Island so many years ago. The tunnel was a funnel for the rounds, and even if he hit the sides, the ricochet effect sent them in the right direction.

A hand grabbed his shoulder and he looked over. Aaron was just behind him and to the side. "They'll figure this out and maneuver," Aaron said.

"Of course," Caleb replied.

He stepped back, allowing another Peacekeeper to step up. Caleb gave him the M-60.

Caleb and Aaron walked back to the first intersection and stepped out of the line of fire.

"How long can we hold?" Aaron asked.

"It's not enough to hold," Caleb said. "We have to punch back to gain time. These aren't NYPD. They're contractors. Which means the Society most likely sent them. That means there's an infinite number of them, but we defeat this first wave, we can gain a little time before they can get the next together."

"That's all we need," Aaron said.

"I always thought the time delay was a stupid idea," Caleb said.

"It's the way things are," Aaron said simply.

"Of course." Caleb picked up a MP-5 submachinegun from a stack of weapons that had been positioned there, just behind the front lines of the battle. "I'm going to flank them. Assault from the side and that should break this assault."

Aaron nodded. "We keep the peace."

Caleb stared at the older man for a moment, whether shocked or agreeing, it wasn't clear from his expression. "Yes. We keep the peace."

Then he began running down the tunnel, away from the firefight. He desired something more personal.

*****

Burns' badge got them into the part of the Smithsonian that wasn't open to the public: the massive storage facilities that were underground. If the curator found Evie's request odd, he didn't show it. Unlike the security guard, he was actually more impressed with her credentials as the curator of Monticello than with Burns' FBI identification. He was a bit put out by her rush, hurrying to keep up with her.

"I wanted to put the painting on exhibition for the fiftieth anniversary," the curator said as he escorted them along a hallway. "I was told it would be in poor taste to exhibit a painting by President Kennedy's lover on the anniversary of his death, but I felt it was giving history its due. We have to accept the glory of Camelot along with its darkness."

"True," Evie said.

He opened up a door; the whooshing sound indicating the room beyond was under positive pressure. "We have several of Mary Meyer's paintings. She was actually beginning to come into her own on the DC art scene at the time of her death. Most tragic to have her career cut short like that."

"I'm sure she was bummed," Burns muttered.

The curator turned to the right. "The art work is along the walls. We preserve as best we can, but budget cuts, the sequester, all of it has had its toll."

"It has," Evie murmured, looking at the paintings as they passed by.

"Here," the curator said. "'Half Light' by Mary Meyer."

"That's art?" Burns asked.

Evie could understand his question. It was a simple, geometric piece. A square with a circle in it, the circle bisected laterally and vertically. The colors were muted: black for the square, then each quadrant of the circle a different color: brown, pale purple, pale blue and a mustard color.

Evie leaned over. "Burns, what do you see here, right at the center where all four colors come together?"

Burns pulled a pair of reading glasses out of his pocket. He put them on, then joined her. "There's a little spot."

"It's not a spot," Evie said. "It's a dot."

"All right," Burns said, straightening and taking his glasses off. "And?"

"Old tradecraft," Evie said. "Something Mary Meyer might have learned from her husband who was in the CIA." Perhaps it was the excitement of her discovery that caused Evie to revert to data mode. "During the Franco-Prussian War, when Paris was besieged, messages were sent via carrier pigeon. Obviously a pigeon can't carry an entire file. Or an entire book. A photographer figured out a way to shrink pictures so that a document could be reduced many, many times. Microdots became very useful in Berlin during the Cold War, after the Wall went up. Which I suppose is ironic," Evie said, snapping out of it. "Given why we're here."

Evie pulled a pocketknife out her coat. "She hid it in plain sight."

"What?" Burns asked.

Evie scraped the dot off the painting, ignoring the gasp of concern from the curator. She held up the blade, the tiny dot on it. "Mary Meyer's real diary."

*****

The digital counter continued to wind down.

00:47:34

12 August 1963

He signed her in as 'Powers Plus One.' The way he always did. As if she didn't have a name. As if her presence at the White House must never be acknowledged.

Mary Meyer had wanted to paint that night. She could see the blank canvas as clearly as she could see Dave Powers getting out of the car and signing her into a place that she

152

shouldn't be; but sometimes emotion won over logic. Jack shouldn't need her like this tonight, but she knew why.

The Secret Service Agents never met her eyes, just like none of the staff did. It's like she was some weakness in their President that they couldn't admit to themselves. Or, more likely, some weakness in themselves to acknowledge the man that led them, the man they idolized, could have such a flaw.

Like he lost value in being just a normal human in pain who reached out to the one person who could share it with him. They all needed him to be perfect, but she was the one person in his life right now who not only knew that he wasn't perfect, but allowed him to just be a man. A man with all his flaws and imperfect dreams and small hopes. She allowed him to be Jack, and she always had, and that's why he reached out for her on this night, of all nights.

She could tell that Dave Powers found her less than and that he felt small sneaking her in on this night when Jackie was on the horse farm in Virginia that Jack had bought her to find some solace in her own time of need. Of which tonight was one of the most painful.

Mary wondered how they could all love him, admire him and yet not know him at all. They loved a man who didn't exist. A figment of their own fervent imaginations needing him to be anything but what he was. Right now she knew with all her heart that he was just like her—a parent feeling the terrible ache of a child in the ground instead of all around you, and demanding some attention that you barely had. All parents feel the constant need of their children, but Mary knew that she and Jack were in the tiny minority of people who felt the black hole of the child no longer there. The pain that is the echoing silence of no demands.

Patrick Bouvier Kennedy had been born by emergency C-section premature in Massachusetts on the 7th of August. He'd died two days later. The funeral had been on the 10th, and Mary had watched the news coverage, her heart aching for both Jack and Jackie. To lose another baby. Arabella, the name Mary knew Jackie had intended for a daughter, had been stillborn back in '56. The baby was buried now and Jackie was off, away from the demands of DC and being First Lady, with her beloved horses in the countryside. But Jack couldn't be away. The demands of office demanded his presence. The demands of life had caused him to call Mary and ask her to come tonight.

She went with Dave through the first floor and up the elevator to his private quarters. When she walked in she saw that he was sitting in a deep leather chair with a drink and a cigarette. He waved off Dave.

She knew the look on his face because she'd been there many times. It was the look of despair on someone who's not allowed to feel it. She couldn't do it because she had other sons, and he couldn't do it because he ruled the free world. For a moment her heart broke for him. For a second she tried to imagine grieving when grief is just considered a weakness and she knew why Jackie was gone and would always be. For a moment she thought of Lincoln who wasn't allowed to grieve in this house, either. There was no grief allowed her, and she started to weep and ran to him and knelt on the floor and buried her face into his crossed legs, and she knelt like that silently crying as she would have done for any sculptor of a saint. He said something to Dave Powers who'd brought her in but she didn't hear it because silencing her own tears drowned out all the words that could have been.

The door closed and they were alone and Jack pulled her up until she was sitting in his lap and he whispered in her ear: "I need this. I need to know that I'm still alive."

Mary knew what he meant, and for the brief time that he gave her she tried to show him that he was living, that he was a man, but that his fears could be gone for the moment. Mary wished with all her heart that she had more than a moment to give but she knew that a moment meant a lot when any moment out of this was pain. A pain so hard that you wonder how people can live at all.

She forgot the blank canvas that brought her a reprieve and looked at him afterwards. "We can't go on like this, Jack."

He buried his face in her hair. "I know. I'm so sorry for using you. I use many people, but I shouldn't use you."

She pulled back. "You aren't using me, Jack. I've been used a lot and it doesn't feel like this. We're using each other and that's so different."

He hugged her hard. "Mary, you need to give me some strength."

She buried her face in his thick hair and whispered: "What do you need me to do?"

"Do you know Khrushchev lost a son?"

"I didn't."

"I've lost a daughter and a son now. You've lost a son. And Khrushchev lost a son. An exclusive and horrible club."

"What do you need, Jack?"

Jack sighed. "I need you to remember something for me."

She pulled back and looked into his eyes. "Why? You aren't thinking of doing something stupid, are you?" Because she'd done many stupid things in his situation, and for a moment she forgot that he was referring to things that were out of her awareness.

And then he got down on the floor with her, a position that hurt him so much with his back that she knew that everything he said was so important that she could never forget a word of it. He grimaced at the pain but he knelt by her and began whispering in her ear.

Mary reached over and pushed her blond hair behind her ear and listened. He whispered for a long time, and she nodded to tell him that she understood. Because a part of her understood exactly and knew at that moment what he was asking her, and more important, she knew how to do it. When he finished she took his face and held it in her hands—the face that was so much bigger because of the steroids, still handsome but swollen to satisfy a part of him that was so ill. She held his face and stared into those eyes.

"I'll do it, Jack."

And for a second she thought she saw a tear and she felt terrible that that tear scared her as much as all the other people who needed him to be something different than just a human being. She turned her face so he wouldn't see the same fear that he saw all day on every other person who mattered to him.

"Mary," he said. "Mary."

She turned back to face him.

"Can you do this?"

"Yes, Jack. Yes, I can do it."

And he hugged her close. "I knew that I could trust you."

And the same fate that was starting to count down his hours went through his embrace and started to count down her fate. But at that moment she didn't know of that and had no idea of the future. She didn't understand then that he was hedging his mortality. And she never understood that he was hedging hers as well. She just knew that she was holding a grief-stricken parent and she did understand that. She did not understand that she'd just sealed her fate with his. She did what he asked in his whispers in her ears.

The gods are kind when they hide the real meanings of such small murmurings.

CHAPTER THIRTEEN
The Present

00:32:30

*****

Through the pain in his head, Ducharme began to sharpen his focus. Or perhaps it was with the aid of the pain. He couldn't separate the pain from who he was any more. He climbed out of the river of sewage ten feet from the massive blades that were chopping through the ditch, which explained the hand he'd encountered. There were lights in the room and Ducharme pulled up his night-vision goggles.

Dripping, Ducharme walked past the blades, weapon at the ready.

What he wasn't ready for was the blow from behind, sending him sprawling. Ducharme dropped the weapon in order to hit the ground and roll, coming up, hands up in a defensive position, trying to determine who had attacked him.

A massive man, a pale figure in the dim glow in the sewage room, towered over him. The man had a gun in his hands, but he acted like it was a distraction as he glowered down at Ducharme.

"You're dead," Caleb said. "You just don't know it yet."

"We're all going to die." Ducharme got to his knees, to his feet. And still he had to look up at his opponent. "Now is as good a time as any."

He went for his pistol and Caleb grabbed his hand, locking it in his powerful grip. "Nice try."

The look of victory on Caleb's face shifted to one of surprise as Ducharme's other hand slammed the Fairbairn into the big man, the narrow blade going right between his ribs and piercing his heart.

As Caleb went to his knees, Ducharme jerked the knife out, picked up his pistol and automatic rifle and continued on his mission.

Caleb blinked a few times, then fell forward on his face with a solid thud, joining all the departed souls he'd dumped in this disgusting part of the sewer system.

*****

"Where is your display on the Cold War?" Evie asked the curator.

"Second floor, northwest corner," the man replied. "But you just—"

He was speaking to air as Evie took off running, Burns trying to keep up.

As Evie swung open the door, she skidded to a halt.

Turnbull was blocking the way and had a gun ready. He had two men flanking him, also with guns drawn.

"Seriously?" Evie said.

Burns drew his pistol and stepped in front of her.

"Seriously," Turnbull said. "Give me the diary."

"You don't think it's important to the current situation?" Evie asked.

"My people are dealing with the current situation," Turnbull said.

"What you think is the current situation," Evie said. "Just like you thought you had Mary Meyer's diary in your little cave. And you didn't. You've been wrong and you're wrong now. So get out of my way."

And with that, Evie stepped around Burns, pushed past a befuddled Turnbull and headed for the stairs. Burns holstered his pistol and sprinted after her. They ran through the Smithsonian until they reached the Cold War exhibit. Evie pushed through a rope barricade to the portion on spy-craft. She carefully inserted the dot on a slide and then placed the slide in the microdot reader.

She was focused on reading when Turnbull and his men arrived. Burns had his pistol out once more, covering her back.

"Relax," Turnbull said. "We're in this together."

"Right," Burns said.

Evie was making tiny adjustments to the knobs on the side of the machine. "It had to be after the Crisis. That's when Kennedy and Khrushchev came up with the plan." She adjusted. "August twelfth, 1963. Just after Patrick Kennedy's death." She was nodding. "Kennedy told Meyer all about it. Leaving some missiles behind. Taking some of the warheads and putting them in Moscow and New York."

"We know all that," Turnbull said.

Evie didn't look up from the reader. "Did you know that Khrushchev told Kennedy that he wouldn't leave nuclear warheads in Cuba? Warheads he couldn't be guaranteed of controlling? That he left some missiles and dummy warheads, and that Castro was furious when he realized he'd been duped?"

"That we didn't know," Turnbull allowed.

"So we don't have to worry about plutonium in Cuba," Evie said.

*****

00:28:15

*****

Aaron checked his watch. Less than a half hour until the world learned that nuclear weapons could not be used without consequences. That no one was safe.

The cost would be high, but in the long run, it would be worth it. They'd kept the peace for over half a century, kept nuclear weapons from being used again after Hiroshima and Nagasaki. A new peace would come out of this.

Future generations would thank the Peacekeepers.

Over half of whom were dead and wavering. The assault was taking a toll. No matter how well Caleb had trained the Peacekeepers, they weren't combat-hardened soldiers like the assaulting force.

Aaron decided on a final course of action. He left his people behind and retreated, making his way to the vault.

26 June 1963

Or go here: http://youtu.be/hH6nQhss4Yc to view Kennedy's speech "I am a Berliner"

"I am proud to come to this city as the guest of your distinguished Mayor, who has symbolized throughout the world the fighting spirit of West Berlin. And I am proud to visit the Federal Republic with your distinguished Chancellor, who for so many years has committed Germany to democracy and freedom and progress, and to come here in the company of my fellow American, General Clay, who has been in this city during its great moments of crisis and will come again if ever needed.

"Two thousand years ago the proudest boast was 'civis Romanus sum.' Today, in the world of freedom, the proudest boast is 'Ich bin ein Berliner.'

"I appreciate my interpreter translating my German!

"There are many people in the world who really don't understand, or say they don't, what is the great issue between the Free World and the Communist world. Let them come to Berlin. There are some who say that communism is the wave of the future. Let them come to Berlin. And there are some who say in Europe and elsewhere we can work with the Communists. Let them come to Berlin. And there are even a few who say that it's true that communism is an evil system, but it permits us to make economic progress. 'Laßt sie nach

Berlin kommen.' Let them come to Berlin! Freedom has many difficulties and democracy is not perfect, but we have never had to put a wall up to keep our people in, to prevent them from leaving us. I want to say, on behalf of my countrymen, who live many miles away on the other side of the Atlantic, who are far distant from you, that they take the greatest pride that they have been able to share with you, even from a distance, the story of the last eighteen years. I know of no town, no city, that has been besieged for eighteen years that still lives with the vitality and the force and the hope and the determination of the city of West Berlin.

"While the wall is the most obvious and vivid demonstration of the failures of the Communist system, for all the world to see, we take no satisfaction in it. For it is, as your Mayor has said, an offense not only against history but an offense against humanity, separating families, dividing husbands and wives and brothers and sisters, and dividing a people who wish to be joined together.

"What is true of this city is true of Germany — real, lasting peace in Europe can never be assured as long as one German out of four is denied the elementary right of free men, and that is to make a free choice. In eighteen years of peace and good faith, this generation of Germans has earned the right to be free, including the right to unite their families and their nation in lasting peace, with goodwill to all people. You live in a defended island of freedom, but your life is part of the main. So let me ask you, as I close, to lift your eyes beyond the dangers of today to the hopes of tomorrow, beyond the freedom merely of this city of Berlin, or your country of Germany, to the advance of freedom everywhere, beyond the wall to the day of peace with justice, beyond yourselves and ourselves to all mankind.

"Freedom is indivisible, and when one man is enslaved, all are not free. When all are free, then we can look forward to that day when this city will be joined as one, and this country, and this great Continent of Europe, in a peaceful and hopeful globe. When that day finally comes, as it will, the people of West Berlin can take sober satisfaction in the fact that they were in the front lines for almost two decades.

"All free men, wherever they may live, are citizens of Berlin, and, therefore, as a free man, I take pride in the words:

"Ich bin ein Berliner."

CHAPTER FOURTEEN
The Present

Ducharme reached an intersection. A train was rumbling to the right. The sound of automatic weapons was to the left.

He turned left and bumped into a man scurrying down the tunnel.

"Freeze!" Ducharme yelled.

The one-armed man raised his one arm. "I do not have a weapon."

"Where's the bomb?" Ducharme demanded.

"I'm Aaron," the man said. "And you are?"

"You're an original Peacekeeper," Ducharme said. "One of the first two with Bathsheba. Where's the damn bomb?"

"Your name, sir?"

"I'm the guy that's going to start hurting you if you don't lead me to the bomb."

Aaron gestured with his one hand. "This way."

"Quicker," Ducharme said, shoving the muzzle of his weapon into Aaron's back.

*****

"Mary Meyer received a copy of the message Mrs. Kennedy gave to Mikoyan," Evie said. She was writing on a notepad, her eyes still on the machine, reading. "It's in code. Five letter groupings."

"Does it say what the message is about?" Turnbull asked.

"Hold on," Evie said. "I'm working as fast as I can."

*****

Aaron reached the first door and slowly worked through that. Eventually they came to the inner room.

00:25:10

Ducharme stared at the large metal box and the digital countdown. "How do I stop it?"

"You don't," Aaron said.

Ducharme realized something: there was no more firing. He took a flashbang off his combat vest, stepped into the doorway and tossed the grenade into the tunnel beyond, summoning help.

Thirty seconds later, the first TriOp man edged in, weapon at the ready.

"This it?" the man asked.

"Yes," Ducharme said. "We need bomb disposal personnel ASAP."

"Already en route."

"It won't do you any good," Aaron said, and then he lunged for the switch in the control room for the poison gas.

Ducharme shot him twice, the rounds punching him in the side and up against the wall. Still Aaron tried to go for the button again and Ducharme finished him with a round to the forehead as the bomb disposal unit rushed in.

"We've got one, if not three, nuclear warheads in there," Ducharme said, pointing at the steel box. "And that's the countdown," he added, pointing at the monitor.

*****

"Oh, no," Evie whispered. She slowly straightened from looking through the scope at the microdot.

"What?" Turnbull demanded.

"Jackie Kennedy told Mary about the message and gave her a copy. It was for Khrushchev to update him on the Sword of Damocles. The Peacekeepers were moving the bombs out of New York City."

"To where?" Turnbull asked.

"Here. DC."

"Where here?" Turnbull said, pulling out his phone. "DC is a big place."

"That's what's in the code," Evie said.

"Can you break it?" Turnbull didn't wait for an answer as he began making calls, getting forces alerted in the area.

*****

The whine of a metal saw filled the vault, making it impossible to speak or hear anything else. Ducharme wasn't optimistic about the bomb squad getting into the container in time. And even then, he wasn't sure how well-versed the NYPD Bomb Squad was in disarming fifty-year-old atomic bombs. Made in Russia.

Ducharme made his way to the surface, knowing that walking distance wasn't going to matter if the bombs went off, but he needed to be able to communicate, and that wasn't possible underground. As soon as he emerged from the Fulton Station he called Evie.

She sounded distracted when she answered. "Yes?"

"We just went under twenty minutes on the timer," Ducharme said. "The bomb squad is—"

"The bombs aren't in New York," Evie said. "They're here in DC and I'm trying to figure out where."

Then the phone went dead.

*****

Evie stared at the five letter groupings. If it was a one time code then she was screwed along with the rest of Washington: a code where the message used something like a specific page from a book that only the sender and receiver knew about and a trigraph transcribed the message.

But it couldn't be, she realized. Because it had been sent to Khrushchev and also given to Mary Meyer. She very much doubted that Kennedy had shared something like that with both of them.

"PT-109," Evie said.

"What?" Burns asked.

Turnbull was still on the phone getting forces moving, ordering a radiological team airborne, although if the bombs gave off a signal, they certainly would have been detected long before now.

But one had to try.

"PT-109," Evie said. She was googling something on her phone. "After they were run over by that Japanese destroyer and swam to shore, Kennedy sent a message via some natives. He carved it on a coconut shell. But after that, the coastwatchers used a code—a very basic code—called the Playfair Cipher. It's rather simple."

"Decode, don't explain," Burns suggested.

"Explaining helps me," Evie said, but she had her cell phone next to the piece of paper on which she'd listed the five letter groups. "You use the alphabet in a five-by-five square, removing one letter, usually the J. Then you break the message into two letter blocks and you go over and then down, and you've got the letter for the message."

And then she fell silent as she rapidly began decoding the fifty-year-old message.

MOVING BOMBS PEACEKEEPERS REMAIN IN NY AS DIVERSION BOMBS NOW IN WASHINGTON PROPANE TANK ETERNAL FLAME

Turnbull was looking over her shoulder and shouting orders as the part about the Eternal Flame was scrawled out. He ran from the room, leaving Evie and Burns alone in this corner of the Smithsonian.

Evie looked at the FBI agent. "I hear they have an excellent new exhibit on Qhapac nan: The Way of the Incas. It's about their road system. Let's take a look since we're here already."

*****

Baths checked her watch. Five minutes. It was time. She got off the bench and walked toward John F. Kennedy's gravesite. The Eternal Flame flickered in the late afternoon sun. The Flame had been emplaced at the insistence of Jackie Kennedy shortly after his assassination. The Kennedy Clan had wanted their favorite son buried in Massachusetts, but Jackie had brought Bobby Kennedy out here to Arlington, and the two agreed he would be buried here in Virginia, overlooking Washington and the Pentagon. Then the family had objected to the concept of an Eternal Flame, thinking it might be too showy, but once more Mrs. Kennedy had been adamant.

They put together a hastily improvised flame, consisting of a tiki torch and a propane tank, for Jackie Kennedy to light at the end of the funeral service on the 25th of November 1963. Robert and Edward Kennedy symbolically simulated lighting the flame after her.

Only Jackie and Bobby Kennedy knew the real reason a permanent flame would be installed. First, though, Mrs. Kennedy had her two deceased babies disinterred and brought to Arlington to be buried near their father. She read that Abraham Lincoln had been buried next to his dead son, Willie, and she knew that her husband had had a strong desire to be buried with his family.

It took the Corps of Engineers a year to finally complete plans of a permanent flame along with a permanent gravesite. It took another two years for those plans to come to fruition.

It wasn't just because of concern about the aesthetics.

A private firm, one that was composed of Peacemakers, built the terrace on which the permanent site would be completed. They built one nuclear weapon into that terrace, with a control panel underneath one of the flagstones that lined the entire area and an access panel through which they could get to the bomb.

Baths walked up to that flagstone and knelt.

Over the years, the Peacekeepers came back every eighteen months in the name of doing an inspection of the grounds and made sure the weapon was still functional. Twice they had to unearth the bomb and replace it with one of the spares, which they took back to New York and cannibalized.

Each time they did the inspection or work, a detachment of Green Berets from Fort Bragg arrived to form an outer perimeter to keep the site secure. They had no clue what was going on behind the tall white temporary fences that were erected.

The Peacekeepers were down to one functioning bomb: the one in place.

Baths put both hands under the lip of the flagstone and used all her strength to lift it and shove it to the side. She checked her watch. A minute and a half. She wondered if the time made any difference now or if she should just initiate. The blast would take out the cemetery and reach the Pentagon, which had been Jackie Kennedy's main intent.

Baths reached forward to hit the initiation.

Just as the sniper hanging on a monkey harness out of the AH-6 helicopter fired. His round hit her in the base of the skull, almost decapitating her.

12 October 1964

Mary Meyer looked up and down the Chesapeake and Ohio Canal Towpath, but Jesus Angleton had yet to show himself, which was unusual. He was a man of punctuality, among many other qualities.

A large man came striding down the path and Meyer felt a moment of apprehension as no one else was in sight. But the way he was walking indicated he had a destination in mind and she stepped aside.

He pulled the gun out of a pocket of his coat.

"Someone help me!" Meyer cried out, taking another step back and putting her hands in front of her face, a natural reaction.

The man shot her in the heart.

As she crumpled to the ground, the shooter showed his professionalism by firing another bullet into the back of her head.

Then he walked away.

A quarter mile later, he turned off the path and rushed to a waiting car.

Angleton was waiting in the driver's seat as the shooter got inside.

"Done?"

"Done," Racca replied. As Angleton pulled out into traffic, Racca dared to look at his boss. "What did she do wrong?"

"She simply knew too much."

13 October 1964

"Ah, Anastas," Khrushchev said, picking up a glass of vodka and downing it. "I am sure you will survive this too, as you have survived so many other purges."

Mikoyan stood on the other side of the Premier's desk. "Meyer was killed in Washington."

"Another casualty of the Cold War. A pity."

"What was in that message I brought to you from Mrs. Kennedy?" Mikoyan demanded, feeling cocky now that the winds of change were blowing once more in Moscow.

"Her well wishes for my continued health in light of what happened to her husband," Khrushchev said. "I'm old and tired. Let them cope by themselves. I've done the main thing. Could anyone have dreamed of telling Stalin that he didn't suit us anymore and suggesting he retire? Not even a wet spot would have remained where we had been standing. Now everything is different. The fear is gone, and we can talk as equals. That's my contribution. I won't put up a fight."

On the next day, the 14th of October, the Presidium and Central Committee accepted Khrushchev's 'voluntary' retirement for reasons of 'advanced age and ill health.'

It was better than the traditional bullet to the back of the head.

CHAPTER FIFTEEN
The Present

Turnbull put on the diamond-encrusted medallion of the Head of the Society of the Cincinnati. While politics was important, the Society inevitably bowed to practicality. Finally solving the mystery, and danger, of the Sword of Damocles, was a coup that rivaled the best that any Head had ever achieved.

He sat at the desk that had belonged to Lucius as long as he had been a member of the Society. He noted the false diary of Mary Meyer, abandoned by Evie and Burns in their rush to get to the Smithsonian. He reached out and picked it up. Then he shoved it in a drawer.

The Philosophers had a new head, too. And Evie Tolliver might be quirky, but she was a worthy adversary.

She was also a worthy ally, and that thought gave Turnbull pause.

With a sigh, he got up and headed to the vault that held Hoover's files. He had to get more familiar with them now that he was Head.

*****

"Heavy lies the head that wears the crown," Ducharme said, looking down at JFK's grave. They were inside high white fences, alongside a tornado of activity as the bomb was being removed.

"Actually," Evie said, "that's a famous misquote. The original phrase comes from Shakespeare's *Henry the Fourth*, Part Two. 'Uneasy lies the head that wears a crown.'"

"Right," Ducharme said. "I got it wrong."

"You got the spirit right," Evie allowed.

Ducharme laughed. "We're making progress, Evie. We're making progress."

166

"Progress toward what?" she asked, truly puzzled, and he gave up on that line.

"At least the Sword never fell," Ducharme said, nodding toward the hole where specialists were working on the bomb.

"I've always wondered," Evie began, but fell silent.

Ducharme walked into it, knowing he was. "Wondered what?"

"Who really killed him?"

"Come on," Ducharme said, leading her away from the grave and into the cemetery. "Back to where it started." They went to the graves of Charlie LaGrange and his father. The earth was still raw. Ducharme went to one knee and reached into the dirt at the foot of one grave. He retrieved his commando dagger. He took the one Cane had given him and weighed it against his original.

"Roughly the same," Ducharme said.

"Are you going to bury both?" Evie asked.

Ducharme stood. He held out his dagger to her. "I think we're going to need both."

The End

FACTS KENNEDY

OIeg Penkovsky was a real person. It is uncertain whether he was a traitor or patriot to the Soviet Union, but he was executed either in the manner depicted in this book or by firing squad on 16 May 1963.

Anastas Mikoyan did represent Khrushchev at JFK's Funeral. They did talk in the Rotunda and she did mention the Endeavor that her husband and Khrushchev had been involved in.

Green Berets were flown up from Fort Bragg to be part of the Honor Guard.

The United States did emplace a battery of 15 Jupiter Missiles in Turkey, well before the Soviets tried to put missiles into Cuba. They were supposedly withdrawn as part of the resolution of the Cuban Missile Crisis.

The Soviet General on the ground in Cuba had authority to use the nuclear weapons under his command, an almost unheard of granting of powers.

Khrushchev's son, Leonid, was either killed in action as a pilot or executed by Stalin. The records are unclear.

Khrushchev's Speech on 25 February 1956 denouncing Stalin turned the Soviet Union on its ear. It's reported some delegates left the 20th Party Congress and committed suicide.

No one has a complete map of the warren underneath New York City and no one knows all of it. The City Hall station is used as a turnaround for the #6 train, but has not been active station since the end of World War II.

Mary Meyer did know Timothy Leary. It's reported she dropped acid with President Kennedy.

Jesus James Angleton was one of the most intriguing characters of the Cold War. The movie *The Good Shepherd* starring Matt Damon is loosely based on his life. He was the first one in Mary Meyer's house searching for her diary after she was killed.

25 November used to wildly celebrated in New York City as Evacuation Day until Lincoln started Thanksgiving.

In 2009 Contractors accounted for 48% of the Department of Defense workforce in Iraq and 57% in Afghanistan.

The USS Beale incident only truly came to light thirty years later. Strangely, though, the 1965 movie, *The Bedford Incident*, mirrored these events.

A black man was arrested for Mary Meyer's murder, but his attorney got him acquitted as there was no evidence.

Half Light, painted by Mary Meyer, is in the Smithsonian Archives.

My wife was present as a young girl in Berlin and heard Kennedy's Ich Bin ein Berliner speech.

Kennedy's autopsy original notes have been lost.

The removal of Kennedy's body from Texas before an autopsy was performed violated Texas law.

Mary Meyer was Mary Meyer. She lived by her own rules until she was murdered.

ABOUT THE AUTHOR

NY *Times* bestselling author **Bob Mayer** has had over 50 books published. He has sold over four million books, and is in demand as a team-building, life-changing, and leadership speaker and consultant for his *Who Dares Wins: The Green Beret Way* concept, which he translated into Write It Forward: a holistic program teaching writers how to be authors. He is also the Co-Creator of Cool Gus Publishing, which does both eBooks and Print On Demand, so he has experience in both traditional and non-traditional publishing.

His books have hit the *NY Times, Publishers Weekly, Wall Street Journal* and numerous other bestseller lists. His book *The Jefferson Allegiance,* was released independently and reached #2 overall in sales on Nook.

Bob Mayer grew up in the Bronx. After high school, he entered West Point where he learned about the history of our military and our country. During his four years at the Academy and later in the Infantry, Mayer questioned the idea of "mission over men." When he volunteered and passed selection for the Special Forces as a Green Beret, he felt more at ease where the men were more important than the mission.

Mayer's obsession with mythology and his vast knowledge of the military and Special Forces, mixed with his strong desire to learn from history, is the foundation for his science fiction series *Atlantis, Area 51* and *Psychic Warrior.* Mayer is a master at blending elements of truth into all of his thrillers, leaving the reader questioning what is real and what isn't.

He took this same passion and created thrillers based in fact and riddled with possibilities. His unique background in the Special Forces gives the reader a sense of authenticity and creates a reality that makes the reader wonder where fact ends and fiction begins.

In his historical fiction novels, Mayer blends actual events with fictional characters. He doesn't change history, but instead changes how history came into being.

Mayer's military background, coupled with his deep desire to understand the past and how it affects our future, gives his writing a rich flavor not to be missed.

Bob has presented for over a thousand organizations both in the United States and internationally, including keynote presentations, all day workshops, and multi-day seminars. He has taught organizations ranging from Maui Writers, to Whidbey Island Writers, to San Diego State University, to the University of Georgia, to the Romance Writers of America National Convention, to Boston SWAT, the CIA, Fortune-500, the Royal Danish Navy Frogman Corps, Microsoft, Rotary, IT Teams in Silicon Valley and many others. He has also served as a Visiting Writer for NILA MFA program in Creative Writing. He has done interviews for the *Wall Street Journal*, *Forbes*, *Sports Illustrated*, PBS, NPR, the Discovery Channel, the SyFy channel and local cable shows. For more information see www.bobmayer.org.

OTHER BOOKS BY BOB MAYER

"Thelma and Louise go clandestine." *Kirkus Reviews on Bodyguard of Lies*

" . . .delivers top-notch action and adventure, creating a full cast of lethal operatives armed with all the latest weaponry. Excellent writing and well-drawn, appealing characters help make this another taut, crackling read." *Publishers Weekly*

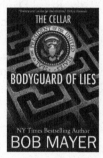

"Fascinating, imaginative and nerve-wracking." *Kirkus Reviews*

THE PRESIDENTIAL SERIES BY BOB MAYER

THE GREEN BERET SERIES

"Mayer has stretched the limits of the military action novel. Synbat is also a gripping detective story and an intriguing science fiction thriller. Mayer brings an accurate and meticulous depiction of military to this book which greatly enhances its credibility." *Assembly*

"Will leave you spellbound. Mayer's long suit is detail, giving the reader an in-depth view of the inner workings of the Green Machine." *Book News*

"Mayer keeps story and characters firmly under control. The venal motives of the scientists and military bureaucracy are tellingly contrasted with the idealism of the soldiers. A treat for military fiction readers." *Publishers Weekly*

"Sinewy writing enhances this already potent action fix. An adrenaline cocktail from start to finish." *Kirkus Reviews*

HISTORICAL FICTION BY BOB MAYER

SHADOW WARRIOR SERIES

"Sizzling, first rate war fiction." *Library Journal*

"A military thriller in the tradition of John Grisham's The Firm." *Publishers Weekly*

"The Omega Missile comes screaming down on target. A great action read." *Stephen Coonts*

"What a delicious adventure-thriller. Its clever, plausible plot gives birth to lots of action and suspense." *Kansas City Journal Inquirer*

THE ATLANTIS SERIES BY BOB MAYER

"Spell-binding! Will keep you on the edge of your seat. Call it techno-thriller, call it science fiction, call it just terrific story-telling." *Terry Brooks, #1 NY Times Bestselling author of the Shannara series and Star Wars Phantom Menace*

PSYCHIC WARRIOR SERIES

"A pulsing technothriller. A nailbiter in the best tradition of adventure fiction." *Publishers Weekly.*

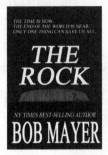

AREA 51/NIGHTSTALKERS SERIES

"Bob Mayer's *Nightstalkers* grabs you by the rocket launcher and doesn't let go. Fast-moving military SF action—just the way I like it. Highly recommend." *B.V. Larson*

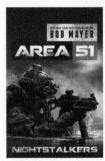

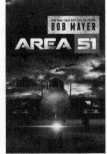

NON-FICTION BY BOB MAYER

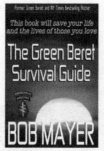

BOOKS BY BOB MAYER AND JEN TALTY

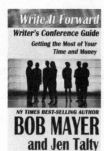

CPSIA information can be obtained
at www.ICGtesting.com
Printed in the USA
FSOW03n0724100118
43253FS